Helen Jacey is the found
creator of the feminis
Investigations. The first n

published in 2018. Helen has developed numerous projects for international film and television companies. Her biographical BBC 4 radio drama about Jean Rhys *Miracle Postponed* was short-listed for a Mental Health in the Media Award. Renowned for her expertise on feminism and the creative process, Helen has worked with film institutions and leading brands throughout the world. Her widely acclaimed screenwriting book *The Woman in the Story: Writing Memorable Female Characters* (Michael Wiese Productions, 2nd ed. 2017) was the first to focus on gender and female representation.

Helen grew up in South London. She gained an MA in Screenwriting from The London Institute, 2001, and a PhD in Screenwriting from the University of the Arts London, 2010. She has taught screenwriting and creative writing at several British universities.

Visit Shedunnit Productions:

Website:
www.shedunnit.com

www.instagram.com/shedunnitproductions
www.facebook.com/shedunnit
www.twitter.com/shedunnit

Praise for Helen Jacey's writing:

'No writer has more intricately explored what contemporary writing for and about women means today. In Elvira Slate, Jacey has created a slick 40's sleuth that could inspire the toughest 21st century feminist – and a binge-worthy boxset of the highest order!'
– Celia Walden, US Editor at Large, *Daily Telegraph*

'Elvira Slate emerges as the new heroine of LA noir."
– Terence Bailey, Author of *The Sara Jones Cycle*

'In Elvira Slate, a fierce female ex-con with an attraction to trouble and nothing to lose, Jacey has created a criminally compelling character I'd follow anywhere – at a safe distance.'
– Jennifer Steil, Journalist and Author of
    The Ambassador's Wife

'Welcome back, Elvira. We've missed you.'
– Stephen Wyatt, Writer *Classic Chandler*, BBC Radio 4
    and Author of *The World and His Wife*

'Elvira Slate navigates the criminal underworld of forties Hollywood according to her own moral compass. Full of a fiery ferociousness first developed as a kid surviving as an orphan in London, entrenched during her years as a gangster's moll, and perfected during a stint in Holloway prison – she is the noir anti-heroine we've long been missing.'
– Savannah James-Bayly, Associate Producer,
    Queens of Mystery

By Helen Jacey:

ELVIRA SLATE INVESTIGATIONS:

Made Moll (novelette)
Jailbird Detective
Chipped Pearls

Chipped Pearls

Elvira Slate Investigations Book Two

By Helen Jacey

Shedunnit Productions

In loving memory of

Lucy Scher
1965-2018

1

'Well I never. If it isn't Jemima Day.'

The voice hasn't changed. Not a bit.

We meet each other's eyes. I know her face as well as the scar on my belly. Both are faded with age, both trigger memories of hell. A searing pain of rage and helplessness.

I give a slight nod and head for the hotel entrance lobby.

Do I make a run for it? Walk out on the case?

No. That way leads to ruin, and fast. Not just financial, but my reputation as well.

But she's spotted me and she will be the destruction of Elvira Slate entirely. Lauder's words echo in my mind. "You realize how many of your compatriots cross the pond?"

Damn it! He wasn't kidding.

She's chuckling now, behind me. Her breath wheezes. 'Like that, is it, duckie? Too good for your old chum?'

There's really no choice. I turn around. 'Hello, Maureen.'

'Hello, Jemima. Or is it Elvira now?'

Maureen's eyelids, papery like scrunched silk, are raised as high as they can probably go these days. She's wearing an unfashionably long tea dress, all pink and white daisies. Her wide-brimmed, pale pink hat is loaded with luscious taffeta roses.

The last I heard, years ago, she was doing a long stretch. She must have served her time and landed on her feet to roll up here. Resurrected in a flouncy dress, on the arm of a mobster, and now coiling around my neck.

Her green eyes twinkle at me. 'You know, we all thought you

were a goner. And here you are safe and sound in California. Thanks to our blessed Lady—Mary, Mother of God.'

Her eyes swivel upwards as she makes the sign of the cross. 'How I prayed you were safe! Look at you! All grown up into an elegant lady!'

A dry lump lodges in my throat as I wait for the punch line.

If she's the same old Maureen O'Reilly, it won't take long.

Sure enough, her thin red lips split into a coy smile. 'There was a lot of readies on offer for news of your whereabouts. If you'd like to stay looking so well, you and me need to have a little chat, don't we?'

2

Ten Days Earlier

I read the telegram.

GREETINGS FROM VIENNA STOP YOUR FRIEND DECEASED STOP INFLUENZA DURING WAR STOP NO OFFSPRING STOP YOU OWE ME TWO STOP MERRY CHRISTMAS STOP.

Hardly words of comfort and joy, but at least Lois had a sense of humor.

A photojournalist and like me a resident of the Miracle Mile Hotel, Lois Schulz had recently touched down in Vienna to take pictures of a butchered city and its people. She was on assignment for *Family Times*, a new women's magazine. Lois's remit was to find heartwarming stories of families struggling in the aftermath of the war: hope emerging from the ruins of Europe.

Before she left, she had reluctantly agreed to try to track down a certain Sophia Spark, whose last known whereabouts were Vienna. 'A few days is all I can spare. Fifty bucks a day.'

I told her if she did find Sophia, on no account could she use her in one of her stories. This was a confidential mission.

The "two" in her telegram meant it had taken her only two days. Lois had been quick, and now had the results I needed. In one way it was a relief—I was in no hurry to fly back to Europe poking around rubble for long-lost daughters.

But in another way, it was a disaster. Sophia Spark was dead, leaving me to deal with some pretty big implications.

The late Tatiana Spark's last wish was for me to find Sophia, her long-lost daughter, and give her the ultimate Hollywood happy ending—a large inheritance and a new life in the Pacific Palisades, California.

For my efforts in locating Sophia, the Spark estate would pay me a hefty stipend to help me start up my detective agency.

I sat down heavily behind my desk, gazing out of the window. To hide from clients what he considered was an ugly view, my secretary Barney had installed venetian blinds in a dark wood and placed an over-enthusiastic cheese plant on the ledge. He instructed me to keep the blinds down, but the slats open. Instead, I kept the blinds rolled right up and moved the plant near the door.

I found the permanent view of the fire escape strangely reassuring.

I lit a cigarette and dwelt on my fate. Without the Spark money how would I pay my rent for the office suite-cum-apartment and Barney's salary?

It covered a lot else. Like the gold-and-black lettering on the marbled glass of the office door which declared my profession.

Elvira Slate, Private Investigator.

Not bad for a former gangster's moll from London, a wanted killer, a suspected spy and probation absconder.

But more than anything else, the Tatiana Spark Trust money had bought me mental space. A brief window in time to process the fact that against all odds, I had escaped the noose. And that as far as Blighty officialdom was concerned, I was dead. Well, Jemima Day was. That was the name on my British birth certificate.

Reborn as Elvira Slate, I had no intention of ever going back.

Swinging my feet up onto my desk, I reread Lois's telegram. Sophia died during the war. That could mean anytime during '39 to now, December '45.

I couldn't wait to find out from Lois how she had got the grisly details. I would need everything she had to present to the trustees so they could decide what to do with the fortune in the bank. But Lois wouldn't be back for a few weeks.

At the end of the day, maybe it was a good thing. Debts to the dead left a bad odor.

And I really should find other clients to fuel my business, so I could cease relying on Tatiana Spark's guilt money. I'd done a couple of what Barney called 'small jobs', but nothing was on the horizon.

Find a new case fast or go bust.

Now I'd just have to find work the way any new detective does. How the hell was that?

There was a cough at the door. Barney's floppy brown hair appeared, a cheeky grin on his face. 'Good news?'

I stalled, swinging my feet off the desk. 'Sorry?'

'Any news from Lois?'

'Not yet.' I shuddered inwardly. He didn't need to know he might not have a job by the time New Year's Day rolled around. It would kill me to tell him.

'You look like you need a coffee. Presto!' He came in, holding a tray with a cup of black coffee. He carefully placed the tray down in front of me. 'So...decided?'

'On…?' My blank stare made him roll his eyes.

'The Christmas tree. Be nice for the clients.'

'We only have one client and she's dead.'

Barney tutted, ignoring my grouchiness. 'We could have a cute little silver fairy at the top. I'll go pick one up at the Farmers Market.'

'A fairy or a tree?' I winked. Barney preferred the fellas. He knew I knew—we'd had too many drinks after I offered him the job, and he had spilled the beans—but now he was turning beetroot.

I cursed my tactlessness. At work, he could forget all about the lie he had to live the rest of the time. He had only opened up to me because he sensed I wouldn't judge and if he was going to quit a stable, if dull, job at *The Chronicle* to join me, he didn't want any secrets. He wanted me to be the perfect boss and this to be the perfect job.

He had told me his beloved parents were busy looking for the right Jewish girl, someone who wouldn't mind a crippled veteran. Barney had lost a foot in France. Life changing but small fry considering his family had lost many relatives in the camps and his mother was in a deep depression, hardly speaking anymore. Barney knew his parents' future happiness depended on his prospects. But for how long could he keep the act up?

In true Barney form, he never let his guilt show. Maybe he had already found Mr. Right and that kept him going.

Or maybe he simply had figured out that if the odds are against you, there's no point moaning about it.

'I don't like Christmas. And you don't celebrate it, so it beats me why we need a tree.' I sipped the coffee.

'Well, you never know who might walk in the door last minute.' Barney reflected, heading back to the doorway. 'And even if they don't, you'll be here all alone for two weeks with nothing pretty to look at. Sad!'

I raised a sarcastic brow. I'd given Barney a full two weeks off because he deserved it.

'I bet you come January, the telephone won't stop. You know, there are more death notices right after the holiday. Busy time!'

Barney's job at *The Chronicle* had been in the personal columns.

'So why should the detective business boom?'

Barney rolled his eyes at my pessimism. 'Imagine the housewife discovering her hubby whispering sweet nothings to his lover on the telephone on Christmas Day? She'll be calling in no time to dig up some evidence to bump up her alimony.'

'But I don't want to do divorce,' I groaned. The plan had been to take on clients who were in a jam, had someone disappear on them, were being bullied, blackmailed, or tricked. Marriage was a fool's game and I didn't have the patience for mopping up the mess of other people's delusions.

But did I have a choice?

I met his eyes. 'You know what? Get a darned tree.'

3

Christmas Eve rolled around a few days later. Barney went back home. The hotel was a shadow of its former self. The lobby, where the residents normally sat chatting after work, and where Mrs. Loeb behind the front desk would bark at us for our misdemeanors, was deserted. The sound of women laughing in the elevator was replaced by silence.

Earlier that day I heard the wail of a lonesome saxophone, melding with the distant horns and hum of traffic on Wilshire. But now even that had stopped. Most probably Alberta, who played in an all-girl swing band The Charmettes, and was the housekeeper of Dede Dedeaux, the hotel's owner.

Well, "housekeeper" was a front. Neither had openly declared it, but Alberta and her white employer, Dede Dedeaux, were an item. The roles of maid and boss enabled them to live together without arousing suspicion.

I wasn't exactly chummy with them, but Dede and Alberta knew my identity was a front, too. We had a gentlewoman's understanding not to pry.

I wouldn't bother Alberta anyway, if she were still around. Dede was away skiing in Aspen with her rich family, so this was probably the nearest thing Alberta got to time for herself.

Now the tree sat in the corner of the front office. Barney had really gone to town. All tinsel festoons and glittery decorations. At the top, a little doll of a fairy with a chalkware face, lacy silver wings and a white frock. She was cute with her gold curls and snub nose. If we went bust next year, Barney could keep her because I'd want to sock her in the face.

I gave her a sharp look. 'You better be a fairy godmother because I sure as hell need one.'

Christmas cards covered the surfaces in the office. I flicked through a few. Most were to Barney.

That was fine by me. Everybody loved him.

Then I caught sight of something. At the foot of the tree. *Gifts.*

Barney hadn't said a thing. He'd just discreetly put them there. Avoiding any awkwardness? That was his style.

I picked them up one by one. The contents of the first one were soft. I flicked over the tag. '*Happy holidays to a great boss!*'

A great boss? Sure, one who forgets to buy a gift for her worker. I opened the crisp pink tissue. Inside, a delicate gray scarf, covered in tiny black dots.

A larger gift was from June Conway, my gown designer pal who also lived in the hotel. After a nasty experience six months ago, she had left the hotel for a break from the city. But life in the boonies hadn't suited her. June had moved back in November and opened a dress shop near Olvera Street.

I tore open the wrapping paper. Inside, a deep ruby velvet gown. I picked it up, the fabric slipping through my hands like soft treacle.

I stood up and held it against me. It had a ruched bodice and a high, heart-shaped neckline with soft puckers around the edges. The long sleeves were quite full, the cuffs fixed with a pair of little velvet buttons. You could take out a person's eye with the shoulder pads. The skirt, cut on the bias, fell elegantly to the floor.

9

Inside, a woven label in gold and shades of pink. *A Miracle Mile Gown*, with a little symbol of a palm tree and a woman's profile.

It was sweet June had named her dress shop after the hotel because she felt it had changed her life for the better. It was a hotel with a habit of changing lives.

A note fell out. *'To my dearest Elvira. I hope you need this dress soon! With love and eternal gratitude. Happy holidays, June.'*

As I had zero parties on the horizon, that was optimistic.

The third wrapped gift was a stiff rectangular box. The paper was covered in jolly Santas and tied with a cream satin bow. The tag read, *'This should come in handy. To a prosperous '46. Beatty.'*

Curt and to the point. Beatty Falaise was the closest person I had to a mentor. She was the most powerful female detective in LA and had taken me under her wing and shown me the ropes.

She had gotten me a magnifying glass with a fine ebony inlaid handle. The glass was thick, edged in a shiny brass. It would have its uses, should another assignment pop up.

Until then, I could just examine the worry wrinkles forming on my brow.

I hadn't even sent any of them a card.

What is wrong with you?

I slumped on Barney's chair. I loved these gifts, but I didn't want to feel grateful. I hated Christmas and for good reason.

My most vivid memory of the supposedly festive season was that of a bunch of hateful nuns punishing me and the other orphans on Christmas morning for bouncing on the beds in our deluded expectation we would be showered with gifts. Ever since then, the holiday season triggered the same cynical boredom I felt when I spotted a con artist duping a stooge with an over-used trick. Christmas was a rip-off.

But now, I would have to make it up to each of them somehow. Buy gifts for the first time ever.

I went back into my office.

I lay back and closed my eyes, shoeless on the couch. The only person I really wanted to see was off-limits and belonged to another world.

I refused to think about him.

The French brandy on the side table would make forgetting easier. Surely I should toast the sad demise of Sophia Spark and then forget about her? I didn't want to imagine her life, her lonely past, maybe an even lonelier death in a cold, bombed-out city, coughing up her guts.

I should at least make a toast to her mother, Tatiana, whose deathbed wish I had failed to fulfil. 'Cheers, Tatiana, rest in peace. Sorry for wasting your money.'

At least Tatiana was spared the sad fate of her daughter. Ignorance is bliss, even if you have to die to stay in the dark.

I got up and picked up the bottle, admiring my newly painted red nails. Wasted on me. I began to twist the stopper, but paused. I twisted it right back.

One sip would surely lead to another.

And another.

Hitting the hooch over the holiday would be a good fix for the looming clouds of dread.

But a hangover, puffy face, dark rings, and a foul mood would get the New Year and job-hunting off to a bad start.

I'd take Barney's cue for life, no wallowing allowed. I would be a better woman. Elvira Slate wasn't a soak or an emotional screw-up.

I needed to stand on my own two feet and detective work was still the most viable option for me.

You can do this. You can make this work!

First things first. A holiday survival plan. I got a pen from my desk and started jotting down whatever came into my head.

Every morning, take a bath.
Dress up and put makeup on, even if not going out.
But make sure you do go out every day. Even if just to get a paper.
Keep nail varnish pristine.
Put pin curls in every night. Don't be lazy!
A movie a day for a whole week. Maybe two?
A light lunch. Coffee and a sandwich.
Dinner anywhere not dishing up turkey.
Go to Luigi's Italian!
Hit the town. But once only. Joyce's?
One drink.

I could allow myself a night out but no entanglements. Joyce's was a lesbian joint in West Hollywood, with a mixed clientele that spanned butches to Hollywood studio heiresses, a mixed bag of ages and races. Some men and transvestites frequented the joint, but were generally outnumbered by the gals. According to one rumor, Joyce said girls were less trouble.

I would stop at one cocktail. Joyce's cocktails were generally potent and possibly laced. One would be more than enough if I didn't want to crash the car.

Out of nowhere, the telephone rang. The business line, on Barney's desk. On Christmas Eve? Was he right? Were homicidal impulses already kicking in all over the city?

12

I ran back into his office, and picked up the heavy receiver.

'Hello?'

'Elvira Slate?' A woman's voice. Crisp, educated, more than a little tense.

'Who's asking?'

'Someone who needs a PI, fast.'

'You gotta do better than that. Christmas Eve, in case you hadn't noticed.' My blasé attitude hid my growing excitement.

'All right. This is Sonia Parker.'

She said it like it meant something. My silence put her right. I could hear a withering sigh. 'The defense attorney?'

'If you say so.'

'You play hard to get, don't you? I need someone who can start tonight. Are you available?'

'Depends what for.'

There was a pause, as if she was thinking about how to handle the evasive Miss Slate. 'Starts with 'M'. Why don't you start guessing and I'll tell you all about it when you get down here?'

With that, Sonia Parker gave me a Downtown address and told me to make it snappy.

I hung up, slipped on my blue snakeskin shoes and threw my gray gabardine jacket over my navy wool dress. The jacket was becoming my favorite garment as it fitted most bills: stylish, comfortable and, most important, unremarkable. June had made this for me, too. Its buttons matched the gray perfectly, oval and concave, like somebody had pressed a thumb into soft clay. June had softened the edges of the collar into curves and given the pockets a depth that would take a pistol rather than a lipstick.

June refused payment, typically. We'd gone to a department store and chosen the fabric and satin silk for the lining.

I bet she purchased the red velvet on that day. Sneaky.

I buttoned up to my neck and tied Barney's scarf around my neck. It matched the jacket perfectly, and I knew then he'd chosen it specially.

I opened my gold compact, powdered my nose and rummaged in my purse for my lipstick. *Ruby Dream.*

My nails wouldn't go to waste after all. I fluffed up my hair and put on my gray fedora hat, with its thick black ribbon, tilting it to the front.

I looked the part. A working girl, one that didn't stop for Christmas Eve. Better than my loser reality, somebody with nobody to see and nowhere to go.

I grabbed my cigarettes, lighter, and the battered leather black purse I took everywhere.

For good luck, I popped Beatty's magnifying glass into the purse, next to a small flashlight, my leather gloves and a small case of hairpins.

I was forgetting something.

My pistol.

'M' obviously stood for murder, so I had better be prepared.

I went back to my desk and slid the gun into the purse. I had an underarm holster, but it was bulky and ruined the line of most of my outfits. Holsters were designed for guys with loose-cut jackets who didn't carry purses.

I switched off the lights before walking out, looking at the glowing tree. It was pretty.

I met the fairy's eyes.

'Fast work,' I said.

Just like me, crime doesn't do Christmas.

4

A compact bundle of chinchilla in female form stood before me in the Downtown office. Sonia Parker's short black hair was curled around her pointy face. But she was no pixie. One tough cookie. I could tell that from her hard eyes now looking me over.

A long, dark, bluish-gray satin evening gown flowed down from under the fur coat like liquid mercury, forming a shimmery column over her green satin sandals.

Most definitely a dame with parties to go to.

'Miss Slate?'

I nodded. "Elvira is fine."

'Sonia Parker. Sorry to drag you out on Christmas Eve.' She didn't sound that sorry.

She wore an emerald-cut jade bracelet that jangled as she held out her hand and matching jade and gold earrings. Her iron grip said, *Trust me, I'm a lawyer.*

'Lucky to catch me. Just finishing up for the holiday.'

Sonia gave a wry half-smile, as if I had contradicted something she'd been told. 'Well, crime and good timing don't go hand in hand, do they? We can talk inside.' Sonia's eyes darted around the empty corridor behind me.

The cautious type.

She showed me through the glass door. The gold lettering screamed out *WISE, SPECTOR, BERGMAN AND PARKER, ATTORNEYS-AT-LAW.*

The lettering was far bigger and flashier than mine.

It was dark, but I could see the reception area was plush with a pale thick carpet, low chairs around a coffee table, and a gleaming front desk. The light from the streetlamps and decorations adorning Broadway below bounced off the chrome fittings.

Sonia closed the door and didn't turn the lights on until she'd closed the blinds. 'Windows have eyes,' she said. 'Take a seat. Want a coffee?'

'Thanks. Black.' I looked around. Now the lights were on, I could see the carpet was blue, with a luxurious sheen to the pile. The chairs looked like some kind of walnut, with darker chenille cushions.

'What's the accent? Can't make it out.' She looked at me, quizzically.

I was used to this. I'd never quite eradicate my London twang. 'I spent some time in England, before the war.' My stock response, true enough and sketchy on details.

She absorbed this and left the lobby area through a door marked *Private*. I heard her talk to someone else. Low voices.

Women's voices? The client?

She returned. 'I'd invite you in, but no point in dragging things out if you can't help. I've got a ticker bomb about to explode.'

'Fair enough. Who recommended me?' I asked.

'Dede Dedeaux. Called from Aspen. Luckily I was at home, hosting a party.'

'Dede? Okay.' My landlady! Was she in trouble? I deadpanned, waiting for more.

'Dede's footing the bill. Your contract will be with me. Dede's name stays out of it, now and later, if things go sour. In the eyes of the world, I'm doing this *pro bono*. I'm hoping of course, we don't end up in court. That's where you come in.'

'Big law firm like this, don't you have your own investigator?' I asked.

It was hardball posturing on my part; Sonia Parker didn't look like someone you declined, and Dede Dedeaux, as my landlady, definitely wasn't.

And you're desperate!

'Dede says you'll do what it takes. Besides, it's always good to have more investigators to call on.'

I felt a 'but' coming. And it did. 'But you're the first woman investigator I've used. Hope you are up to the job.'

So she trusted the boys more. But Dede had insisted and here we were.

'So, what do you want me to do?'

'It's very simple. Your job will be to look into matters—and only those matters—which I specifically request you investigate. You will report back. You won't question, you won't hypothesize and most of all, you will not undertake any unauthorized activity. You will work exclusively for me. Your job is to get what I need, when I need it, and you must not compromise the case by any unwise moves. My job is to defend my client.'

So far, so restrictive. I nodded. 'Fair enough.'

'My client is a young woman. A shopgirl and sometime vocalist in an all-girl band. Swing Shift Maisies, I expect.'

I wondered if it was The Charmettes, Alberta's band. I had only seen them play once or twice, but each time the vocalist had been different. Once, it was a tiny white blonde with a massive voice, another time a glamorous black woman who looked like a star. Was the client either of these?

17

Sonia offered me a cigarette from a shiny case. I accepted.

We lit up. I could see tiny beads of perspiration on her cheeks. She immediately placed her cigarette in an astray on a stand to slide out of the heavy fur coat. 'Jeez, too warm for December.'

Actually, the office was a fridge, but I said nothing. I'd spent enough time incarcerated with women to know when they hit fifty, they develop some kind of inner pizza oven.

A male PI wouldn't offer sympathy on any women's issues, so neither would I.

Then again, surely Sonia Parker wouldn't be so obvious about her temperature changes with a guy. Was it a test? To see if I'd get sucked into women's talk?

Without the coat hiding it, the dress was even more divine. The satin draped elegantly, and the neat gathers and pleats worked wonders to refine her chunky physique. Sonia read my thoughts. 'Most people wrongly assume *haute couture* is an indulgent luxury. It's good value for money. I bought this old thing in Paris in 1934.'

'Very nice.' I feigned indifference. How much would a frock like that cost nowadays? At least ten murder cases—the rich types, for whom a decent defense would be small fry.

Sonia went on. 'My client discovered a body. But there's a problem. She didn't call the police. She ran.'

'Why?'

Sonia exhaled, meeting me straight in the eye. 'Panicked. Thought the killer could still be around. The deceased was her beau. A new one, been seeing him for a month or so. Then she called her friend, who called Dede Dedeaux. Dede got hold of me, and here you are.'

'The friend being Alberta, by any chance?'

She nodded. 'You know her?'

I nodded back.

'Then I won't have to introduce you.'

My mind raced. The client calls Alberta who calls Dede who calls her upmarket lawyer friend to handle the case and instruct me. All on Christmas Eve. Seemed like the client was special.

'The fee is one hundred a day, plus expenses. Is that satisfactory?'

One hundred bucks a day? I tried to hide my delight. 'It's fine.'

At that moment, the door opened. Alberta entered, with a cup and saucer. She looked drained and frazzled. Underneath her black swing coat, she wore a red formal gown, edged at the hem with a thick band of white faux fur, and dangling gold Christmas tree earrings. Vibrant red poinsettia flowers and fake holly boughs were pinned to the side of her head. I stood up.

'Hi, Alberta. How are you?' I took the saucer.

'Been better, Miss Slate.' She normally called me Elvira but was clearly keeping up a pretense for Sonia's benefit.

'So...were you playing tonight?'

'Uh-huh. At Joyce's.' Alberta turned to Sonia. 'Dolly's as ready as she's gonna be.'

Dolly. I mentally filed the name.

Sonia nodded. 'No more hysterics?'

'I'm doing my best. She ain't so easy.'

'All right. Well, bring her in as soon as she's rational.'

'Yes, ma'am.' Alberta left the room, glancing at me. If she could have said, *'Who the hell is this bitch?',* she would have.

Sonia turned to me. 'When they arrived, Dolly was out of

her mind, so I've mainly gleaned the facts from Alberta. Dolly found her lover dead in bed with a cleaver in the chest. She panicked like I said, and ran, using the escape. But the concierge definitely saw her entering earlier. She'll be prime suspect as soon as the body's found and the guy's questioned.' She paused. 'To me, a knife in the heart has a personal touch.'

'Unless it's set up to *look* personal.'

Sonia ignored this. I remembered I wasn't supposed to hypothesize.

Better get used to the one-way street!

'Can I ask a question?'

'Go ahead.'

'Was he dead for sure?'

'Let's hope so. Not helping a dying man equates homicide.'

'Do you know who the lover is?'

'Ronald Hunter, big cheese. The Hunters of Pasadena. The family made a pile from munitions. Ronald Hunter inherited the fortune and business.'

I was still clueless about the city's great and good. Or maybe the not-so-good, because in my limited experience, men with money and power were rarely boy scouts.

Sonia studied me carefully. 'Dede mentioned you were new in town. You've got some homework to do about LA's movers and shakers if you're going to make it big here.'

'I'm not interested in making it big, just earning enough to pay my way.'

She didn't comment on my aspirations to an insignificant life.

'Hunter had political ambitions: he wanted to stand for Mayor of Beverly Hills. He fought in World War I. So, a hero.

20

Leaves behind a first wife, a beautiful second wife and a bunch of kids. First marriage, all girls. Second marriage, a young son. But for some reason, Hunter was playing away with a lower-class lady. How he and Dolly even met, God only knows. Then again, nothing surprises me in this town.'

She eyed me. 'Your first task will be to go to the love nest and observe. I want you to make a note of who shows up. Hunter's a millionaire tycoon—somebody is sure to come looking. Maybe someone who knows about the apartment. I want to know who.'

'So I surveil, then tail?' I couldn't exactly ask for anybody's name.

Sonia shot me an irritated look. 'Obviously. While you're there, Dolly and I will go to the police station nearest the apartment to report what happened. Then there'll be fireworks. Don't stick around for when the police and ambulances arrive.'

I couldn't tell her how relieved that made me. Hanging out in the immediate vicinity of LAPD officers on Christmas Eve was definitely not my idea of fun.

The door opened again. We both turned. Behind Alberta, a skinny blonde girl floated in, in a daze. Dolly Perkins was a lost wraith. She was in her early twenties, if that. Her dress was exactly the same as Alberta's, bright red with white fur. The only difference was she had a long white fur stole around her shoulders. She clutched at this like a blanket.

Her poinsettia hair clip was dangling over her ear. Tears had smudged her mascara and the rims of her eyes were bright red, almost the same color as her dress. Her chapped lips were mottled with the remains of scarlet lipstick. Naturally chubby cheeks made her head look somewhat too big for her tiny body.

The mass of messy curls didn't help the lack of proportion.

Disheveled, but definitely familiar. She was the same white singer that I'd once seen at Joyce's with The Charmettes.

Sonia said, 'Hi, Dolly. Come in and sit down. Miss Slate is helping me with your case.'

Dolly surveyed me briefly. Then she glared at Sonia. 'I swear to God, I didn't kill Ronnie. I loved him. And he was going to take care of me!' Her childlike body contorted with involuntary shudders.

'All right. Calm down. Take a seat.' Sonia said, not exactly warm.

Sniffing, Dolly obeyed and sat on the sofa. Alberta joined her. 'Will I go to jail? I can't!' Dolly whispered, staring up at Sonia, and then to me. 'What about the baby?'

'Baby?'

I looked at Sonia for her reaction.

Weariness and surprise duked it out on her face.

5

Dolly was bawling. 'I'm having Ronnie's baby! He promised he'd take care of us, and now somebody's done that terrible, wicked thing to him. Who would do that? Why?'

'How far gone are you?' Sonia barked.

'A month? God's blessed us!'

I focused on my nails. Babies weren't necessarily blessings. They could ruin lives.

Sonia snapped, 'Dolly, Hunter was married. He has kids.'

'I know. But we loved each other.'

Sonia's pen hovered over her notepad. 'All right. Let's take it from the beginning. What time did you get there?'

'Around nine. Ronnie said he had something special for me. A gift.'

'But didn't you have plans to sing with Alberta?'

'Sure I did. I meant to head down to Joyce's. Afterwards. We play kinda late.' She looked a little ashamed.

Sonia looked confused. 'Joyce's? Is that a nightclub?'

Dolly blurted out, 'Yeah, for ladies who like the ladies. I'm not that way inclined myself, but we're all God's children, right?'

I briefly met Alberta's eyes. She was deadpanning. It was an *I know you know, but we're both gonna pretend we don't know* look.

Dolly turned to Alberta. 'I didn't mean to let the girls down. You'll tell 'em for me?'

'Wanda's got it. Don't you worry about that.' Alberta's voice was soothing.

'Wanda's got a real good voice. Better than mine.'

'You're just different. Nobody's better.' Alberta smiled indulgently.

'I'll be there tomorrow! Can't miss that!'

Sonia interjected sharply. 'Best not to count on that.'

'Why?' Dolly looked genuinely surprised. 'I didn't do nothing bad!'

'You discovered a body and there are official steps to follow. That can take time.'

She was bluffing. She could not risk Dolly having a fit of hysteria right now.

'Go on.'

'So I go up by the stairs, don't like elevators. Make me feel like a chicken in a coop! Chitchatted with the doorman. Bogdan, or something. Think he's Romanian. He likes me, friendly guy. The door was unlocked. Ronnie does that sometimes, if he's already in bed waiting for me to do Baby Dolly.' She lowered her lids.

'Baby Dolly? What do you mean?' Sonia asked.

Dolly pulled a coy expression. 'Our little game, I dance for him in something pretty. Skimpy lingerie. But he don't say nothing, figure he's asleep. So I get in bed and snuggle up. Next thing I know, something's all wet. Cold and sticky stuff. Thought he'd gotten sick, or something. Then I feel that horrible great big knife. Stuck right here.' She patted her heart. 'I hollered! His skin was like ice. That's when I knew he's dead! I thought, maybe they're still inside, maybe they're coming for me, too! I fling my clothes back on and just ran. Down the fire escape.'

'Why?' I asked. Sonia turned, amazed I had the audacity to ask her client a question.

Dolly's eyelids fluttered down. 'Had to, is why. Ronnie said nobody could know about us. I promised him I wouldn't tell a soul.'

Sonia interrupted. 'But you said the doorman knew you. Hunter must have been okay about that, so why not ask him for help? He could have called the cops, or an ambulance.'

Dolly's eyes glanced sidelong at her attorney. 'Ronnie was dead, I tell ya! Nobody could bring him back! You blamin' me? I couldn't do nothin'! I couldn't save him!' With that, she burst into tears.

Full-blown hysterics were a second away.

I studied Dolly's crumpled face. An irritating child. Hunter may well have drilled secrecy into her, but the fact Dolly was unable to foresee any consequences to her actions in the heat of the moment was plausible enough. I bet she couldn't do it in ordinary life.

Alberta passed Dolly a handkerchief. 'There, there, honey.'

Sonia's face was blank, the lawyerly brain at work. 'Dolly. I'm not blaming you. But the police will ask exactly these questions, so we have to get the story straight.'

I looked at Sonia. 'May I ask another question?' Sonia flicked her hand impatiently. I turned to Dolly. 'Did you notice anything else in there?'

'Like what? I just ran. I called Alberta from a bar a few blocks along. She picked me up and brought me here.'

'Called her at Joyce's, you mean?'

Dolly nodded. Alberta did the same. Sonia lit up another cigarette, this time not offering them around. Her eyes flicked to Alberta, then back to Dolly. 'Did Hunter mention anything about any troubles with anyone? Family, business?'

25

'No. He said he liked me because he could just have fun.' Dolly sniffed. 'He don't get much with Her!'

'Who do you mean?'

'His wife is who. She don't treat him so good. She got her own life.' She rolled her orb-like eyes meaningfully.

'How did you meet him?'

'At the Tilsons Department Store. I work there. He came in with her. Our boss said he was interested in buying the store!' She looked down. 'Guess he took a shine to me. Told him I'm a singer. Next thing I know, he slips me his card. Said he knew somebody who could help my career.'

'Did the wife see any of this exchange?'

'No. She was busy shopping. Beauty products, I recall.'

'When did this happen?'

'Couple of months ago?'

Sonia jotted a few notes down. 'What about this 'something special'? The gift Hunter said he had for you. Did you find it?'

'No! Like I said, I ran.' Her mouth turned down, and she scowled, focusing on her hands in her lap. It was an odd expression, like a naughty child. Alberta, Sonia and I exchanged a look. Alberta asked. 'What's up, Dolly?'

'I think I done something real dumb.'

Sonia snapped, 'What?'

Dolly put her hand in her pocket and pulled out something flashy and gold. It was a man's wristwatch. 'It's Ronnie's.'

Alberta shot me a discreet *Oh, shit* look.

Sonia got up, walked over to Dolly and took it out of her hands. She held it up to the light. 'I can barely read the inscription.'

I rummaged in my purse, then produced Beatty's gift to me, the magnifying glass. 'Here.'

Sonia took it, without giving any indication she was impressed by me being so well prepared. She scrutinized the wristwatch under the lamp. When she was done, she passed the magnifying glass back to me. Slowly she walked over to Dolly, fixing her with an icy glare. 'How did you get it?'

'I took it.' Dolly looked down. Her caught-in-the-act naughty girl look couldn't get any more Shirley Temple.

'You mean to say you removed it from his dead body?'

Dolly folded her arms, staring defiantly into the distance.

There was a long silence. Sonia didn't move. Alberta clearly didn't relish Sonia towering over her and edged herself back along the sofa, slightly away from Dolly.

Sonia said, 'I asked you something. If you want me to help you, you need to answer.'

Alberta reached out, touching Dolly's arm. 'Girl, you gotta answer!'

Dolly glared up. 'Figure I can sell it and get me a pram, a crib or something. Ronnie said he was gonna get me the best of everything! How's he gonna do that if he's dead? Who's gonna look out for my baby? I can't do it on my own. No folks. Don't hardly earn a cent.'

She could get thousands of cribs with that watch.

Alberta said, 'Oh, Dolly. That sure ain't right.'

Dolly shot Alberta a fleeting look. I knew the expression. *It's all right for you.* Dolly's face crumpled into tragedy again. Alberta looked out the window, as if she was biting her tongue. Wishing she hadn't picked up the phone earlier, no doubt.

Sonia seemed oblivious to the dynamics. 'Which arm did you take it off?'

Dolly frowned, flustered. 'Hell, how should I know?'

'Well, you had time to think about taking it. Try to remember.'

Alberta got up, started to gather the coffee cups. She was finding this painful.

'I don't know!'

'Was he right- or left-handed?'

Dolly looked down, sobbing again.

Sonia finally moved back to her chair, studying Dolly. When she spoke, her voice was silky and cajoling, as if she was talking to a kid. 'Okay, Dolly. Focus as hard as you can. Close your eyes. What side of the bed were you, and how was he lying? Take your time.'

Dolly shut her eyes, imagining. Her mouth turned down. Then her eyes bugged open wide. 'The left. Yes, it was his left arm.'

'You're absolutely sure?'

'Yeah, he was on his side. Can I have it back, please? I'm gonna need the money real bad. I don't wanna have to give this baby up 'cause I'm broke.'

'You know who gave it to Hunter?'

'No.'

'Well, I do. Inscribed here, plain as day. *Devotedly, Linda.* Linda Hunter, his wife, we can safely assume. Don't you think she'll ask the police where it is?' The maternal tone was vaporizing by the second.

'Why? He could've just taken it off someplace before he met me. Or she could think those lying cops coulda took it. Bet those guys ain't above thievin'.'

'Sorry, Dolly. I can't let you keep it.'

'You going to give it back to her? But she's stinkin' rich! What about me?' Dolly whined.

I looked at Sonia. Was she going to just lose the wristwatch?

Sonia stared icily at her client. 'Did you close the apartment door behind you?'

'I think so.' Dolly looked a bit vague. 'Ain't locked.'

'One last thing, do you have any priors?'

Dolly was all indignation. 'I do not.'

Sonia gave Alberta a fake smile. 'Take Dolly into my office for a moment.'

Alberta held the tray of cups. She nodded to Dolly. 'C'mon, Doll. Let's give the ladies some time.'

Dolly stood up.

'You gonna help me, right? Get me out of this jam? You know, I think somebody's been following me!'

'What?'

'A man. Waitin' around my rooming house.' Dolly explained she had seen an overweight middle-aged man, sitting in a green car. Twice. She was vague on details. Sonia sat down, and jotted a few notes. 'All right. Thanks, Dolly.'

With her free hand, Alberta opened the door to let Dolly through. Then she looked back at me, with a *This is bad, isn't it?* expression.

With Dolly's fingerprints on the weapon, a stolen wristwatch and, last but not least, the doorman seeing her in the lobby, it was hardly looking good.

My mind raced. If it had been a premeditated killing motivated by greed, Dolly had plenty of time to hide the wristwatch before she called Alberta. It wasn't the kind of thing you forgot you had on you. Taking the watch was, surely, pure desperation?

I'd been there before, in the past. Wanting to feather your

29

nest any way possible when bigger birds were circling to finish you off. Survival brings out the selfish risk-taker in people. But any half-decent prosecutor could convincingly twist desperation into motive to kill.

When we were alone, Sonia let out a long sigh. 'The prosecution could have a field day. She's broke, pregnant by a man who—it could be alleged—was giving her the brush-off. So she takes vengeance every way possible. Kills him on the spur of the moment, takes a valuable item. To top it all, her prints are probably on the weapon. Unless we pull something out of the bag, she's probably halfway to death row.'

I wasn't sure if I was allowed to join in with her musing.

'Pretty good frame-up, then. What about this guy? Could be suspicious?'

'Could be a neighbor, anyone. Fat, middle-aged, and a green car!'

I wasn't sure I agreed. The real killer could easily be spying on the affair. Or using somebody to do it.

Sonia flicked over the Hunter wristwatch and checked the time. 'You should go. It's coming up to two hours since she left Hunter.'

I stood up.

Sonia followed suit. Then she dangled the watch out, with a curious look on her face. Rather like an imperious mistress ringing a bell for a serving girl.

A look that conveyed, *I'm not done with you.*

And then she said the unthinkable. 'If nobody has arrived, break in and put this back on the body. And wipe any prints off the knife while you're at it.'

6

I knew the private investigator's lot would be risky. To get results, you put yourself on the line. Bluff your way through dicey situations, maybe pay a bribe if the cops find you snooping where you shouldn't. Even better, make friends with the right cops. Have names to drop and strings to pull.

Or you play it safe with divorce cases or missing persons. Cases where honey trapping sleazy spouses is the biggest thrill of the job. Rarely encountering law enforcement.

And then there were the fictional PIs. I'd read enough detective novels in the clink, hand-me-downs from do-gooders. I could never relate to these private detectives. The hero was always a prig, judgmental and moralistic. He or she never had to slum it, to steal to survive, or do a spell in the joint. They showed the cops up as fools, but they were always on the same side. And they could blend in, because society respected them. Everybody was impressed when they made mugs of the cops by cracking the case.

The truth was, I had no idea what kind of sleuth I was. *Ex-con Private Investigator* would not look good on my calling card.

Whatever type I would end up, this case was fast shaping into something well out of my league.

Sonia Parker was asking me to do something blatantly criminal and didn't seem too bothered about it.

Low-key infidelity cases suddenly began to look very appealing.

If I was caught at the crime scene wiping down a blade stuck in a very dead body, or shoving a priceless wristwatch back on

31

the corpse, I was dead meat. In custody, how long before they cottoned on Elvira Slate was a fake? There were no genuine records verifying her existence.

How long could I hold out in an interrogation?

Being at the scene was bad enough, but tampering with the body and destroying or handling evidence? Any two-bit prosecution attorney could make mincemeat out of me. And would Dede Dedeaux be so keen to stump up for *my* legal fees? Would Sonia Parker be on my team?

Interesting question.

Up till recently, I believed I would shoot my brains out rather than let myself get caught. I could not risk anyone seeing my face in the papers. If anyone recognized me as Jemima Day, or Ida Boyd, it wouldn't just be me who faced trouble.

Detective Randall Lauder could also get in deep shit. At best, finished professionally. Worst? He would face a long stretch. He was an LAPD vice detective who had lied to Scotland Yard, telling them Jemima Day was dead, to get them off my back. And with the word out I was dead in Blighty, he had got the mob off my back too. The Little Italy crew had been after me for killing two of their own as I escaped London.

Two birds, one stone.

If I owed anyone anything, I owed him. Thanks to him, I was beginning to like life again, stretching out in the sunshine, feeling free.

Lauder wanted me to be the safe, low-key type of PI. I couldn't blame him. We hadn't yet discussed the big *what if*? What if I was ever caught and questioned?

Now I wish we had.

Sonia's words sliced into my reverie. 'Right now, there's a slim window for damage control.'

I blinked hard. 'Yeah. A window slamming down hard on my fingers.'

She shot me one of her now familiar steely glares. 'So Dede was wrong? You won't do what it takes?'

'I will, within reason. Does this sound reasonable to you?'

'Of course. I wouldn't be asking otherwise, would I?'

I got it. It was a means-justify-the-ends situation to her.

I got up, pacing the room. 'If *I'm* caught, at best I'm tampering with evidence. Second best, breaking and entering. Then what? Then I'm accessory to the fact of murder, after the fact, or whatever the frickin' fact. I'll be replacing Dolly in top billing for prime suspect.'

Sonia looked down, picking at invisible fluff on her grand gown. 'If you're changing your mind, say so. Now. If Dolly's found guilty, they'll let her keep the baby a few hours after birth. Then she'll be executed. I don't know about you, but that doesn't sit well with me.'

Below the belt. I swallowed hard.

It certainly did not sit well.

In my own stretch in His Majesty's Prison Holloway, there had been enough convict mother and baby separations. The women went nuts. The babies howled, endlessly. Dolly in that situation? She'd be destroyed.

And Dolly's baby deserved to start out in life with its doting mother. Dolly was sentimental as hell, and I had a sneaking suspicion babies went for that kind of thing.

Another orphan was not what the world needed. Another helpless brat, learning the hard way that nobody gave a damn.

A triple whammy of sick feelings slugged it out in my stomach: responsibility for Dolly's life, concern for her kid's welfare, and fear for my own and Lauder's lives.

The exact same reason I hated Christmas would be why I would act the sucker now.

A baby changes everything.

The baby was Sonia's trump card but she couldn't know she'd played it.

'Fine. I'll do it!' I snapped. But I didn't have to be happy about it.

One hundred bucks a night would help.

'Good. If this works out the way I want, we could use you again.' She gave me a meaningful look.

'What if the cops are already at the scene? Or somebody's discovered Hunter already? What should I do?'

'Do nothing. Leave. I'll be in touch. And remember to take a good look around while you're inside. Look out for that gift.'

I nodded. 'You know Hunter's address? I mean the family residence?'

'Why?'

I explained that there would be no harm in scouting for any activity at the Hunter residence, whether I could get into the love nest or not.

Sonia thought about this. 'All right. I'll give it to you. But be discreet and don't improvise. I'll call you in the morning, then I'll decide on the next steps.'

7

The dark streets were illuminated with Christmas lights. If I got caught, these could be the last I ever saw.

The engine purred. No grunts or groans tonight. Good. Mabel, my car, was in fine fettle. An old late '30s maroon model, she wasn't really mine, just loaned from my mentor. Sitting inside Mabel was like having a big protective hug from Beatty.

I could do with one of those right now.

Sonia's final and hurried instructions rang in my ears. If nobody had showed up yet at Hunter's, I must act fast. I had an hour, tops: the thirty minutes' drive from Downtown to Brentwood, where Hunter's love nest was; ten minutes for me to do what I had to; twenty minutes for any hitches. She didn't specify what these could be.

When exactly sixty minutes was up, she'd take Dolly to the police station. Dolly would report her grisly discovery and say shock had paralyzed her and being in the family way, she'd taken weak, and had to rest on a bench. Then she had come to her senses and called Sonia. How Dolly and Sonia knew each other was attorney client privilege.

Sonia didn't want Alberta anywhere near the cops, not even to provide an alibi for the duration of three hours, or to say that she had picked Dolly up. 'Next thing you know, they'll be pinning it on her.'

She had shot me a meaningful look. Alberta, being black, could become an easy target.

Dolly had to wipe what really happened from her mind. No

Alberta, no office, no me, no watch. Demanding so much from her seemed high-risk to me.

'Do you think she'll remember all this?' I asked. 'She's pretty cut up.'

And not all that smart, I thought.

'She's smarter than she looks,' Sonia had said, mindreading. Her parting shot had been odd. 'Ronald Hunter was obese. He must have crushed Dolly in the sack.'

With that, she handed me the wristwatch. It was even heavier than I thought. Numbers sparkling with gems— diamonds, maybe—but I didn't have time to admire it. I just stuffed it in my top left pocket.

Now it periodically thudded against my heart, with every turn of the wheel. A dead weight.

I drove on. Luckily, no traffic. I hoped Christmas Eve meant fewer patrol cars on the street.

Only twenty minutes for hitches.

Unexpected traffic. A tire blowing. The fuel gauge out of order.

I was riddled with anxiety, my palms sweating inside my gloves. I tried to calm myself. I had to do this. If I impressed a rich lawyer like Sonia Parker, '46 could be boom time at Elvira Slate Investigations.

But dread persisted like a starving rat, chewing on my innards, turning them to mush.

I looked out and slowed down. I was here. I cruised past the grand apartment block.

All was still, as it should be on Christmas Eve.

Go in and get the hell out.

8

Lush planting edged both sides of the wide tiled path: a mixed bag of cacti, succulents and neat little palms. Well-tended banana trees and yuccas had been jazzed up with Christmas lights, and produced a dramatic jungle effect, like a movie set for a tropical musical. The main door to the lobby was topped with ornate, carved stonework.

The light in the lobby was still on, and beyond it, the obligatory twinkling lights of a big Christmas tree in the lobby. The concierge, the Romanian, might have his feet up on the desk taking a snooze, or so I hoped.

I cut across the planting to get to the rear of the building. Something scratched my leg. Great. A run in my stocking and blood on my leg wouldn't help if I were apprehended.

I dived into the shadows, heading for the small path that led to the rear yard, staying close to the back of the building. My plan was to get in exactly the way Dolly had fled, the fire escape.

I reached the back of the hotel. The fire escape zigzagged up the pale building, like black stitching on white cloth.

On each floor, the metal structure widened into a platform with a door into the building, Further along every platform, there was a second window belonging to an apartment.

My flat gumshoes, that I kept in the trunk, kept my ascent quick and silent. I reached the fourth floor fast.

Something caught my eye. Something wedged in the bars of the metal platform.

A lipstick?

I bent down, prized out the shiny gold tube, and slipped it into my pocket. Lipstick. *Mayberry*, an expensive brand.

I took a deep breath and pushed the door open.

It was dead quiet inside the fourth-floor lobby. Cone-shaped pink frosted wall lights protruding out of brass holders gave a soft peachy glow. There were four doors leading off the main area, all a decent distance apart, each one numbered. I froze, to listen better.

Nothing, except for the indiscreet thud of my heart.

I dashed to number 401. The door was closed as Dolly had said. I tried the handle. Unlocked.

I pushed open the door, reaching for my flashlight, then closed it behind me.

It was gloomy inside, but the lights had to stay off.

Windows have eyes.

Using the flashlight, I tiptoed along the hall, peering into each room, every muscle tense. The whole place reeked of expensive functionality. The bathroom was spacious. White marble tiles, a towel crumpled on the floor.

Thankfully, no overpowering smell of death.

I stood outside what could be the bedroom. I took a deep breath, and stepped inside. The drapes were shut. I pointed the flashlight at the bed, bracing myself for horrors.

And there he was.

His vast torso illuminated in the moonlight like a harpooned white whale. I approached the bed.

The wound around the knife had dried, leaving bloodstains, dark ribbons like the laces of a corset, trailing over his expanse of chest. The blood gave off a stale odor similar to a butcher shop.

I heaved, but somehow held it back.

A white sheet only partially draped his lower half. For a large man, his penis was shriveled and tiny, lolling across his dark and shiny scrotum.

I moved closer to the bed.

Hunter's eyes were open. His lashes were thick, pale and blunt, his eyelids papery. In her panic, Dolly didn't close his eyes. There was something innocent about them. The mouth was open, the dark tongue sagging back into his head. It sure looked like somebody knew where to strike and how.

Dolly had spindles for arms. There was no way she could thrust a knife in with such force. This was a guy's doing, or a very strong woman.

I studied Hunter's face again.

Who killed him? Who hated him that much? Did he somehow deserve this?

Stop dreaming. Put the watch back on and scram!

I quickly slipped the watch on his wrist. Hunter's body was in full rigor mortis, horribly convenient for the task in hand. While my gloves prevented me touching his skin, they slowed me down. I didn't look at him again as I fumbled with the clasp. Then I wiped down the handle of the knife with the sheet.

As I got up, I noticed something on the floor. A handkerchief? It was white, good quality silk, with a dark and elegant embroidered monogram with the letters R.A.H. Bloody fingerprints covered it like polka dots. Dolly's?

I picked it up and snuck it into my purse. Found in my possession, I'd be done for. Leaving it there was out of the question.

My flashlight danced around the walls. I couldn't see anything remotely gift-like.

But I saw something else.

The word *LIER*, scrawled in large, messy writing on the walls, in what looked like thick crayon. Somebody couldn't spell.

Dolly hadn't mentioned this at all. Had she even seen it?

Lier. Somebody jilted or cheated on? *A crime passionel*?

I went closer, shining light on the letters. Lipstick? I had my own hankie in my purse, so I blotted it on the letter *L*. Later I could check if it matched the lipstick I'd found.

Now I was in possession of two handkerchiefs, both laden with incriminating evidence.

BUZZ!

The intercom! My heart flipped over. Someone could be on the way up right now!

Time to bolt.

I slipped out the way I'd entered.

At the bottom of the escape, I snuck along the rear of the building to the side path. Voices came from the front of the hotel, stopping me in my tracks.

A woman whined, 'Where *is* he?'

A young man answered, 'Snoozin', probably. Let's get outta here. Mr. Hunter won't like it anyway, us burstin' in on him.'

'No, no. I have to try!'

'Sugar, you don't. She ain't worried for real.'

'But she said he told her he'd be home at eight.'

'She's playin' you! She wants you to keep tabs on him.'

'She sounded real upset. Even called me at home. I was eating with my folks. That's why I called you, when he didn't answer.'

The young man said, 'Upset, huh? Well, sounds like she put on a fine performance. Because from what I hear, she's got her own thing going on the side. Sugar, she used to be an actress, for Pete's sake. Look, I'll buzz again. No answer, we shoot back to my place!'

'But she gave me a message, I should tell him.'

'Maybe he's got business to finish off before the holiday. He said he'd call me when he's ready to leave. Come back to my place and wait. I'll keep you nice and warm.'

There was a moment while she thought about it. 'I guess you're right. But no funny business, Brad. I mean it.' She sounded tense.

I peered around the edge of the wall. A couple hovered outside the building's entrance.

She was short and curvy with curly hair under a bonnet-style hat. The guy, Brad, was wearing a uniform with a cap. Hunter's driver? He wasn't much taller than the girl but he was muscular. His arm was creeping around her shoulders, and he was whispering in her ear.

She looked cornered.

'Hey, what's that?' The girl said suddenly, taking the opportunity to wriggle away from him.

I dived back, pressing myself back against the wall. Had she heard me?

'That smell!'

I looked down. She was heading for a clump of flowers at the corner of the building. If she came too close, she'd see me. She'd used the plant to get away from him.

After a while she said, 'What if he's had an accident? He gets dizzy spells, you know.'

41

'How many times! Leave him be. I'm getting a dizzy spell just lookin' at you.'

'Oh, Brad, quit it!' She was irritated again. I didn't blame her. Brad was a persistent jerk.

'C'mon. Let's go.'

Suddenly she cried out, relief filling her voice. 'Look, there he is! Let's ask him if we can check on the boss.'

She ran away. I heard a rap on glass and the swing of a heavy door. Voices. And then silence. The door swung shut.

The doorman had let them in.

Time to go.

I waited ten seconds. Then I sprinted through the front garden and jumped over the wall. I reached Mabel and jumped in, panting.

I opened my purse and pushed both hankies through a hole in the lining I'd never had repaired. I tried my best to spread them out so they wouldn't make a bulge.

Now take off!

Mabel chose that moment to wheeze and cough. 'Great timing!' I cursed and tried again. She spluttered to a start. I patted the walnut wheel. 'Baby, you're kinda long in the tooth to be a getaway car, but don't let me down.'

Intrigued, I couldn't resist a peek through the rear-view mirror.

Nothing.

But in minutes, Hunter's staff would be knocking on the door to his apartment. When Hunter didn't answer, all hell would let loose.

Relief washed over me. I'd done it! I had information for Sonia. Hunter's *modus operandi* for his infidelity. That his wife might be suspicious. That the oversexed driver wouldn't put it past Linda Hunter to have an affair. And finally, the secretary was young, anxious. Keen to please.

Dolly would now be giving her story to the on-duty officer at some precinct.

Showtime.

9

It was only when I stopped at the first red light, I realized my whole body was shaking and my limbs were like jelly. Now I regretted saying to Sonia that I'd scout the Hunter residence, which was in Bel Air, an area I hardly knew. I just wanted to go home and curl up in bed after downing every drop of liquor I could get my hands on.

Was there somewhere nearby still open? I could knock one drink back and then lurk outside Hunter's for a while. But I wasn't dressed for any swanky nightclubs around this side of town. And I didn't have time on my side.

I spotted a liquor store and pulled up. I wasn't beyond swigging from a bottle in a brown bag, in the dark of the night.

Not classy, but needs must.

A young crowd were filling the place, noisily ordering bourbon and vodka. They'd already had a skinful. Probably movie industry types, the world at their feet, joking with the storekeeper who wore a Santa hat.

You should be like them, young and having fun.

The girls were in party frocks. One shot a pitying look at my working girl clobber. I didn't blame her. To even the score, I gave a quizzical look at her revolting green eye shadow, which clashed with her rosy skin.

I quietly ordered a bottle of scotch and slipped out.

Back in Mabel, I peeled off the brown paper and took a couple of glugs. Droplets trickled down my chin. So much for my resolve to have one swig, but what the hell, I *was* working, wasn't I? And I'd survived the unthinkable. The liquor had an immediate effect. My eyelids felt like lead. The after-effects of shock and tension were flooring me. I leant back, closing my eyes for a second.

I jolted upright, my stomach lurching.

How long had I been asleep? I checked my wristwatch. Thirty minutes!

What the hell are you doing!

I was parked beneath some street Christmas decorations. I grabbed the map to locate the Hunter residence. The gleam from the decorations enabled me to just make out the main arteries and the side streets.

Beatty's magnifying glass came in handy for the second time in one night.

I sped towards Bel Air, gazing in awe at the vast mansions behind the high clipped hedges. Every house was piped with fantastic Christmas lights. Glittery globes of splendor hung from white diamond festoons spanning the landscaped gardens.

Dreamy, idyllic scenes on Christmas cards, now come to life.

It wasn't hard to find the Hunter residence. A crowd of reporters jostled outside. There were a couple of photographers with cameras and flashes at the ready.

News had traveled fast. The law had somehow alerted the press. And my snooze on the job meant they had beaten me to it.

Cursing myself, I got out, quietly shut the car door, and lurked on the opposite side of the wide street. I stood underneath an ancient yew tree that cast immense dark

45

shadows. A murky specter, I could safely observe proceedings from here.

The chances of anyone coming or going from the house now to face this mob were slim.

The Hunter residence was an imposing pile with castellated towers. Arched gates protected a long gravel drive. The golden tips of the dark gates shone in the dark, and a family crest was molded in gold metal on the gates. The letter H was prominent in the design. The vast stained glass windows were edged with millions of red twinkly Christmas lights, all the more dramatic against the violet night sky.

The house wasn't that old, but it was meant to look like it was.

I tensed as two LAPD prowl cars screeched up. A uniformed officer jumped out, followed by his partner, who didn't look so enthusiastic. He yawned, tightening his belt over his considerable girth.

Working on Christmas Eve was a bummer.

The cops in the second patrol car didn't budge. Back-up muscle.

I needed to blend in. Joining the press wolf pack was for my own protection now. I brandished my pen and notebook to look more the part and moved out of the shadows.

A couple of reporters glanced at me, but not for long. All eyes were on the cops.

'Hey, you considerate men and women of the press, show's over.' The first cop put his hands on his hips in front of the gates. He didn't want to be here. 'You heard me, folks. Scram.'

A volley of questions flew at him like arrows. 'How long was Hunter dead?' 'Got the perp?' 'Who's the prime suspect?' 'Where's Linda Hunter?' The voices clamored like hungry seagulls.

'Show some goddamned respect and beat it. You wanna spend Christmas banged up?' He was red-faced. The press grumbled but got the message, slowly dispersing. I was among the first to move away.

'El?'

What?

Only one man in the world called me that. I turned.

Randall Lauder.

His expression was inscrutable. He was in a smart lounge suit with his usual snazzy tie.

As magnetic as ever.

Had he just shown up? Or had he slipped out of the side gate of Hunter's mansion, while the press surged on the cops? Why would a City Hall vice squad detective be talking to the spouse of a murder victim on Christmas Eve? I hadn't seen his car, but then, I hadn't been looking.

'Fancy meeting you here.' Said with a half-smile.

'What the hell are you doing here?' He growled. His eyes roved over my outfit.

'Working a case.' I hoped he couldn't smell the scotch on my breath. I stood back a little.

'What case?'

'A new one.' I shot him my best W*hat's it to you?* expression.

'For who?'

'Sonia Parker. You know, the defense attorney?'

His eyes glared at me. 'I know who Parker is.' *And I don't like her*, was the implication.

'It's work. What's the problem?'

He looked away, glancing at his watch before surveying the dispersing reporters. He was tense, assessing the risk of being seen with me. A couple of reporters were still haggling with the cops, but in a good-humored way. But if me and Lauder stuck around, somebody might butt in and expect an introduction.

He grimaced slightly. His voice was low. 'Follow me. Now. No stupid games.'

'Sure.' I answered, coolly. Damn. My scouting was over for the night, and I had nothing to add to Sonia's update, except a certain vice cop I knew was at the premises.

Should I even tell her about Lauder? Name him? That very much depended on what I got out of him.

I hopped into Mabel. Lauder got into a real shiny beefcake of a car. Promoted? He'd had a string of successful busts in the last few months; one major case had been entirely due to my help behind the scenes.

I didn't resent it, or the flashy car. Lauder could be bumped up to President of the USA off my hard work and I'd still be happy for him.

Maybe things were looking up for both of us, career-wise.

We both knew the drill. I'd follow him, at a distance. If he lost sight of me, he'd wait until I caught up. I gave it a full two minutes before I pulled away.

He drove westward, towards Hollywood. And then beyond, turning southwards, to one of the many tatty corners of the ever-sprawling city. Here, the streets were flanked with billboards and shopping malls. The sidewalks were edged with lanky palm trees.

This was a side of town the Hunters of this world would never venture, unless to buy up the land and pull down the frame houses, moving communities on and out, to build blocks

48

that the ordinary people couldn't afford. It was a side of town where the property magnates' hops, chauffeurs, maids and housekeepers lived modestly.

Jemima Day had died in the rubble of blitzed London. She was reborn as Elvira Slate in this side of LA.

Whatever ambitions I'd once harbored to break free and become someone better, someone classy, fate had brought me right down to earth. Being a private eye with offices in the Miracle Mile Hotel was as high as destiny would let me rise. And Elvira Slate still didn't feel like she belonged there.

Get over it, honey.

At one set of lights, I redid my lipstick—only to realize I'd accidentally used the one I'd found outside Hunter's place. Yuck! I shuddered.

I wiped it off quickly and stashed the tube down the lining of my purse.

Finally, Randall turned into the empty lot of the Astral Motel. The front office was dark, the blinds pulled down.

A *No Vacancies* sign hung in the door.

The Astral. I'd lived here for a while after Lauder bust me, and it felt like coming home.

Lauder was already at the door of Room 12, his key at the ready.

I followed, a little nervous. He was going to grill me, then read me the riot act. I stepped in as he closed the blinds and turned on a low lamp.

'Drink?' he asked.

I nodded.

He headed for the kitchenette at the end of the living room. He pulled a half-empty bottle of scotch and a couple of tumblers out of an otherwise bare cupboard. He filled them generously.

I didn't sit down on the couch, but chose instead to lean against the wall.

Lauder handed me a glass. Our fingers touched. 'Merry Christmas.' His eyes, blue as ever, bored into my soul, and another part of my anatomy.

'I don't do Christmas,' I announced, meeting his eye. 'More of a New Year's Eve kind of girl.'

'All right. To 1946.' He replied, his eyes locked on mine.

We chinked glasses and knocked the liquor back in one. Lauder took my empty glass, placing both on the counter.

'Why were you there? No lies, no secrets, no half-truths, remember?'

'A job. Relax, nobody saw me.'

'You were standing with the goddamn press!'

I met his eyes. 'Do we really have to do this now?'

Lauder came closer. He knew what I meant. He pressed me against the wall with his body. His hands roved down and pulled up my skirt. My hand slid between our wedged bodies to feel his cock. In seconds, we were pulling off each other's clothes, devouring each other's mouths.

Suddenly the sight of Hunter's corpse flashed through my mind, the pale ivory whale beached on a crumpled bed. Particles of his dead body swirling in the air were coating me, spreading onto Randall, infecting us. Hideous! I jerked away. 'I've got to take a shower.'

Lauder laughed. 'So do it. I'll meet you in bed.'

10

Randall Lauder was my off-limits lover. The one person I wanted to see at Christmas, the one person I tried to not ever think about when I wasn't with him.

Our romantic life was strictly black market.

And here we were now, in Room 12 of the modest Astral, hungrily making love as if it was tightly rationed candy.

In the course of a few months, we had gone from mutual hatred, to distrust, to confusion, to gratitude, settling at professional respect mixed with lust. One night, after too many drinks, the physical desire that had been there the whole time was unleashed. In one way, we had so many sordid enmeshments, sex was the most straightforward of the lot. I picked up the slack for Lauder's sex drive, and he did the same for mine.

I was a convicted felon, after all, and he was an ambitious vice detective, engaged to a hoity-toity uptown girl, who was saving herself for marriage. He hadn't ever told me that, I'd gleaned it elsewhere, but surely he knew I knew.

I'd never meet the parents. His life was totally off-limits— The Fiancée, the department—and I would never probe.

I didn't want to know, anyway.

My life was a totally different story. He knew everything and our deal was that my life was to stay an open book.

Lauder was the only reason I could live as Elvira Slate. He wasn't the first guy to help me out of a bad situation, but he was the first to put his good reputation on the line to save me from the noose.

The one-way nature of our relationship didn't prevent him from being up there with the best lovers I'd had. Maybe it helped. Turns out screwing a guy who knows all your dirty deeds and could bring you down if he wanted is kind of a turn-on.

But obviously, I could take him down too, so maybe he got the same buzz as me. Not so much love-hate as lust-fear. And having great sex softened the edges of being permanently in his debt.

More debt. I was drowning in debt.

Debt to the dead: Tatiana Spark.

Debts to the living: Randall Lauder and Beatty Falaise.

I focused on what we were doing. Sex was frantic but intense. Everything he did felt right. He wasn't the most generous lover, but I was a taker, too. It wasn't too intimate, or sentimental. Our bodies trusted each other more easily than our minds. They knew how to stroke, push, and move in unison. And tonight, he felt better than ever.

It had been two weeks since our last rendezvous and neither of us lasted very long. He climaxed first and pulled me on top of him while he was still hard. My body felt like a desert bloom opening up under intense heat.

Merry Christmas, Elvira!

I lay back in the twisted mass of bedclothes, a fat grin on my face, my eyes shut.

Lauder was breathing heavily, next to me. I opened my eyes and noticed now he'd lost weight. Was he overdoing it, working all hours?

I bit my tongue. Those questions were The Fiancée's prerogative.

His hand fumbled for mine. 'So...what's the deal?'

'Parker's helping somebody.' I needed to tread carefully. He probably knew more than I did. I couldn't very well tell him what I'd already been up to: consoling the suspect, shoving wristwatches onto the victim, removing evidence, and stashing blood-sodden hankies and evidence in my purse.

'And I need the work.' I sensed the waves of disapproval rolling my way.

'Why? Spark case keeps you fed and watered.'

'Sophia Spark is dead. I just found out. *Ipso facto*, money dries up with my final report to the trustees. I don't want to go bust come January, do I?'

Lauder thought about this. 'You sure she's dead?'

I met his eyes. 'As sure as I can be. Unless I get on a plane and try to dig a death certificate out of bomb dust.'

We both knew travel to Europe was not an option. Ever. Lauder had approved of me asking Lois to do it.

'How did she die?'

'Flu.'

'Rest in peace, Sophia Spark. But you gotta quit this case.'

'What? No! Why should I?'

'Don't act dumb.' Now he sounded just like the old him, the one I easily hated.

It was okay for him with his cushy job. I had a business to run. Besides, how could I just drop Dolly now? Going to Hunter's had been a crazy risk but worth it. And I'd made a hundred bucks in one night. Pull out now, I'd be history as far as Sonia was concerned. And Dede? She wouldn't be renewing the lease to a flaky tenant who walked away from a well-paid gig. Even if I wasn't evicted from the hotel, I'd be lucky to get a missing cat case sent my way.

'You know I can be very discreet,' I said.

He guffawed, rolling onto his side to look up at me. 'I also know you take chances. Like tonight, loitering with that pack of wolves. The *Hunter* homicide? Know how big this is? You, snooping for the defense? Get real. There's nowhere you can go on this case where Flannery or the press won't be sniffing around.'

'Who?'

He leaned over the bed and pulled his jacket towards him. He dug out a packet of cigarettes. 'Dale Flannery's leading the case and he's like that'—he put two fingers together—'with the DA. Golden boy of the department, with a run of convictions.'

The way he said 'Dale Flannery' sounded bitter. He pulled out a cigarette case and offered me one. Extracting it, I asked, 'A run of convictions? Oh, the usual type who doesn't give a damn if someone innocent goes down?'

'Suspect looks good for it. Fled the scene.' We lit up. So he knew a lot.

Infuriating. It was already sewn up. And Lauder's tone was high-handed. 'I see the LAPD hot wire's been humming, all right.'

He shrugged.

'Parker thinks it could be a frame-up.' I instantly regretted saying it. It was a lie; I had no idea what she really thought. Lauder knew something, that's why he was there, and however much he resented this Detective Dale Flannery, he certainly had no loyalty to me, to Dolly, or whoever I was working for. I had been totally indiscreet, breaking all Sonia's rules. I had revealed to Lauder, a cop, that she had instructed me.

'When did she ask for your help, by the way?'

I tensed up. 'A little earlier. Called me.' That was all he would get.

Change the subject, and fast!

I stroked his arm. 'So you're gonna bankroll me? Swish hotel suites don't come cheap. Nor secretaries. Remember Barney quit his job for me?'

He turned to me, his voice gentle. 'What have you done for Parker so far?' Funny. We were both trying to cajole the other.

'Just had a butcher's at the house, where you found me.' I lied.

'A what? Oh, "butcher's". Your limey slang again.' He rolled his eyes. 'Well, put your bill for "'aving a butchers" in the post.'

'Your accent sucks.' I pulled away, flicking ash onto the tin tray on the nightstand. Lauder's attempts to rein me in were antagonizing me, but he couldn't know it.

As I'd already broken Sonia Parker's rules, I may as well do it in style. A calculated indiscretion could swing it. 'Dolly Perkins is innocent. And she's knocked up.'

Lauder was genuinely surprised. 'By Hunter?'

I nodded. 'Between you and me, she loved him and she wouldn't hurt a hair on his head.' I asserted, crisply. 'Jail's no place for someone in her condition.'

'If she loved him so bad, maybe she should have called an ambulance.' He raised a sarcastic brow.

He definitely knows everything!

'She wanted to protect his reputation.'

'Oh, the thoughtful type.'

We sat up, shoulder to shoulder, puffing away. 'Other than screwing around, was Hunter a monster? His bullet factories doubling as gambling rackets or something?' I joked.

'Why?' He looked slightly irritated at my persistence.

'Well, why would you bother showing up on Christmas Eve

if his murder wasn't connected to something you're already sniffing around?'

'Why ask? You're done. Over. Period. So mind your own fucking business.'

Damn! I felt my check flush with anger. 'Whatever you're looking into has to be connected. It could be linked to the frame-up! You could help Dolly get off!'

'*Dolly*? You pals or something?'

'Of course not! Parker briefed me quickly.' I busily inhaled, avoiding his eyes.

'It's over, El. The case. And this conversation.'

My blood was now at boiling point. He wouldn't shut me up like this. 'What if the wife sprung for the setup? She could've easily found out about Dolly. Maybe Hunter has done this before. This way, she gains. She isn't humiliated. Why don't you tip your pal Flannery off about that?'

Randall snapped. 'First, he ain't my pal. Second, I'm not interested in Hunter's murder. Now quit it, or do I have to lock you up?'

I glared at him. 'What? What did you say?'

'Figure of speech.' His voice was flat.

'Charming. What, haul me in on a bogus Code whatever, bang me up for the night?'

'Shut the fuck up!' Lauder exploded.

There was a long silence. We'd both gone too far. Mutual regret filled the air like smog.

When he spoke, he sounded almost placatory. 'You've got to see sense. A singer has a hotshot attorney? She's got rich pals bankrolling her.'

'Maybe it's *pro bono*.'

'Get real. How much is she paying you?' He just wouldn't believe it.

'Fifty a week,' I lied.

'PIs are a dime a dozen. Press are gonna be all over Hunter's case. What if they take a picture of you, huh? Someone "has a butchers"? The mob maybe? You realize how many of your compatriots cross the pond?'

I froze. 'Like who?'

'Like people you don't want to know you're alive and kicking. Do I have to spell it out? Please, El. I gotta trust you'll walk away.'

For the past few months, the dread of somebody recognizing me had been locked away in a little box with the lid on tight. And now he was ripping it off. He didn't name names, but he didn't have to.

He looked at me, his eyes intense in the dark. 'Just stick to the nobodies. Safe cases. For both our sakes.'

This was the most desperate he had ever sounded. I was conflicted. I let out a heavy sigh. 'All right. But since we're being totally straight with each other, tell me something. If the worst happened, and I'm picked up, what do I do?'

Lauder exhaled. 'If it's mobsters, do what you gotta. Cops? I'll handle it. Stay silent. At all costs. Plead the Fifth, if it comes to that.'

'Oh, great. A real good look in court. Or I could just kill myself before it gets that far?'

'You're not the type.' But he glanced at me, and I could see the doubt in his eyes.

Faced with Holloway Prison or hanging, yes, I'd shoot myself. Would I do it to save Lauder?

Probably.

'It's funny. You said I was a natural investigator. You got my permit. But first job I get is off limits.'

'Something else will show up. If you run out of dough, I can cover fifty a week. Not like she's paying you a hundred a night.'

Damn. My lie had instantly backfired.

Lauder got out of bed. He looked down at me. 'I didn't want it to be like this. Are we done?'

I nodded. He was leaving on an order, and I didn't like it, either. I also didn't like the thought of facing Sonia Parker and telling her I was quitting.

But you've got no choice.

He grunted, picking up his pants. 'What are you doing tomorrow? Got plans?'

'Nothing special.' I didn't want his sympathy. I wouldn't ask about *his* Christmas Day; I could see it anyway. Some grand Hancock Park mansion, a beautiful tree next to a roaring fire, and The Fiancée in some flowing gown. And Lauder, acting the prodigal son-in-law.

It made me want to retch.

'Mrs. Falaise inviting you?'

'Beatty's gone sailing. And I wouldn't go even if she asked. I'm looking forward to being by myself. Hotel's nice and calm. I just don't like Christmas.'

He was rummaging around in his pockets for something. I never tired of looking at his physique. He was muscular but his long legs and broad shoulders always looked skinny. Now he reminded me of a white gopher.

I flinched inwardly. I didn't want him to go. I didn't want to share him. Sexually, he was mine.

At least for now.

I hated him, too. Ugh! What a mess.

Rule Number One for female ex-felons. Don't sleep with a cop who knows your past.

He found what he was looking for, stood up and handed me something. 'Then I won't say Merry Christmas.'

A small gift wrapped in tissue.

Another flinch. 'What on earth is that?'

'What does it look like? Open it.'

Why's everybody buying you gifts? Why is he giving you a gift?

Luckily it was dark, because I blushed. 'Well, I haven't got anything for you.'

I tore the tissue open. Inside, a gold necklace lay coiled on the white paper, with a single pearl on the fine chain. Shouldn't this go to Her? What was he up to?

I met his eyes. I said, awkwardly, 'It's pretty.'

'Put it on.'

Did I want to? Did I have a choice? Lauder came around and lifted my hair. The clasp clicked. He stepped back and put a side lamp on. He admired it, smiling fondly. 'It belonged to my favorite aunt, Jessie.'

'Jessie for Jessica?'

'Yeah. She reminds me of you.'

'What, a nutjob?'

'Just quit it for once, will you?'

I fondled the pearl. It felt surprisingly heavy, suspended on the chain. 'Thanks.'

I should be more gushing. Is that what he expected? Wrong girl. And I was still bruised about being kicked off the case. He gave me a quick smile, before he started getting dressed. His braces dangled as he pulled on his shirt. I watched as he buttoned it up, slid his jacket on, and knotted his tie. When was he going to take a shower? I wouldn't suggest he did now.

I wanted my scent on him, as much as he wanted this chain around my neck.

'I'm going away. Two-week vacation. Skiing in Colorado. Sure looking forward to getting out of the city.'

What? I felt like a bee had stung me, a burn that takes you a second to process that something is happening and that something is pain. What was he doing, mentioning his other life? Skiing? Colorado? Cavorting in the snow?

You don't want to know!

He glanced at me.

'You okay?'

'Sure.'

He bent down and kissed my lips. 'So long.'

I watched him head for the door. The motel door slammed shut.

So long.

11

Nine o'clock in the morning and the sun was bright. My first Californian Christmas Day.

I'd got back to a very silent hotel in the early hours, knocked back a couple of brandies, and fallen into a deep slumber. Sonia's call would be the closest thing I got to a good morning kiss.

Now, all over the city, kids were tearing presents open. Happy families everywhere, or maybe LA at yuletide was more like Barney's version. Heart attack and infidelity city.

My only experience of family Christmases were during the few years I lived with Gwendoline, my foster mother. She would shower me in pointless gifts: an easel and a set of watercolors, a potter's wheel, acting classes. I was overwhelmed; the gifts felt too good for me, but I played along. Her dream was for me to be the daughter she always wanted, to follow in her footsteps as an artist, or a performer. But I hated the limelight. I had no eye for art, my lines came out wooden and I was probably tone-deaf.

Gwendoline wasted a lot of money on a lost cause. Luckily, she remained blind to my weaknesses. She died happy, not knowing I would inevitably have let her down.

Just like Tatiana Spark.

I got up and made myself a coffee in the kitchenette and returned to bed.

I sat up, pulling the pillows up behind me. Why hadn't I just shut up shop and left for the holidays? I could be in Miami by now or, even better, Havana. I'd have checked into a seafront hotel and be downing tropical cocktails. By night, I could gamble my pennies away. At least I'd have some fun before going bust.

And I would have missed Sonia's call.

But I didn't go. Because I owed Tatiana Spark, and until her case was solved, no way could I blow the stipend on vacations.

At least I didn't have a turkey to baste.

I noticed the brass pendant lamp with the primrose yellow shade. A bulbous and ugly thing, dangling from three rusting chains, and probably installed when the hotel was built in the early '20s.

I'd told Barney not to bother fitting out my room, it was a waste of money. I'd given him an allowance for the main office and my back office. He'd done great with a painting, a piece of modern art from an artist friend in Venice Beach and furnishings from an insurance firm that was closing down.

Would it all prove a waste? Lauder had just snapped off my lifeline. How on earth did he think I was going to limp on? Take his money, and I would be little more than his whore.

I dreaded breaking the news to Sonia. By now, Hunter's death would be front-page news, even on Christmas Day. The press would be waiting to descend on anyone and anything connected to the case.

I thought of Dolly—incarcerated, and likely to stay that way.

The incriminating pieces of evidence were still in my purse, by the side of the bed. I reached over and extricated them.

Maybe I should just burn them anyway and bin the lipstick? I was off the case, and nobody needed to know.

But I was curious. I pulled the lid off the lipstick tube. A stub of squished scarlet wax remained. The rest was messily encrusted inside the lid, smearing my fingers. The color was identical to that on my hankie. And it had been dark, but I was certain a similar shade had been ingrained on Dolly's lips.

If it was a setup, somebody had been able to get pretty close to Dolly to pinch the lipstick. I wondered what Sonia would make of it.

Then I went into my bathroom. Barney never came back here, preferring to use the facilities for male guests, which were on the ground floor. I found my screwdriver and undid the back of the chunky scales, which I never used. I stuffed the blood-stained handkerchiefs inside the mechanism and screwed the metal back on. Then I washed my hands, vigorously, rinsing away all remaining traces of Hunter's blood.

Then I did it again, just to be on the safe side.

I ran a long, hot bath, chucked in a handful of violet scented bath salts and washed Lauder from my skin.

Five years in the joint could convert a cat to loving a hot soak. I lurched upright, remembering I still had the necklace on, splashing water everywhere. Ruining Lauder's heirloom already! I pulled at the chain around my neck, squinting at the pearl.

An odd gift indeed in our relationship. A necklace? Did he think I needed to class myself up? That my jewelry, on the rare occasions when I did wear it, was too cheap?

I examined the pearl more closely. It was smooth as satin, creamy and luxurious. Where did it come from? Was it lucky or unlucky for the pearl to end up on my neck?

With me, it stood a good chance of being knocked around by life.

TRING!

Sonia, it had to be. I jumped out of the bath and grabbed a towel, half hoping it was Lauder, to tell me he had canceled his holiday, broken off his engagement and was heading over now to spend the day with me.

Stop it!

Sonia's voice was crisp and a little tense. 'I trust things went okay?'

'Uh-huh. All good.' I sensed Sonia was speaking in code in case of nosey operators, so I would do the same.

'Anything of interest?'

'Yes. We need to talk.'

'I want to hear all about what happened, so I'll stop by tomorrow. I'm on my way to the boondocks to visit my folks.'

A damn good seeing-to is what happened. And an order to quit your case.

'I need to you do one thing. Go pay our girl a visit. She needs...reassurance, you know? So, *Alice*, when you get there, just say the truth. Give them your name, Alice Lucas, junior attorney at the firm. I appreciate you're with your family today, but it's kind of important. Say you're in my team. I left some of the firm's cards with your hotel caretaker.'

Cards? Alice Lucas, junior attorney? What the hell?

The penny dropped. Only an attorney could visit a felon. Sonia was telling me to visit Dolly as junior attorney-at-law Alice Lucas. Today.

No choice but to break the news. 'I can't... We've really got to talk.'

'What's the problem? You said you were free today. This is critical.'

64

'I know, but...'

I just couldn't say it. The words 'I quit' just couldn't come out.

There was a long pause and a longer sigh from Sonia.

'I know last night can't have been...fun, especially on Christmas Eve, Alice. It was a lot to ask for a new associate. I'll pay you double time.'

'It's not about the money.'

'Well, what? Are you sick?' She was losing patience with me.

'No, I'm fine.'

'Well, I wouldn't ask if this wasn't imperative. I cannot emphasize enough that she needs to retain her...composure... and remember no...chitchat...without me present. I need to go to my parents' facility. They literally have weeks to go. It's their last Christmas Day. I'll be back later, so I want her to see a friendly face.'

Sonia sounded torn, but she was a tough nut. Maybe there was a play underneath it all.

'Sorry to hear that.'

'We've all got to go sometime, but I'd rather some didn't go prematurely and unfairly.' *Like Dolly*, she was implying.

Dolly's smudged mascara and her plaintive wailing came back to me. Sonia was right to be concerned. Dolly could be out of control and easy prey for a circling Detective Flannery. Presumably he wasn't supposed to question Dolly before Sonia got back but that didn't mean he wouldn't try.

'Okay, I'll go see her.' I heard myself saying.

What are you doing?

'I'll call you later. We'll meet tomorrow.'

On that heart-warming note, she hung up.

65

I'd quit tomorrow. Face-to-face was always better. Lying came so easy to me. I'd give her some line about flying to Vienna for another case. Then, to avoid bumping into Alberta, I'd jump on the Sunset Limited to Florida.

That would be my reward for my good deed in checking on Dolly and telling her to keep her mouth shut.

Anxiety came back, a knife twisting in my guts.

I would be voluntarily walking into a police station.

Happy Christmas, Elvira.

12

Career girl's clothes had colonized my closet.

The dismal palette of grays, blues, mushrooms and blacks outnumbered the few pretty frocks and blouses I owned. June's red velvet gown now looked rather lonely amid the dull crowd.

What would Alice Lucas wear? She needed to be convincing and forgettable at the same time. I wanted the cops at the police station to let her in without batting an eyelid.

Alice would be a boring girl with no interest in clothes. I pulled out a crisp dark brown wrap dress in brown wool. Covered brown buttons were diagonally sewn across the body, over the hip. With a brown felt hat, I'd be suitably dull. Seamed stockings, and low brown brogues.

I looked at myself in the mirror. A sensible girl.

Should I wear the pearl necklace? A talisman to ward off any evil cops.

I put it back on.

To top it off, I put on my tortoiseshell glasses and stuffed my curls into a hairnet. The red polish would come off. Alice wouldn't bother with it, or with make-up.

I'd pretended to be many things in my life, but attorney was a first. My outfit would be my armor against my fears.

Fear I was breaking Lauder's command. Fear I would bump into reporters. They'd surely be prowling now, following the unfolding case, noticing new faces enter the station.

Fear they could hound me as someone close to the case, just as Lauder dreaded.

Fear we would both go down.

Fear I'd get there and be paralyzed. Alice Lucas wouldn't sip from a flask of French brandy, but Elvira Slate would. I filled my small pewter flask in the kitchen.

Elvira would drive the car down; Alice would get out.

To my relief, nobody was outside the police station, a solid, square building.

Still, the absence of reporters did nothing to dispel the sick feeling in my stomach as I headed towards the entrance.

Suddenly, the main doors were flung open as a female bum, an old woman, was manhandled out of the building by a cop. He was young and harassed-looking, she was a growling, shaggy, graying thing. An ancient wolf. They struggled down the steps. She was in layers of dirty clothes, but something stuck out. A white fur stole was draped over one shoulder, the end of it dragging on the steps. I'd seen it before, just last night.

A *fake* white fur stole.

Dolly's?

No mistake. But how had she got it?

The cop growled, 'Go home, Annie! And I don't wanna see you round here anytime soon.'

Now on the sidewalk, Annie was grabbing on to him for dear life, yelling. 'That's what I keep tellin' ya. I got no home! Kicking an old lady out on the street, real nice that is. You treat you own mom this bad?'

'My mom don't glug a bottle or two of hooch every day!'

She lowered her voice, plaintive. 'Gimme some of that nice milk you got inside, Officer. What do you say? The special stuff. Else I'm just gonna get the shakes! Then I'll be good.' She tried to put on an amiable expression.

'You dried out last night. Why don't you make it last? You're lucky it's the holiday or else I'd throw you back in the slammer!'

'You fucking asshole! You're all the same.'

'Oh, that's a nice way to talk. Very ladylike.'

'You don't care about me. I'm gonna die in the gutter. What do you care?'

The cop raised his brow at me. *See what I gotta put up with?* Annie disgusted him. She was old, hair grew out of her chin, and she stunk to high heaven. I smiled back, more out of relief he saw me as an ally.

Thanks, Annie, for making me look like the respectable one.

Out of nowhere, the cop gave Annie a shove and turned around to mount the steps into the building. Annie staggered, losing balance, and fell on her knees.

The officer was already in the doorway, heading in.

I felt for her. He didn't have to do that. I had a horrible feeling he pushed her because I had shown up. Impressing a younger woman with macho bravado.

Think again, asshole.

I ran over to her. 'You okay?'

Annie was cursing inwardly, picking herself up. She rubbed her arm where she'd fallen. Her knees were grazed, her thick stockings ripped. Her unlikely hat, a small red pillbox with a net, had managed to stay on her unwashed gray hair, scraped into a messy bun. A section of the hem of her old long dress was hanging down.

Annie shrugged off my arm, shooting me a vicious look. 'What in hell you starin' at?'

'Relax! I wanted to check you were okay.'

'Oh, screw you, too!' She staggered off.

I watched her go. Annie probably had her fill each day of pity as well as hate. Do-gooders like Alice Lucas probably just rubbed salt in the wound.

I could end up a bum. I was full of bad seeds, just waiting to sprout like the hair on Annie's chin. Somehow, I was managing to cling on to the bottom rung of society's staircase, with the help of Beatty and Lauder. They thought I was worth it. And I had the assets of youth and an okay face. Annie had nothing going for her. She could die on these streets and everyone would say, 'She brought it on herself.'

I walked into the main lobby of the precinct, praying I looked the part. *Alice Lucas, junior attorney-at-law.*

The lobby was dingy, the purgatory to jail hell. The walls, which needed a good coat of paint, were dotted with faded signs that no one had bothered to take down. One listed air raid instructions. Another was a poster for the Red Cross.

Give Gladly.

A tiny Christmas tree made out of wire and thinning tinsel had been shoved in a dull metal bucket. Somebody had bent the tip where the fairy should go. The sand the tree stood in was topped with cigarette butts. The air was stagnant with years of exhaled nicotine smoke and a distinctly masculine odor: sweat, cheap aftershave, and something leathery.

Eau de Tough Guy.

A wooden staircase led upstairs with a sign: *Detectives and Commanding Officer. First floor.*

The uniformed cop I'd seen earlier went into a side door on

the left, next to a front desk. He appeared on the other side of it. A half-drained tumbler of milk was on a smaller desk behind him. Up close, his cheeks were flushed, a sure sign he'd been drinking on the job, confirmed by rum fumes.

'Can I help you, Miss?'

'I would like to see someone you're holding. Dolly Perkins.'

He looked me up and down. 'Why?'

I passed him my card. 'I work for her attorney, Sonia Parker. We need to check on our client.'

He shrugged. 'You can't. She ain't here.'

I blinked. 'Where is she?'

'Gone.'

'Released?'

'Nah, she don't get that kind of lucky.'

'Where, then?' Surely not the County Jail already?

'County hospital. Got sick in the night.' He opened a record book. 'Left here at three a.m. by ambulance. Approximately.'

'Sick? What happened? Is she okay?' I was totally alarmed. 'You didn't tell Miss Parker?' It was rhetorical. Sonia had no idea.

'Not my shift. You wanna know more, ask at the hospital.'

Was this bribe time? Surely there was some kind of record of the details. No, Alice Lucas didn't do bribes. That could lead to trouble. But I was totally out of my depth now. I wanted to run, but needed to stay authoritative. 'We really should have been informed.'

'Yeah, well, consider yourself informed now.'

I stared at him. Sonia must have a sixth sense, with her worries for Dolly. 'Is the investigating detective aware of her situation?'

'Yeah. He knows.'

I stared at him. 'This is way out of line.'

He shrugged. 'So write to the commander. Go to jail ward. They might let you see her. Can't guarantee it, though.'

Jail ward. Another high-risk visitation for a job I wasn't even supposed to be on. I had no way of getting to Sonia. She said she was going to call me. I could just go back and wait in my office and let her find out later.

'Are we done here, Miss?'

I must have been staring into space. He had his rum-spiked milk to get back to. 'Yes, sir. Thank you for your time.'

The cop grunted something I couldn't make out, his eye already on his glass. I gave him a tiny smile and left, confident he'd forgotten Alice Lucas already.

I turned around and headed towards the daylight streaming in through the glass panels on the main doors.

I'd made it. I should be relieved, but this situation stank. They hadn't even bothered to call Sonia. And if Dolly was ill, or medicated, God knows what she'd be babbling. Was Detective Flannery already down there, sitting by her bed with a recorder? As Dolly had gone during the night, he'd had all morning to get at her alone in a weakened state.

Could she be dead?

13

Out in the street, I scanned the area. Annie the bum might know what really happened, especially if she'd been locked up with Dolly. No sign of her.

She couldn't be far. I ran across the lights and along the next row of closed shops. I stopped, relieved. There she was, rummaging through the contents of a trashcan. The end of the white stole was already grimy with filth, dangling in the gutter. As I got closer, I could see there was something darker, as if it the edge of the fur had brushed brown paint. Dried blood?

I slowed down and sidled up to her. 'Hey. It's Annie, isn't it?' I said. 'I need your help. Were you in the cage last night with a small blonde girl? Name of Dolly Perkins?'

Annie stood up, totally ignoring me. She clutched an empty bottle as if was pirates' treasure, holding it upside down.

'Looks like a whole lot of nothing in there.' I said. 'Tell me what happened. Maybe I can help you out.'

Now she looked at me with bloodshot, puffy eyes. 'Scram, why don't you?'

'I got liquor in my car. A whole flask of it. French brandy, good stuff.' Alice Lucas was disappearing by the second.

Her eyes lit up greedily. 'You ain't kidding?'

I said, 'Do I look like I'm kidding? Tell me what you saw, maybe I can give it to you, call it a Christmas gift. You were locked up last night? Did you see Dolly? Little bitty thing. Hair about this long. That fur stole you're wearing sure looks like Dolly's.'

Annie scratched her head, eyeing me. 'She gave it to me.'

'She did? Why would she do that?'

Her hand went to the fur stole, protectively. 'Finders keepers.'

'I thought you just said she gave it to you?' She was crazy. A whole waste of time. 'Can you just tell me what happened?'

Her eyes flicked around. I knew that look. She would say anything for a drop. But I needed facts, and fast.

'Where's your car?'

'Tell me what you know, first. If I believe you, you get a drink. And I'll let you keep the stole.'

'It's mine now. Sure don't need furs on death row, huh?'

'Did she tell you that?'

'Heard she's on a murder beef.' She gave an odd smile. What remained of her teeth were little yellowish-gray stumps. She was further along the path of self-annihilation than I'd realized, but maybe I could trigger an iota of empathy for Dolly.

'You look like a real kind person. You can help me help Dolly. I need to know what really happened. Those cop jerks won't say.'

Annie frowned, confused. She wasn't used to being taken seriously. 'That's too bad,' she mumbled.

'Come on, tell me what you know. Let's sit over there.' I pointed at a bench. I took her arm to guide her. It was bony, a worn spindle under the dirty layers which were her only padding against the cold.

We sat down. Annie started to speak without really looking at me. 'I'm tryin' to get some shuteye, then they throw her in the cage. She's bawlin' her eyes out. I'm thinking she's needin' a fix. Told her them cops ain't gonna do a damn thing, no matter how loud she hollers.'

She tailed off.

'Then what happened?' I nudged her to continue.

'I don't remember. I'm thirsty.'

'Annie. Tell me!'

'She's cryin', yellin', says she's knocked up, she's gonna lose the baby. There's blood all over.'

She broke off again, maddeningly.

'Then what?'

'Sure could use that drink.' She coughed plaintively.

'Later. Then what, Annie?'

'Then she stops yelling. I guess she blacks out. Finally, a cop shows up, ambulance gets here, takes your girl away.' Annie's hand poked my arm. 'Hey! Deal's a deal.'

'All right, all right.' Dolly had almost certainly miscarried. If she survived, she would be devastated.

I helped Annie up and we staggered over to Mabel. Annie bent down to rub her sore knee. I got the flask out of the glove compartment.

'I dished! Hand it over!' Annie's hand shot out.

The flask was good quality and it'd be a shame to lose it, but wasn't I supposed to be cutting back? Giving up the flask was eliminating temptation.

And Annie had kept her word.

'All right.'

Quick as a flash, she grabbed it off me. Anticipation of a hit seemed to be an instant cure for the shakes. She twisted the lid off and knocked the contents back in one slick move, like a hustler potting the black in one.

'Make it last, why don't you?' I said sarcastically.

Annie waved me to shut up with her other hand as she glugged.

'You really on the street? No family?' I said, as she finished guzzling.

Annie narrowed her eyes, wiping her mouth with a grimy sleeve. 'My son's over Alhambra way. His wife hates my guts. Feelin's mutual. He ain't got no backbone. Just like his useless pa.'

'Maybe you don't help your case. Takes two to tango.'

'Family? Who needs 'em? Rot in hell for all I care.' Annie wobbled off.

I half-watched her, too caught up with the mental images of what Dolly had gone through during the night.

The sand timer of legal process was draining fast. No baby, no stay of execution if Sonia lost the case.

But what if Dolly herself hadn't made it?

Damn.

Annie wandered off. I called out, 'How can I find you again?'

'Oh, I don't go far, feet too bad.' Annie's eyes suddenly brightened, tossing the empty flask in the gutter. 'Won't be needing that no more.' She tottered off, flinging the stole around her neck like a defiant starlet. She yelled back at me, 'Tell her Annie says hello!'

Annie knew what I was doing before I did.

I was going to jail ward.

14

The officer gestured at my purse. 'Purse. Open it.'

My heart pounding, a knot tightening in my stomach, I undid the clasp and handed it to him. I tried my best to look calm as he poked around.

So far, so good. My second risky visit of the day as Alice Lucas.

The fact the cop was letting me inside meant Dolly had to be in an okay condition.

You wouldn't know the jail ward was even part of the hospital. Security doors divided the general population from the sick and incarcerated. Another uniformed guard stood by these doors. He hadn't once taken his suspicious eyes off me.

'Wait through there. The nurse will escort you.' The cop had finished with my purse. I headed towards the guard, who began to unlock the door, still eyeing me.

He held the door open for me, and I felt his glare boring through my back.

I was inside. Back in a jail. My heart pounded and I could barely breathe. The guard locked the door from the inside. It struck me that I was a prisoner in here until he decided otherwise. I just wanted the whole thing over and done with.

What the hell are you doing this for?

I waited in the cold corridor. The place was cheerless, devoid of any sign of Christmas celebrations.

It was windowless, the air stagnant. The smell of jail wards everywhere, disinfectant mingling with the desperation of the criminal class. Funny how in Holloway, girls would feign fevers, flu and migraines to get to lie in the cold brass beds of the medical wing. The food was slightly better there and at least you could get out of your cell for a while.

I didn't want to be here. I wasn't supposed to be here.

Christmas Day was going from bad to worse.

A frazzled nurse came out of a door on the right and closed it behind her.

The guard spoke. 'Visitor for Dolly Perkins. You got ten minutes.' He said the last part to me.

'I might need longer. She's my client.' I frowned, trying to conceal the dread inside with a professional demeanor. My hands and face were clammy with sweat.

'Ten minutes,' he repeated.

'This way, Miss. I'm sure she'll be pleased to have a visitor.' The nurse led the way.

When the guard was out of earshot, I asked the nurse. 'Is Miss Perkins okay?'

'She's doing just fine. Most women survive miscarriages if they're treated fast and the cops brought her as quick as they could.'

No, they did not.

'So...she lost the baby?'

The nurse shot me a *Have you even been listening?* look.

I tried to look apologetic. 'Sorry. My boss asked me to step in today. It's not the best of days, to be honest.'

'I've been working since six this morning. And it's Christmas. But if criminals don't stop, we can't.'

'How do you know she's a criminal? They haven't charged her yet.'

She gave me a withering look. 'She can't be decent if they had reason to arrest her on suspicion of homicide.'

I ignored this. 'Is she sedated? Can she talk?'

'Oh, she's talking all right. And no sweet talk. She's only had something for her stomach cramps.'

'Have any detectives visited?'

'Not yet.'

If she started at six, the nurse might not know what went down last night.

She stopped. 'This one.'

The women's ward had four iron-framed beds, small metal cabinets, and not much else. A gloomy dump.

Dolly lay in the corner on her side, facing the door. Her hopeless eyes were blank, one of her thin arms lying across her recently vacated womb. Somebody had cleaned off her makeup; she looked about fifteen years old. And in her faded striped pajamas, every inch the inmate.

A manacle tethered her leg to the bed.

I made my way over towards her. Dolly's dull eyes glanced at me. 'Leave me alone, will ya?' Miserable, but not doped up. She rolled onto her other side, the chain clinking, to face the wall. The hair at the back of her head was a yellow, matted mess. Her pajama top slid up. I caught a glimpse of a long purple scar on her back. An old welt? Instinctively Dolly's hand slipped back around and pulled the top down. She muttered to the wall. 'That beauty's compliments of my step-daddy.'

I pulled up a metal chair. 'That sucks.'

'You bet.'

'Turn around, Dolly. I heard about the baby. I'm very sorry.'

She pulled her knees to her chest. 'They let it die!'

And you didn't call anyone for Ronald Hunter, I thought. Karma's a bitch.

'I'll make sure Sonia knows about it. Look, I don't have long. Has anyone questioned you in here?' I kept my voice low.

'I don't care what happens to me. I'm through with it all.'

I glanced behind me. Luckily, the nurse was outside the door, talking to another nurse. They were laughing.

I hissed at Dolly. 'Don't talk like that! Answer the goddamned question! Has the detective visited you? You say anything to that nurse, anybody? Turn around, will you?

Slowly, she rolled back around. Dolly shook her head without looking at me. So far, so good.

'I ain't said nothing to nobody.'

Maybe Flannery couldn't be bothered to leave his own Christmas celebrations to quiz someone whose conviction was already looking like a slam dunk. As Lauder had said, Dolly seemed guilty as hell. Cut and dried. Flannery could crucify her at his leisure.

I could relax, too; the risks of running into him today were low. 'You sure?'

'Think I'm that dumb?'

Was that a tear rolling down her cheek? I resisted an urge to sit on the bed and console her. I said, 'I've been there too, exactly where you are now. Hating the very air you breathe. Feeling your life's over. But guess what? One day, things get better. The nightmare will fade.'

Who was I kidding? I still remembered exactly how she felt as if it was yesterday. Washed up, betrayed and friendless.

'You been in jail?'

I resisted an urge to share. 'Been in a some jams, sure.'

She absorbed this. 'Unless you been banged up, you got no idea. So quit pretending. I know what's gonna happen to me, so quit your pep talk, an' all.' Her voice was devoid of emotion.

'Sonia's a real good attorney. You've got to hope for the best and keep your mouth shut. You haven't been charged yet, so sit tight.'

Now she met my eyes. 'If they kill me, I'll be closer to him, won't I? My baby son. Born on Christmas Day.'

There was no answer to that. She surveyed me. 'You got kids?'

I shook my head.

'So you ain't got nowhere better to be today? All on your lonesome?'

Now it was my turn to avoid her eyes. 'We care about you, Dolly, and we're doing our best to help you. So try to remember that, all right? And for the record, I'm going by the name of Alice Lucas, Parker's assistant. So forget about my other name, if anyone asks.'

Dolly sat up. She wiped her big eyes. 'It's all right, Alice. I remember who you are.'

She sounded more rational. I wanted to pat her hand, give her a hug, but something made me hold back. 'Well, so long.'

Dolly gave the briefest of nods.

I was facing my worst fears being here, but I couldn't expect gratitude.

I got up and headed to the door where the nurse was still chatting.

'I'm done here.'

The nurse stepped aside and let me through. I turned back

to Dolly. 'Merry Christmas' seemed wildly inappropriate. 'Goodbye, Miss Perkins.'

Silence for an answer.

The nurse shot me a *Some people!* look, rolling her eyes in Dolly's direction. Outside in the cold corridor, the nurse said, 'It's a blessing a girl like that lost the baby.' She locked the door.

The judgmental bitch was wrong. If I knew one thing, it was that Dolly would have loved her child.

But "Alice Lucas" grimaced in answer. The nurse took it as agreement.

I walked out into the winter sunshine, feeling the sun on my skin and the breeze through my hair. I was free, while Dolly was incarcerated and wanting to die.

I wanted to detach.

I'd done my bit and now all I had to do was tell Sonia I was off the case.

Job done.

I burst out laughing in the street.

It was uncontrollable relief. A nervous reaction. I must have looked and sounded like a crazy woman.

15

Back in the Miracle Mile, I had one desire. To get into bed and sleep till Sonia's call woke me.

On my way back, I'd bought all the papers, but they sat unopened on Barney's desk. A headline screamed: *Ronald Hunter, Munitions Magnate, Murdered in Cold Blood.* I couldn't face reading them yet.

I pulled off the hairnet, slipped out of my clothes, leaving them strewn over the floor. Then I showered, ridding myself of jail dust and misery. After, I sprayed myself with perfume and grabbed the bottle from the drawer and, towel around me, poured myself a generous measure.

I found a pink nightgown and put it on. It was a pale peach affair made of silk satin, with lilac bouquets all over. It was perfection. I'd bought it for romantic rendezvous with Lauder, but there was never time to put it on.

So now I would just enjoy wearing it, and that was enough. *Only for you.*

I fumbled at the pearl around my neck. The ball and chain. Randall was fond of me, but where fondness ended and controlling began, who knew? Lust was a common symptom of both conditions.

I got into bed and pulled up the sheet and eiderdown.

Giving me the present, mentioning his trip, Lauder was crossing a new threshold. It was as if he was trying to rationalize his two lives. I was the mistress who got a few hours in the Astral; The Fiancée got nice trips—and now I had to hear about it. I wondered if she, too, was getting a necklace at Christmas. Furtively giving me a family hand-me-down, while getting her diamonds that he had to take out a loan for on his modest cop's salary.

A little mention here, another there, soon I'd have to accept his other reality. But not *her*. Miss Hoity-Toity would be spared hearing about my sordid existence.

Why had he told me about his darned vacation? He'd broken the rules for a reason. I didn't know why and I didn't like it. Most of the time, I kept him off my mind. My body, he could do what he liked with, and vice versa. I just didn't want him ramming his fancy life into my head.

Shut up!

All of a sudden, I wanted the necklace off. I undid it and slipped it in the side drawer of the nightstand, along with sleeping tablets, and a slushy romance novel June had pointlessly lent me.

If Lauder wanted our affair to continue, he could shut up about his private life and quit with the gifts.

Girls like me and Dolly didn't get skiing trips with the rich and famous to revel in the powdery snow. We rotted in jail. Lauder's indifference to the likelihood Dolly had been framed was disgusting. He should know that she could be innocent, and that she might never see the light of day again. Dolly hadn't killed Hunter, but she was easy prey for the DA and Flannery. She would be gold-digging trash in the eyes of the law—no more, no less.

For Dolly, Christmas Day would simply become the anniversary of the worst day of her life.

However long she had left.

And then there was Ronald Hunter. What picture were the press now painting of him, the great patriot, and his affair with a good-time girl from the wrong side of the tracks? Surely they couldn't hide the fact he was sleeping with Dolly? Or would a rich family like his just be able to cover it up?

I bet they would feed the public a lot of lies about Dolly. Just like those Hollywood movies, where some good wife type triumphs over the wayward girl who is out to steal her guy. Usually, the girl would be a model, a dancer, or a gangster's girl and winds up in jail unless she eats humble pie and embraces loneliness and repentance.

Who she really was or what she really wanted out of life, the movies never said. She was just a 'wrong 'un', and that meant she had to pay.

No, I had to read the rubbish. I got out of bed, and stomped to pick up one of the papers in the office. I flicked through a few pages.

Beyond the headlines, there were photos of the apartment block. *Killed in cold blood; Found alone in his private office.* No mugshot of Dolly, but maybe the cops hadn't released it yet. I scanned down the page. 'A suspect has been arrested and is being held, pending further investigation.'

That was all.

Lower down, I was confronted with a picture of Lauder's rival. The smug face of Detective Dale Flannery. He had a strong jaw, and thin, mean-looking lips. I could see him in a Western, as a sidekick to the hero. His hair was probably fair underneath the hat. He was quoted as saying the police were making fast progress on the case.

I read on.

A lot on Ronald Hunter; his achievements, his factories, and his plans for a foundation for veterans. There was a picture of younger brother Rufus, who had taken over the business in the last couple of years.

Then some pictures of Linda Hunter, on their wedding day and a studio portrait. She could be his daughter. Her face was pretty enough, but there was something dull about her eyes. Perhaps the look that comes from having money, good looks and a lack of imagination.

So Flannery was biding his time. It would play to his advantage to let the press build a big, damning story on Dolly.

I went back to bed and stared at the ceiling.

I so badly wanted to help her.

Wait!

I was free; I had to remind myself of that fact. And Lauder, however pissed I was at him now, was fundamental to my better life. I could never forget that. But neither could I forget who I was trying to become, and what I needed to do.

Control by any man, even if it was for my own protection, was just not on the agenda. Particularly now.

I was a big girl. I could be careful. I'd done it before, with nobody telling me what to do. Even Lauder's recent promotion was partly due to the fact I'd ignored his commands.

Lauder needed to think he controlled me as it made him feel safer. I would do what I wanted, and he would stay blissfully ignorant. I would do nothing to shatter his charmed life.

I was a private detective, I liked my work, my new life, my secretary. And I was going to help Dolly Perkins.

16

I was back on the case without Sonia Parker knowing I had even left it, and without Randall Lauder knowing I hadn't quit it.

Sonia called that evening as she had promised. She would meet me first thing in the morning for a full debrief. We could meet at Hal's Diner on Olympic. I didn't know the place, but I said I'd meet her there.

Before she hung up, I asked her if I could visit *'our baby girl's friend, you know, the one who was with her'*.

Sonia twigged immediately I meant Alberta. 'What do you want to do that for?'

'They are good pals. Could prove useful?'

Sonia gave a grunt of affirmation but asked me not to reveal anything about the 'problem', even to pals. She was referring, of course, to the case.

'But she can know about our friend's...health, right?'

Sonia reluctantly agreed. 'That's all she needs to know.'

Dede Dedeaux's place sprawled over the entire fourth floor, an oasis of African art, potted palms, modern art and furnishings. She was very well-heeled, thanks to a hefty inheritance from her plantation-owning predecessors.

Now she splashed the money around on legal fees for underdogs like Dolly. She'd also stumped up the money for June to have discreet medical attention after the sexual assault.

Alberta opened the door, wearing a navy wool coat with a fur neckline, and a purple pillbox hat. Underneath the coat, a shimmery floor length purple gown. She was clearly on her way out, a small purse in one hand, and her saxophone case in the other. An expression of concern and irritation flashed over her face. 'How's Dolly?' She immediately read my expression, holding the door open only a few inches. 'What's wrong? Something bad?'

'Got a couple of minutes?'

'Yeah, sure.'

Worried, Alberta let me into the spacious lobby, pointing the way into the airy living room that overlooked the city.

The art had changed since I was last up here. Now, a series of monochrome photographs of women, some black and some white, from the turn of the century and earlier, ran along one side of the room. Their voluminous Edwardian dresses looked rather quaint, yet powerful at the same time. Were they Dede and Alberta's relatives? I wouldn't ask because I wouldn't get a straight answer.

In the corner, a beautiful blue spruce tree glittered with silver baubles, tinsel and crystal lights. It outclassed ours in the office below. There was a tiny cross on the top. It faced a tall wooden African sculpture in the opposite corner of the room, made of huge curved shapes, some kind of fertility goddess, I guessed. The tree and the sculpture seemed symbolic of the little I already knew about Dede and Alberta's life.

I relaxed into the plush leather couch, imagining what it must be like to inhabit such a palatial pad. Pretty darned good, and I could get used to it. Alberta stayed standing.

I broke the news about Dolly's miscarriage and that she was recovering in the County hospital. Alberta froze, genuinely shocked.

'Oh, my Lord. Is she okay?' She sat down, heavily, on the edge of the sofa.

'Physically, I think so. Mentally? Not so good.' Were Alberta's eyes moist? I couldn't really tell, but she was definitely cut up.

'Thinks she'll be closer to her baby if she dies.'

'Poor Dolly. I need a drink. Want one? Scotch okay?'

'I'll pass. I'm on my way out to find something to eat.'

'I got some leftovers if you want. Custard cream pie?'

I said thanks but no thanks. I didn't fancy anything sweet. If she'd said eggs and beans, we'd be in business.

Alberta went over to the glass and ebony bar and pulled out an expensive bottle of Scotch. This was nothing like the lowly maid act she put on in Sonia's presence. 'Sure hope this Parker lady can fix this. Supposed to be the best in town.'

'I hope so, too. You didn't want to go skiing with Dede?' It was a personal question, but I was curious. If Alberta didn't mind me seeing her so free and easy at home, maybe she would open up to me now.

'No. Dede's people bring their help, so I don't need to be there. And I really don't like it up there. Too cold, too white and too expensive for me.'

She wasn't opening up, but she wasn't closing me down entirely. Playing the maid around Dede's privileged family must get tiresome.

'Can I ask a few questions? About Dolly. Just trying to figure her out.'

'I'll tell you what I know, but I been racking my brains for anything that could help. Trouble is, I got nothing.'

'Sometimes you don't know what you know.'

'How's that?' Alberta stopped pouring, staring at me.

'Well, you're her pal, and she trusts you. She may have told you things that could help us, even though they seem like nothing special to you. Details.'

Alberta thought about it, shrugged and finished pouring her drink. 'You mean something that could lead to the person who framed her?'

'Maybe. But we don't know anything for sure.'

She glared at me. 'But we do know she's been framed? Somebody's mad at Hunter and used Dolly.'

'It certainly looks that way, but early days yet.'

Beatty Falaise, my only educator in the detecting business, had taught me that at the start of a case, assume nothing. Going on assumptions was like driving on empty. And Sonia had asked me not to divulge much.

Alberta snorted with derision. 'Oh, so somebody just happened to walk in on him in bed, stab him in the heart, and a couple of minutes later, Dolly shows up? They must have known about him and her! They knew when she was gonna be there.' She took a seat and knocked her drink back fast.

'Does anybody have a beef with Dolly?'

'Nobody.' Alberta shifted uncomfortably in her seat. 'Dolly's harmless. A big kid. You thought about the wife? Maybe she found out about her man and Dolly. Maybe she couldn't take it anymore. So she flips. She bumps him off, or pays somebody to do it, and punishes Dolly the same time.'

This was exactly what I'd said to Lauder. Hearing it from Alberta confirmed Linda Hunter was definitely worth investigating as soon as Sonia Parker gave me her blessing to do so. 'Maybe, but anything's possible. But we just can't assume anything right now.'

Alberta hid her irritation at this. 'So what else do you wanna know?'

I asked about how she knew Dolly. She explained she'd known Dolly for two years. Dolly had been hanging out at various clubs on Central Avenue. Being white, she had stuck out and she also been seen with a few jazz players. 'Dolly's kind of a flirt, she loves to get attention from anybody. She got friendly with Sol, he's a trumpeter. Jewel's brother. Nice guy.'

'Jewel plays in The Charmettes?' I asked.

'Sure does. Reeds.'

I blanked. 'Reeds?'

'Reeds. Clarinet.'

I nodded. My musical education had been virtually non-existent.

'Sol says to Jewel, Dolly can sing, so why not let her jam with you? So she did. Turned out fine. She don't sing with the band at Sugar Hill, but there's plenty of other places.'

'Were Dolly and Sol an item?'

Alberta raised her brows. 'She was sweet on him. He kinda liked her... but nobody needs trouble. I mean, judgment.'

'Yeah, world's shitty place.'

'And she don't need one person's love, she needs the whole world to love her. The way she comes up with all these big ideas.'

'Like what?'

'Oh, like she don't just work in the Tilsons Department Store, one day she was gonna buy the whole place! Crazy stuff like that. All talk. Dreams but no idea how to make 'em come true. The way I see it, to a rich fella like Mr Hunter, a girl like Dolly would be like a toy, just a cute little plaything. He probably did promise to take care of her, in her situation. Another reason she wouldn't kill him!' Alberta winked.

The picture she was painting of Dolly made me feel uneasy. I'd have to warn Sonia. Any character witness she used who knew Dolly would have to be pretty convincing on the stand that Dolly wasn't a flirt or needy. That might take omitting some truths.

I asked where Dolly lived. Alberta said a boarding house near Compton.

'So, all the Charmettes get along with her?'

'Sure. The ones who know her. Some don't.'

I looked confused. Alberta explained. 'The Charmettes, we mix up the lineup from time to time. We can play as a ten-piece, or a sextet, or just a quintet. Other times, we'll just meet up and jam. All in all, I guess there's about fifteen or twenty of us. Depends who's available. Like I said, Dolly only sings now and then. Like at Joyce's.'

'So who else is on vocals?'

'Wanda, mostly. Carmen and Jewel can do harmonies. Wanda was in the Honey Duchesses, toured all over, they were a real good band. We just stick to the city. Joyce, she pays well and her crowd loves us. Other places, we can't play with a mixed lineup. We ain't exactly the International Darlings of Swing.'

I stared at her, blank. Her eyes were laughing. 'You don't know who I'm talking about, do you?'

'I'm not very knowledgeable about music.'

'You like swing music? You look like you oughta.'

I grimaced. 'I haven't been out much the past few years.'

One day you will tell her about your long incarceration, won't you? You know you want to. You want her to know the whole truth.

Alberta studied me hard, sipping. 'Maybe you should try. Life's kinda short not to have any fun.' I doubted she would approve of the only way I was having a little bit of fun. Screwing an LAPD cop on the side.

I said, 'So you had no idea about Hunter?'

'No. Dolly kept that real quiet.' Alberta's eyes widened. 'There's something else.'

'What?

'She makes promises and then she don't follow through. One time, she said a pal in New York would help us make a recording. Didn't happen. Another time, some lady or other was gonna make formals for us for free, in return for singing at a wedding. Sure enough, didn't happen. I think Dolly makes up stuff so we like her and let her sing more.'

Sonia would have to question Dolly about a lot of things. The mystery job offers, any boyfriends, why she made promises only to let people down. Sonia would need to get ahead on anything that the DA might spice up to make Dolly look even more morally dubious or chaotic. A girl that up till recently preferred the company of a racially mixed group of jazz musicians? That could be painted as crime of the century. And singing in a band who played regularly at lesbian clubs? Dolly should be burnt at the stake.

I pointed at the sax case. 'You're playing tonight?'

'Uh-huh. Private party, at Joyce's.'

I wondered what that meant exactly. The club was already

the epitome of private. 'Wasn't Dolly supposed to sing tonight? Before the arrest?'

'Yup. Wanda's covering it. It'll be a sextet. Carmen on drums, Bertha on bass, Jewel on reeds, Wanda on vocals and trumpet, Zetty on trombone. And yours truly, tenor sax. Why don't you join us? I can give you a ride.'

'No, I shouldn't.'

'You really gonna stay at home on Christmas night?'

'Why have you and Dede got Dolly's back like this?' I asked out of the blue.

It was the closest I'd come to acknowledging their coupledom.

Alberta didn't flinch. 'Something real lonesome about her. She was adopted, and they died. She ain't got no one in the world so we're helping her out.'

We're helping her out. It was the closest yet Alberta had come to saying they were an item and she had a say in how they spent their money. And I felt a surge of comradery. With her and Dede because of our secrets. With Dolly, because we were both orphans with a double abandonment in our childhoods. She might be my helpless little sister.

But still, they were giving a lot, just out of pity for somebody. 'Dolly's lucky to have such good pals.'

She glanced at her watch and stood up. 'Change your mind? There'll be plenty of food and you can meet the girls. Then you can see for yourself nobody hated Dolly!'

I gave a short laugh. 'Never said I didn't believe you.'

'You detective types, you don't trust nobody. Come on, what do you say?'

It was obvious she wanted me to meet them to rule them all

out. But just because Alberta trusted the band didn't mean I had to. Dolly languished in hell, and here were some of the females that she regularly hung out with.

Any one of them could have nabbed her lipstick.

'All right. Why not?' It certainly beat sitting at home next to the radio, trying not to think of Lauder's vacation.

I stood up. 'Just don't say I'm an investigator. Joyce knows, but nobody else needs to.'

I wanted to be free tonight. Dancing, killer cocktails, fun.

Alberta seemed to read my thoughts. 'You gotta dance tonight, for Dolly's sake. Because she can't. And if all this goes bad, she might never again.'

We met each other's eyes. I nodded. 'I'll give it a shot.'

She looked my outfit up and down. Unimpressed. Black slacks and beige pullover, things I'd slung on for a simple night with a takeout. 'Wait here.' She bounced out of the room.

A few minutes later, Alberta came back with an entire outfit: a dress, in a shimmery golden fabric, a black-and-gold striped jacket, a gold feathery tilt hat and gold backless shoes. She bundled the lot into my arms. 'Go change in the bathroom. But hurry.'

I hesitated. It was all brand new!

'Dede buys a pile of stuff she never wears. Then before she's even tried it out, she don't like it no more. Fickle lady. You may as well have it for tonight. Then I'm gonna donate it to the needy.'

She didn't know it, but she already was.

17

The slick moves of my dancing partner, a tall girl called Cheryl, made my re-introduction to dancing seem effortless.

When she'd asked if I wanted to dance, Cheryl told me she was Irish, and that her girlfriend was a midwife, who was unexpectedly called in to do a shift on the maternity ward.

She wanted to make it clear a dance was just a dance. Fine by me. I had enough complications right now.

On stage, the band's wailing horn section let rip. All the members wore silky purple gowns identical to Alberta's, with high necklines and mounds of ruby sequins over the shoulders and waistband that gleamed like fresh pomegranate seeds. Their dresses swayed in tune and the flowers in their hair, sprays of fake purple and red orchids with silver veins, bounced in rhythm as the horn section took it to the top.

The singer, who had to be Wanda, had a liquid satin voice that wafted me to another world. I closed my eyes, letting myself go.

If Lauder could see me now, jitterbugging with a woman!

The song came to an end, and the crowd went wild. I turned to Cheryl. 'Thanks for going easy on me.'

'Pleasure. Find me later if you want to do it again.'

On stage, Wanda took a long bow, a grinning ball of energy. 'Well, thank you very much, ladies and gentlewomen! I wrote *My Particular Guy* myself and it's all about the best kind of love. Forbidden love, y'all know what I mean?'

Everybody cheered. Wanda beamed. Confident and

charismatic, she was a five-foot-tall powerhouse, totally in her element. She was stunning, with warm brown skin, now moistened with perspiration, and jet-black hair that was curled, coiled and oiled.

Then I noticed something odd. The stage bandstands didn't say *The Charmettes*. They said *Wanda and her Charms* in curly lettering. Alberta hadn't mentioned anything about playing in another band tonight.

Wanda went on. 'We love who we love, and nobody can do a thing about it. Ain't that right?'

The crowd exploded.

On stage, Alberta's eyes landed on me, and she gave a half-smile. Wanda beamed at her fans. 'We're gonna take a break now, but we'll be back real soon! Then I want everybody on their feet.'

I headed for the bar through the throng.

'Well, look what the cat dragged in. Miss Slate?' It was a warm, polished voice. One that I knew all too well.

I turned around. Joyce, the club's proprietress, had a wry smile on her face. 'What a charming surprise. You're here for pleasure, not business, I hope?' Her dark eyes twinkled at me. 'You're certainly dressed for pleasure.'

She could be describing herself, fabulous in a long dark blue velvet gown and a bucketload of diamonds at her neck, ears and wrists. A diamond tiara glittered on top of her black hairdo, which was parted in the middle with elaborate braids forming curls on either side. She evoked a hybrid concoction of European shepherdess, Native American and Cleopatra. Joyce had been born in the wrong body, but now she was her true self.

'Officially off duty,' I lied. 'Alberta invited me along. We live at the same place.'

'The Miracle Mile? Nice digs. Let me get you a drink. A cocktail, created especially for the occasion.'

'Christmas special? If it's eggnog, thanks but not thanks.'

Joyce tutted. 'Do I look like an eggnog girl? No, this is a wonderful cocktail to celebrate my birthday.'

'Many happy returns.'

How old was Joyce? Fifty? Sixty? I had no idea. She was ageless in a way.

'I make a point of celebrating Christmas just like the Europeans do—on Christmas Eve. That means today is only ever all about me.' She gave a superior smile.

Joyce looked around and her eyes fell on one of her many glamorous waitresses. She held up two fingers and the girl nodded and pranced off in the direction of the bar, worked by female bartenders.

Tonight, all the staff were dolled up in gold lamé pant suits, covered in silver stars. Their hair was in elaborate buns with small silver top hats perched on top. They could have walked off the set of a musical.

But they didn't make musicals featuring lesbians. And they probably never would.

'Join me in my booth. I want to hear all your news.'

News? We didn't exactly move in the same circles.

Joyce's plush booth occupied a prime spot at the edge of the dance floor. I looked around. The place had definitely had some kind of makeover with a cream and purple pearly theme. Faux columns edged the walls, ivory and purple satin drapes hung around the back of the stage. The table tops were now a dark marble on which stood small brass lamps with deep purple shades, lending a soft light. It was more sophisticated than decadent. Even the resident drug dealer that I remembered had disappeared. I said, 'Looking swanky. Did you...er...get busted?'

'No. I like to run a tight ship in these uncertain times, so a couple of features you may recall have been relocated or discontinued. My clients have enough trouble as it is. Being closed down wouldn't do anyone any favors.'

I nodded. The waitress soon reappeared with a brass tray carrying a cocktail in an elegant glass and a flute of bubbles which she presented to Joyce, who smiled graciously. The waitress handed the cocktail to me. The drink was a creamy white, with a dark streak through the top.

'I haven't thought of a name yet, but I invented it. Try it.' Joyce nodded to me. Why wasn't she partaking of her own concoction?

'Happy birthday,' I said. We chinked glasses, and Joyce smiled again, watching while I sipped. The drink was soft, like fluffy vanilla ice cream laced with something orangey and floral. The dark streak tasted like a boozy treacle with chocolate undertones. 'Deadly.'

'Have to say, I'm quite proud of myself.' Joyce leaned back, pure satisfaction spreading over her face.

'You're right. You need a memorable name for it.'

'I'm thinking *Wolf's Eye*. It kind of looks like a white eye with a long dark pupil.'

I looked at down at my glass. The treacle streak was slowly blurring into a wider band. Brown was bleeding into the white.

'Why not name it after you? It's your birthday, after all. How about...*Joyce's Bliss*?'

'Ooh, *Joyce's Bliss*. Once tasted, never surpassed. Perfect! That settles it.' She looked at me, impressed.

We chinked glasses again. Now I was in her good books, I couldn't resist a little probe. 'So...you heard about Dolly Perkins?'

Joyce looked at me, askance. 'Of course she didn't do it. Dolly Perkins! How ridiculous.'

So Alberta had told Joyce and possibly the band too. Considering our story was that she hadn't been with Dolly that night, wasn't it a risky move to talk to anyone at all about Dolly being in a jam? But Dolly had called the club, and Alberta had left for a while.

Alberta was convinced everyone liked Dolly. But if Dolly had enemies in the band or at the club, who could be involved in the frame-up—maybe by stealing the lipstick, even if it was at the real killer's behest—it was dangerous to talk.

If Flannery got to hear Alberta *had* been with Dolly, she could be in the firing line.

I nodded towards the stage. 'The stage bandstands. New name?'

'Wanda's been itching to launch her own band for some time. You can't blame her for wanting to get some distance ahead of the scandal breaking. Dolly's bound to be all over the papers soon.'

'Smart move, then.'

'Just bringing forward the inevitable,' Joyce said, enigmatically.

Wanda wasn't just itching to launch her own band; she'd been busy preparing for it long before.

'Kind of suits you, too, I guess, if the name's switched?'

'I'm never one to mind anyone switching anything.' Joyce gave a pointed look. 'So long as somebody plays at my birthday, I'm happy.'

'Do you know Dolly well?'

'Not well. A funny little thing. Nervous energy, a little too keen to please. You always worry for girls like that, don't you? But boy, can she belt out a song, and from such a tiny body. Where Piaf is Paris's little sparrow, Dolly's our very own Los Angeleno yellow warbler.'

Sadness flitted across her eyes. 'Well, could have been. I guess she's finished now. Even if she gets off, this will follow her like a ball and chain.'

Joyce sipped her champagne.

'How long did The Charmettes play here?'

'On and off, since I opened.' She peered at me over her champagne flute. 'You're asking an awful lot of questions for someone on her night off.'

'Just curious.'

'Hm. Once a nosey parker, always one, I guess?'

'A professional habit. Hard to shake off.'

Her eyes suddenly bored into mine. 'Or are you in fact helping Dolly?'

I lowered my glass, avoiding her gaze. Had Alberta said anything about my involvement when she returned to the club? Surely not. I was between a rock and a hard place. I couldn't spill to Joyce, but could I outright lie?

A halfway house answer would do. 'Being incarcerated isn't fun. Particularly when you're innocent. If I could help, sure, why not?' My voice sounded sufficiently blasé.

Joyce studied me. 'You know, I can never quite make you out. Do-gooder or meddler? Well, as I'm in such a good mood, I'll cut you some slack.'

Joyce's eyes were already flitting elsewhere. She politely told me she had another guest to see, and did I mind if we ended our little chat? It was a polite way of kicking me out of the booth.

I wished her happy birthday again, finished my drink, and reluctantly got up from the comfy seat.

Joyce's voice sang out after me. 'Remember, everything's on the house tonight for my nearest and dearest. Maybe that will include you, one day?'

I laughed, but didn't look back. A suave man in a tuxedo passed me, heading for Joyce's booth. He had a pencil thin moustache, greased silver hair like a sheet of aluminum, and perfect skin. His face split into a good-natured grin, revealing gleaming teeth. Joyce's particular guy? I resisted the urge to look around and watch their greeting.

I merged into the maelstrom of noisy women.

No sign of Alberta, or any of the musicians in their purple frocks. I needed to pee, and found the bathroom.

In the mirror, I was a new woman in the golden dress. Across the top and shoulders, pale gold and black beads were embroidered into fern-like frond patterns. The same pattern was repeated around the hips. The jacket was a stiff little bolero, with three gold tassels as fastenings. The stripes turned out to be ribs of gold brocade across the chest. The high-heeled gold shoes fitted well enough for one night if I did the straps up tightly. I fluffed my curls and pinned on the hat. It was a black and bronze turban, with a big gold centerpiece encrusted with a polished striped slab of tiger's eye.

I found my darkest red lipstick and powdered my nose.

'Not bad for an ex-con,' I announced to myself in the mirror.

I left the bathroom and turned into a small corridor lit by small glowing wall lamps in the shape of ice cream cones. From a partially open door, I could hear a discussion. I paused near the door.

Wanda was saying, 'I wanna do it, so you girls gotta tell me if you're in.'

One woman said, 'If it pays like you says it will, why the hell not?'

Another said, 'Count me in, too.'

'Santa Barbara? Where we gonna stay? She gonna put us up?'

'Yeah. The deal is our own rooms, doubling up of course, new formals, and a bus with our name on!'

'You mean, *your* name on it. Now we're just the Charms.' This was Alberta. 'You work fast, girl. I only told you last night. How's Dolly gonna feel?'

'She don't have to find out.'

'Course she's gonna find out.'

'We gotta look out for ourselves now. I don't want no cops grilling me about Dolly Perkins and her dead boyfriend. None of us need that shit. What I do want is to make some good money for a change.'

Alberta spoke again. 'How did you find out about this party?'

There was a beat. Wanda sounded coy. 'Zetty's boss. Tell 'em, Zetty.'

There was a long silence.

A woman spoke. She had a deep, husky and thick accent. European. Italian? I couldn't tell. 'I work for her. Very rich. Everything Wanda says is true. She wants us to play. Money no

103

problem for her. I tell Dolly. She was excited. Now she can't sing. So Wanda do it.'

Alberta said, 'I feel bad for Dolly.'

Wanda's voice took a plaintive tone that didn't suit it. 'I want to tour, I want a recording contract, I want to play in concert halls one day. This party, if it pays well, it gets the show on the road.'

'Good timing for you, then, ain't it?' Alberta sounded sarcastic.

'Everything happens for a reason. God's plan.'

Alberta said, 'Zetty, you're Dolly's best pal. What do you think?'

Zetty said, 'Dolly will be disappointed. But maybe we give her a cut to help her.'

Some grunts of agreement. Wanda said, 'How about that? Whatever happens, Dolly's gonna need dough.'

Alberta sighed. 'This boss lady okay, Zetty?'

Zetty said, 'Yes.'

'All right. Count me in, I got time on my hands and I like to play. Anything after that, we'll see.'

Wanda said, 'You made my day, girl!'

There were shouts of 'All right!' 'Let's do it for Dolly!'

I figured now was a good time to walk in. I pushed open the door. Six surprised faces and a collective shimmer of violet silk spun around.

A Mediterranean-looking woman with heavy eyes looked familiar. Where had I seen her before? A waitress at Luigi's? I couldn't place her. Was this Zetty?

Wanda wasn't smiling at me. 'Lost? This room is for band members only.'

'I'm looking for Alberta... Oh, there you are!'

Alberta smiled. 'This Elvira, she's a pal.' Her hand waved around. 'Wanda, Zetty, Jewel, Carmen, and Bertha.'

'No offense, I might not remember your names. Those cocktails sure are potent.'

'I saw you dancing out there.' Alberta laughed.

'You ladies play real good.' I addressed that to Wanda.

Wanda looked me up and down coolly. She said to the others, 'Joyce's cake time, ladies.' As she led the way out of the door, she said to me, 'No offense, whatever your name is.'

I waited until Alberta was last to pass me. She spoke with a low voice. 'You get any of that?'

I nodded. 'Most of it.'

She said, 'Poor Dolly.'

On stage, Wanda stretched out her arms and made an elaborate bow to the audience. She spoke into the microphone. 'We all know it's a special night for a special lady. So I wanna hear some noise.'

Everyone clapped and roared. Most of the partygoers were now at the tables with the low lamps, as waitresses cleared their plates. The dance floor was empty. I grabbed a plate and stacked it with cheese pie and grapes. I sat at the bar and picked at the food.

'One, two, three, let's go!'

The band started to play as two women dressed in green pixie outfits pushed out an enormous tiered cake towards Joyce's booth.

The whole club burst into song.

Joyce feigned delighted surprise. I bet she'd been in on the whole thing.

I looked around. It felt good, being here.

Further down the bar, my dancing partner Cheryl was ensconced in her lover's arms. They looked happy.

I suddenly missed someone I could hold. Someone who would give me cake and sing on my birthday.

Snap out of it!

I had work to do and I had to stay sharp. I finished my drink and slipped out.

18

Sonia had huge dark rings under her eyes. She was furious about the cops' handling of the miscarriage. 'You know where to find the old soak again, if need be?' I told her Annie was well known by the cops and it shouldn't take much to locate her.

Sonia grunted and perused the menu. I did the same, deciding not to ask how her dying parents were.

Hal's Diner was packed out, each turquoise vinyl booth filled with noisy, hungry brunchers. I bet most, like me, were relieved Christmas was over.

Sonia had chosen a booth near the window, in the corner, so we couldn't be overheard. She was already here when I arrived, a different fur coat to the previous chinchilla hanging on a clothes tree near the booth. It was a pale cream sable fur.

Sonia had quite a death count in her wardrobe.

Today, she wore a vibrant blue crepe dress, the cuffs and belt edged in a darker blue silk. A trio of little dark blue velvet buttons at each wrist matched the blue silk and velvet flowers across the bodice. In daylight, her hair was a steel gray, not black, which set off her coral lipstick very nicely. Her jewelry consisted of large cut stone blue earrings set in gold, and a matching bracelet. A huge sapphire ring weighed down her finger.

The whole look was effortlessly stylish and expensive and totally out of place in the humble diner.

I had thrown on black pants, a simple crepe blouse, June's gray jacket, and a beret, thinking a diner shouldn't warrant too much effort. While I felt underdressed next to her, I had a sneaky suspicion Sonia would approve of my simple work attire.

She wouldn't want to be outclassed in the style department.

She looked up as a middle-aged waitress strolled up, holding her pen and notepad.

'Life treating you good, Paula?' It was strange to see Sonia actually smile brightly, for once.

The waitress gave a wry smile. 'Every day's a good day Miss Parker, so I ain't complainin'. What can I get you?'

'I'll take the special. Eggs over easy. Bacon on the crispy side, the way I like it. Three pancakes. Drizzle of maple syrup. Oh, a large pot of coffee.'

Paula the waitress jotted this down, turning to me. She had a tattoo of a flower coiling up her arm with a few hearts and black cats thrown in for good measure.

I felt a pang, instantly remembering Kettle, my cat back in London. He had died while I was in the slammer. One day, I'd get another kitty. But not now. I still missed Kettle too bad.

'Same as her, but eggs sunny-side up, no bacon. And no bacon fat to fry the eggs.'

Sonia and Paula both stared at me. Sonia said, 'Didn't have you down as a health freak.'

'I'm not. I just don't like meat. At all.'

Paula jotted something down. 'Can ask but no promises. Sunny-side up, no bacon. Eggs cooked separate.' She walked off towards the kitchen.

I nodded after Paula. 'Former client?'

'A *pro bono* case. Told her to thank me in waffles.'

She lowered her voice. 'Hal's staff have all done time. He's a rare individual who thinks time served is the punishment, not the rest of their lives.'

I glanced at Hal, a stooping and balding man in an apron, chatting to a customer who sat at the counter. This one was bony, in a shabby pinstriped suit, and dented hat. He was shoveling up the food on his plate and talking at the same time. I bet he'd just been released.

'Society doesn't think like that, though, does it?' Sonia flicked ash into a large ceramic ashtray.

I shook my head. This conversation hit a nerve. The world, as I well knew, treated criminality like a birthmark. Something you were born with, something that defined you, and something that would never go away. Something people would always judge you by.

A few, like Hal, believed redemption was possible. That a person could do good.

I'd met another person who thought the same when I was inside. The prison governor, Lucinda Seldon. My first ever contact with someone from the establishment who saw me as a person, beyond the criminal. Back then, I'd thought she was a sucker.

Now I admired her.

And the Hals, the Sonia Parkers and the Lucinda Seldons also knew that the rich could get away with murder because they had the money and the contacts to pay for the best defense.

I thought of Lauder, marrying into this golden world. He told me once that I'd proved to him an ex-con could do good. I knew he hadn't initially wanted to help me, but somewhere deep down, he knew I wasn't rotten to the core.

Sonia was studying me, curiously. 'Still here?'

I roused myself. 'Sorry, I was just thinking I recognized Hal from somewhere. Got one of those faces.'

'Fill me in, everything since I dropped you at Hunter's.' Sonia leaned back, arms folded, her pen poised.

I did my best, reliving my moments second by second. Sonia didn't flinch when I told her about wiping the blade or describing his body. When I recounted seeing *Lier* scrawled on the wall, she finally made a movement, pursing her lips and writing something down. 'In lipstick. You're sure?'

I opened my purse and passed the lipstick over. 'Wedged in the back staircase. Rather too carefully, so no way could it be kicked away.' I explained how I'd dabbed some of the writing off the wall with my hankie, which I then produced from my purse. Sonia undid the lipstick and pushed it up. She held it against the stain.

No doubt. In this light, too, it was identical.

She slid to the lipstick back to me. 'Keep it safe. I'll ask Dolly what brand she wears.'

'If she uses this one, surely it proves it's a setup, right? Anyone close to Dolly could've lifted it.' I put the lipstick back in my purse.

But who? Other than The Charmettes, who else was in Dolly's life?

'The prosecutor will have no problem pinning the writing on her. Lipstick plus rage plus bad spelling.'

'Will they do a handwriting test? Get an expert to compare?'

Sonia met my eyes. 'You do your job, I'll do mine.'

I went on to explain that I hadn't managed to find out much

more about Dolly, other than Alberta felt sorry for her, that her adoptive parents were dead, that Alberta had assured me Dolly was on good terms with the rest of the musicians, even if she annoyed them with empty promises.

I explained about Wanda's opportunistic move on Zetty's businesswoman boss for a gig that Dolly wanted to sing at. 'So should I look into her?'

'Wanda or the businesswoman?'

'Er...either.'

'The only point in that is if I think there is a chance this Wanda framed Dolly to get her out of the way just for a well-paid gig. A highly implausible scenario, unless Wanda's a psychopath. Did she appear particularly insane to you?'

I didn't appreciate the hint of sarcasm. I conceded she didn't; that Wanda looked and sounded like a woman who wanted to give fame and fortune her best shot.

'Nothing wrong with ambition.' Sonia declared. 'Let's get back to everything else you've seen and done. Then we'll plan your next steps.'

This was investigating by numbers. Sonia's numbers.

I leaned forward. 'I found a blood-stained handkerchief with a monogram. R.A.H. And I took it.'

'Where is it?' I explained it was safely hidden.

'All right. Keep it that way.'

Again, no real indication if I'd done a good thing or not. Did she lavish her male investigators with praise?

Toughen up, will you!

Ignoring my need for approval, I told her about Hunter's people being outside. 'The girl sounded nervous. The chauffeur, he's called Brad, is a full-fledged jerk.'

I explained how Linda Hunter had phoned the secretary that night to find out about Hunter's whereabouts. How Brad seemed to dislike Linda Hunter and hinted she was also having an affair.

Sonia took this in her stride. 'Hunter's wife's acting name was Linda Reeves. She only made two movies before the studio let her go. But she comes from money. Texan family. Tobacco, as I recall. There's at least a thirty-year age difference between her and Hunter. She can only be in her late thirties. He's by far the wealthier.'

'Kids?'

'Yes, a boy. I told you this already.' She sounded irritable at my forgetting.

I nodded. 'Maybe Hunter stepped out one too many times and Linda finally flipped. She could have paid somebody to get close to Dolly for the lipstick, watch her movements and do the hit.'

Sonia gave me a *'Don't go there'* look.

I spluttered. 'I know it's not my call, but shortlisting suspects can't start too soon, can it? I just want to help.'

Sonia relented. 'Sure, jealousy can make a person go crazy. So Dolly says Linda makes Hunter unhappy, where does that lead us? If she's that fed up, divorce would be on the cards. Linda Hunter could simply hire a good private detective rather than resort to cold-blooded murder. A few snapshots of Ronald Hunter *in flagrante*, she would walk out of a bad marriage richer than she walked in. A vengeful murder? Highly unlikely.'

I laughed inwardly. I knew exactly the right investigator for Linda Hunter if she wanted to expose Ronald.

Beatty Falaise.

'What if she's got a lover and Hunter found out? Then she might get nothing.'

'We have no evidence of that.'

'*Yet*. I could look into her. You said the case had a personal feel.'

Sonia listened but I could tell she didn't buy it. 'I just don't like her for it. Gut feeling. I don't know her, but she looks like the sort who would turn a blind eye to her husband's affairs, particularly if it means she doesn't have to service him.'

As Sonia continued to dismiss my theory, I switched off, examining my red nails. Starting to flake already. I envied Sonia's perfect coral manicure. On my way back, I could try to grab a manicure if any place was open. Would I get the same red polish? I liked it. It reminded me of a car I'd once seen, a beauty owned by a certain successful screenwriter.

Paula returned with our substantial specials and coffee. As she put my plate down, she said, 'Eggs for the health nut.' But she was winking, so I smiled.

Between mouthfuls, Sonia asked me about Hunter's mansion. I was reluctant to tell her about seeing Lauder. Even less so my napping on the job.

But I'd already told *him* about Sonia. Surely I owed her more than him, as far as this case was concerned? It couldn't hurt, if I was careful how much I told her. 'I saw a cop leave the house. I think he works for LAPD vice squad. I don't know him, but...'

'A vice cop?' Her eyes lit up. 'How do you know?'

'Er...I think I saw his picture in a paper. He busted some blackmail case a few months back, maybe?'

'Odd. Maybe his buddies in homicide were thinly stretched

and he was doing them a favor by breaking the news to her.' She prodded a hash brown. 'Alternatively, this could really be something. You don't recall his name?'

I shook my head. 'Let me ask around. I'll see if I can root him out.'

'Good. I'm sure your own cop contacts can help us here. You do have some, surely?'

Dammit! She thinks you've got your own insiders!

I swallowed, nodding convincingly, focusing on carving off a corner of waffle.

Sonia said, 'Well, I have news, too. Dolly was taken from jail ward back to the precinct this morning. I've been summoned for later this afternoon's questioning. When we're alone I can ask her about the lipstick then. She's been discharged to be charged, I expect.'

'Oh, no.' She'd saved this key development till last, I noticed.

'Actually, I find the charge is a defining moment. It sharpens the focus.'

Sonia issued instructions for my next steps. I was to go to Dolly's digs, a boarding house in Compton. The landlady was a Mrs. Olsen. I was to talk to anyone there and try to work out who had access to Dolly's room.

'What about Hunter's firm? Should I snoop around that side of his life?'

Sonia shrugged. 'Not yet. Ronald is the eldest and the controlling shareholder, but apparently, he's let Rufus run the show. Best buddies, by all accounts.'

'What about Hunter's political ambitions? A rival bumping him off?'

'The election's several years away. And a mistress as unlikely as Dolly would be an easier way for any opposition to discredit him. They'd just leak it to the press. This is America. We still like our political leaders scandal-free.'

I felt frustrated, every path blocked. If Sonia had a suspect or a strategy, she would never share it with me. That much was clear. And theorizing would soon become tedious anyway, always getting a negative in answer.

But I knew that to defend Dolly, she would have to prove it was a frame-up and, ideally, find a suspect with motive and provide some evidence. That meant letting something slip to me at some point soon. If she didn't buy the wife, the brother, or political rivals, who the hell did she buy?

Finally, she said something that did surprise me. 'I just wish I had a way to get you into the funeral.'

Wait a minute!

My nails. Bright red.

I felt a flush of excitement from actually being able to act on my initiative. 'You said Linda Hunter used to be an actress?'

Sonia nodded. 'Why?'

'Hunter's funeral. I might know someone who can get me in.'

19

Martell Grainger was writing her *pièce de résistance*, the life story of Tatiana Spark. It would be her first biographical screenplay, a break from her long and well-remunerated tradition of schmaltz.

And only she could write it because she had insinuated herself as Tatiana's friend before the latter's sad demise. Tatiana had apparently shared the most intimate details of her life with Martell. The main theme was maternal guilt, naturally. Tatiana, in her later years, was riddled with remorse for putting fame and fortune ahead of her illegitimate child, Sophia, and then leaving her back in Europe in the care of a childless couple who may or may not have survived the various invasions, first by the Nazis, then the liberating Russians.

As the young Tatiana's star rose, so would her anguish that her daughter didn't know her and might be enduring a terrible life.

Martell had the complete support of her wealthy producer, Lyle Vadnay, and together they obtained the blessing of the trustees to make the movie, on condition Sophia Spark was located and approved the ending.

After all, the movie would inevitably reveal some of the harsh realities of Sophia's life, and the yearning for a reunion. Martell, in previous conversations, had indicated that should Sophia prove to be dead, this would actually help her get script approval from the censors. It would be the ultimate cautionary tale for any female member of the audience who dreamt of putting her selfish need for work first. She would watch a woman die, never finding her daughter, who would grow up only to tragically die young, never knowing her mother.

Leave your kids, you may never see them again.

The movie would be a tearjerker and a huge hit.

After I said goodbye to Sonia, I rang Martell from a payphone at Hal's Diner. I assumed she'd be away like the rest of her set, skiing somewhere 'cold, white and expensive', as Alberta had put it. But, amazingly, Martell was in and couldn't hide the fact she was pleased to hear from me. Normally, she called me. She would put in a weekly call to Barney, bugging him about my progress on the Tatiana Spark case.

'Happy holidays. It's your favorite detective.'

'So, you've got news?' Martell didn't beat about the bush.

I asked if I could pay her a visit. She invited me directly over.

I had to play it carefully. Martell was a deal-maker, the ultimate strategist, and pushy as hell. If I wasn't careful, she'd get what she wanted and I'd come out with nothing. Assuming she knew Linda Hunter, she could take me to the funeral, but only if I gave her something valuable in return.

And thanks to the tragic twist of events in Vienna, I had just the thing she was most desperate for.

Closure.

The marble statue of Venus was decapitated, a clean break to the neck. Her head lolled by the plinth below, eyes staring morosely into the velvety emerald turf.

'I don't know what I was thinking, giving the boys baseball bats. Still, live and learn. They've gone back to Daddykins.'

117

Martell surveyed the damage, hands on hips. She turned to me. 'He's far too strict with them, so when they come here, they just go wild.' She shuddered. 'Thank heavens Phyllis was here. She is the only one they listen too.'

Phyllis, Martell's longstanding housekeeper, was at the far end of the garden, setting out drinks on a table with a bright white cloth. She moved with the over-careful movements of the exhausted. I wondered if she had been deprived of Christmas with her own family to look after Martell's brats.

Her sons being here meant that Martell's ex-hubby must have finally caved in. Having deserted a bad marriage as a banker's housewife in Pasadena, Martell had fled to Hollywood to pursue a career as a screenwriter. Her ex had punished her by depriving her of access to her sons for many years.

And as a divorcee, Martell hadn't wasted one second of her freedom. Compensation for her maternal loss was a stellar movie career, churning out slushy romances. And when her sister died, giving her charge of her effervescent niece, Pammie, Martell found a daughter figure she could indulge.

Her magnificent residence was Perpetua, a Beverly Hills villa. I'd only visited a few times, but each time the grounds seemed more magical.

A headless Venus couldn't ruin the charm of the place for me.

'I hope you've come bearing good tidings. It is Christmas, after all. Come have a drink.' she said.

I noticed how her auburn hair was a shade lighter, but still as glossy, with thick curls tied up with a simple silk bow, giving her a girlish look. She was immaculate, as always, in a pale green silk dress and suede shoes in exactly the same shade. She seemed to co-ordinate with the clump of pampas grass swaying in the distance behind her.

She escorted me to the patio where Phyllis had been moments ago. She had left a silver tray with two crystal goblets and a vintage white wine in a chiller, and a fluffy shawl neatly folded over one of the seats. It was a perfect Californian winter's day, surprisingly warm and balmy, with a slight breeze.

'How's Pammie?'

'Wonderful! She's started acting classes. Naturally talented, but I thought some training wouldn't hurt.'

Lucky Pammie, having an aunt who could open doors with a snap of her fingers.

All those broke girls from the Midwest, arriving on buses with dreams in their hearts, and cents in their wallets, who didn't have a relative with connections. They risked ending up prey to men who expected sex in return for a helping hand up the ladder.

But the rungs were rotten, and the hand was already groping somebody else's ass.

We sat down. Martell poured two generous glasses of wine and handed me one. 'So hit me with it.'

'Sophia Spark was located in Vienna. The bad news—she's dead.'

Martell very carefully put her wine down. She was not one for spontaneous outbursts and the cogs were already whirring. 'Oh. How did she die?'

I nodded. 'Pneumonia.'

'Pneumonia? How awful.' Martell had the decency to try to sound rueful and pull a sorry face. Maybe some part of her did care, for a second. But she couldn't help the way she was wired. Martell always came first, what Martell wanted a close second, and coming up third, Martell getting the best out of any situation. Spending time thinking about others was a waste of precious Martell time.

Sophia's death was the best ending from Martell's point of view and knowing about it also meant the brakes were off the movie. Martell would be getting on the line to producer Lyle Vadnay as soon as I left.

'To think what a life she could have had. Oh! The tragedy. I can't bear it.' It was a good performance, amusing in its own way. Martell sipped her wine. 'Are you absolutely certain?'

'It's exceedingly likely. And no kids.'

'None?'

'Apparently not.'

'So, after the holidays, you'll be notifying the trustees?'

I lit a cigarette. 'Possibly.'

This annoyed her, but she tried to hide it. 'But you said you're certain? Why wait?'

I exhaled a long plume, hoping to achieve a blasé effect. 'I figure I should probably wait for my source to return. She may get a copy of the death certificate, something more conclusive to show them.'

A flash of irritation in her eyes. 'And when will that be?'

I shrugged. 'She's on a real big assignment. She's following troop demobilization for a major magazine feature.' A lie, but Martell didn't know.

'You know, Elvira, I have been very patient. This investigation has taken you almost two months. I have no idea why you didn't just jump on a plane and go there yourself. I'm sure with your skills, and trust's resources, you could have found this out far sooner.'

Clever move. Imply I've been incompetent and not running on all cylinders, to manipulate me into doing her bidding now. She was touching a nerve because I actually did feel guilty that I couldn't go to Europe, and I hadn't wanted to waste Tatiana's funds doing nothing.

Don't let her get to you!

I reminded myself the trustees wanted to honor a dead woman's wishes to provide for her child and, possibly, grandchildren. The movie was not their priority, only Martell's. She knew it, but that wouldn't stop her bullying like this. Life had taught me one thing: ruthless bullies won't stop with any dirty tactics until they're forced.

I met her eyes, picking up my glass. 'I could tell them, for sure. But we both know it would be wrong to give unconfirmed information. So it makes sense to wait for my reporter pal to get back with facts and, let's hope, proof of death.'

'You don't look like a checkbox kind of girl.'

'I just want to do things properly.'

Martell's eyes glinted coldly. I was, until she got her way, Against Her.

'I suppose you're on a retainer? The longer this whole darned business takes, the more it benefits you?'

Ouch! Martell had pulled another low-down move. I bristled. 'That's irrelevant. I want this done as much as anyone else involved. But I need to be professional. That means getting verification.'

It was time to make my play.

I swallowed some more wine. Delicious and emboldening, the way wine should be. 'I appreciate the picture depends on this notification, and you're kind of stymied until then. Professionally, I mean.'

'Me? Baloney! I'm positively drowning in offers of work. But this movie is the one I feel a sense of duty towards. Just like you.'

She was shameless. Making out she was doing the dead Tatiana a favor by making the movie.

'Well, I guess the odds are heavily against Sophia turning up alive. So maybe I could alert the trustees.'

Her perfectly plucked brows raised like little arches. She could smell victory, but she wasn't going to let her guard down. 'My sentiments exactly. I really think they deserve that.'

'You know Linda Hunter?'

'*The* Linda Hunter? As in Ronald Hunter's wife—I mean... widow? Rest in peace. How dreadful is that news?'

I nodded. 'Know her well?'

'She had a bit part in one of my pictures. She's not exactly in my inner circle, but we go to some of the same parties. I left a condolence card as soon as I heard. Why?'

'Know anyone who would want to kill Ronald Hunter?'

Martell gasped, but looked amused. 'Do I what? Good heavens, no! What a question!'

'So, happily married?'

'What on earth are you getting at? You think Linda Hunter did it? Preposterous.' Martell studied me. 'You're investigating, aren't you?'

'I'm not at liberty to say.'

'Gee, aren't you full of surprises today!'

The risk of talking to Martell suddenly hit me. If she even casually mentioned to anyone the tasty morsel that she knew the defense's PI, then it might not take too long for the creep Flannery to learn about some Elvira Slate, digging around for the defense.

'You're working for the defense, of course.' I didn't indicate yes or no.

Martell refilled our glasses. 'Aren't they holding some woman?'

The press hadn't mentioned a woman. The papers had said "suspect". Martell, as usual, had inside information somehow. I mulled. There was a good chance Detective Flannery had informed Linda about Dolly. He would have quizzed her on what she knew.

And maybe a distraught Linda had confided in someone Martell knew.

'Could be. You think Linda Hunter has a lover on the side?'

'How on earth did you get this impression?'

'Does it matter?' Sonia might want to close that avenue down, but I was itching to know.

Martell gave a superior smile. 'Curiosity killed the cat. If she is, she is. I have no idea, to be frank.'

'What's she like?'

'To be perfectly honest, sweet, but dull. And can't act for toffee. Most girls who want to make it cotton on fast that a pretty face isn't enough. An actor is born with the gift, or they are not. I don't think Linda ever worked that out. Problem of being born into money.'

'What about him? Hunter?'

'I don't like to speak ill of the dead.'

'But you met him?'

'Uh-huh. Put it this way, we didn't have a lot to say to each other. I'm not his kind of woman.'

What did she mean exactly? That she was too old? Too threatening? I couldn't say that to her. 'Like…intelligent?' I suggested.

'A man like Hunter wants someone on his arm to laugh at his jokes. I got divorced to get away from all that.'

I had to laugh. 'So will you go to the funeral?'

'The reception, afterwards. Everyone will be there, if they aren't away. Why?'

'Think I could tag along? As your pal, or something? A great storyteller like you could easily invent a reason.'

She leaned back. 'Oh, you're in a very nosey and demanding mood. You want my help, you gotta spill, honey. Let's not pretend you're not working for the defense.'

Our eyes locked. Now for the bait. I leaned forward, enticingly. 'How about I tell the trustees on 2nd January that Sophia Spark is dead and my evidence is on its way back from Vienna? Then the screenplay can be finished with their blessing and you don't have to wait for any certificates. You take me to the funeral, and don't say a word to anybody about why you *think* I want to be there, and that's what I'll say to the trustees.'

Martell mirrored my position, looking straight into my eyes. 'Looks like you got yourself a deal.'

That was quick.

Martell held out her hand and we shook. Her skin felt as soft as silk.

I added, 'This stays between us. I wouldn't want to have to tell the trustees I got some new information, meaning I can't guarantee Sophia is dead. That I have to go to Vienna after all, and figure it out for myself. Which could take a long time.'

Martell swallowed a laugh. She picked up the cashmere shawl that Phyllis had left over the back of the chair and pulled it around her shoulders. 'You've toughened up. I remember the first time you came here, just a little mouse. And you look better, too. More color in your cheeks, more flesh on the bones.'

Enough flattery. I needed to pin her down. I said, 'I want a guarantee.'

'Honey, you're rock solid from where I'm sitting. I just want to make the movie. Why on earth would I tell Linda Hunter or anybody else I'm helping the defense? Of course I won't breathe a word.' She looked at me. 'I'm sure I can come up with some persona for you.'

'Sounds good.'

'Besides, knowing you're snooping will make a dull affair more interesting. Maybe you will catch a rat amongst the lilies.'

'Maybe. But unlikely.'

'So now we're in cahoots, who's the woman, the suspect?'

'A nobody.' I shrugged it off.

Martell mused. 'A nobody, huh? No surprise. Who men marry and who men like to have fun with aren't always the same type of girl, in my experience.'

I flinched at her words, thinking immediately of Lauder.

'Wouldn't know. Never been married, never been duped. And I intend to keep it that way.' I smiled, standing up.

Martell also stood up. She escorted me back towards the French doors that led inside.

In her lobby, she said she'd call as soon as she knew the funeral date. It was likely to be soon. She looked down at my modest attire. 'Be sure to look the part.'

I assured her I'd dress to impress, but I could use a heavily veiled hat if she had one. She said she had just the thing.

20

'What do you want?' It was a woman's voice with a strong accent. European, but I couldn't place it exactly.

I stood on front porch of the shabby boarding house, looking around for the source of the voice.

A woman stood just below me. She must have come from a side entrance at ground level. The matronly type, in her fifties, her graying blonde hair tied back in a scarf. A white pin-tucked apron covered her ample bosom. Her sleeves were rolled up, her hands covered in flour. Her eyes were a clear and bright blue, her cheekbones wide and high.

Standing on some bleak Scandinavian hinterland, she wouldn't be out of place. This had to be the landlady, Mrs. Olsen.

I told her I was a friend of Dolly Perkins. Was she Mrs. Olsen?

'Yes, but Dolly is not here. You want to leave a message?'

Dolly was still unnamed by the press. Maybe Mrs. Olsen had no idea she was involved.

I stomped back down the wooden steps. One cracked, a rotten one. The boarding house was a large old house in Compton, and it had taken me a while to find. There were signs of female occupancy in each window on the upper two floors. Delicate underclothes drying on makeshift lines, little pots of miniature roses, even a mannequin with fabric draped over it.

If I'd come to stay at a down-at-heel place like this when I first got to LA, rather than the upmarket Miracle Mile, would my destiny have taken a different route?

No June, no Lauder, no Beatty.

No Elvira Slate.

But I'd never have stayed in a low-rent dive. I had been hell-bent on a glamorous life, despite my dwindling funds. And with no intention of getting a job, ill-gotten gains were on the horizon.

What life was teaching me fast was that delusions of grandeur have a habit of biting you in the ass. 'Know when she's back?' I said.

She shook her head. Plumes of flour danced into the air from her bosom.

I pulled a face. 'Dang! Dolly said she'd lend me a gown for a do tonight. I'm here to collect. Can I go to her room?'

The hooded eyes narrowed. 'You are musician?'

'Yeah. I play the drums.' I said, for no good reason at all.

What? Are you crazy? The drums?

She concealed a smile. 'The singers, I do not mind. Dolly sings like angel. A drummer? Never come here if you need a room.'

'Oh, I'm in no need of lodgings, ma'am.' The fact she was warming up to me was an advantage. 'Could I just grab the frock?'

Mrs. Olsen frowned. 'I don't know.'

'You can trust me. You know, Dolly told me she's behind on the rent, in a dry spot. Say I give you last week's rent. That proves I'm legit, right?'

Total long shot.

'You want to pay her rent?'

'Sure. Why not? Dolly's a pal. She can pay me back when she's flush. Said her fella's got plenty of money.'

127

'I do not know about that. No men allowed here.'

I opened my purse. 'How much she owe?'

'Fifteen dollars.' Mrs. Olsen wasn't one to look a gift horse in the mouth.

I took out a stack of dollar bills and counted fifteen. I handed them to her.

'Does she have a roommate?'

'Willa. But she is not here. This way.' She led me back up the rickety stairs. At the door she produced a key from her apron pocket and opened the door.

We entered into the sparse hall of the boarding house. A line of blue painted doors had little white numbers. The wood floor was thick with layers of old wax. To my amazement, Mrs. Olsen handed me a small key.

'Dolly is in room eight. Lock the door after you.'

I opened the door. There was just enough light to put your mascara on without messing it up. I flicked the light switch on for a better look around.

The room was surprisingly large, with twin beds with painted metal frames and two closets facing each bed. The beds were covered in faded cerise-colored candlewick bedspreads with garlands of blue and yellow roses. One bed was neatly made, the other rumpled.

At one end of the room, a large window was covered by heavy festoon nets that were prematurely gray. The drapes on each side were made from simple blue and white floral linen. On the opposite wall, adjacent to the unmade bed, a pale blue painted dressing table and a mismatched dark wood stool with a padded yellow velvet cushion. The dressing table was strewn with the usual scent bottles, makeup, brushes, powder puffs, hairpins and lacquer. A pink cut glass vanity tray was filled with trinkets and cheap costume jewelry. A battered silk corsage of red and pink flowers lay on its side.

Half the room was clean, tidy and smelt of lemony floor wax.

The other half was a trashcan. I bet it was Dolly's territory, and she had claimed the dressing table.

Discarded dresses were hanging over the open door of the closet facing the crumpled bed.

All the kinds of things Dolly would wear.

I just couldn't see her spending much time here.

I got to work, searching for any kind of clues about Dolly's life.

Inside the closet, a jungle of clothes. A fake fur swing coat, black, mid-length, with a high neck; a row of summery dresses; several satin and sequined formal gowns in various shades of pink, lilac and ivory. A couple had stains around the hem, suggesting Dolly didn't splash out on dry cleaning until things got bad.

I rummaged through anything with pockets. I extracted a heavy gold plated lighter, a man's, with the initial S. S for who?

On top of the wardrobe, a stack of hat boxes. One was full of stockings, like a tangled mass of snakeskins. I grabbed a handful, lifting them out. At the bottom, a small card with writing on caught my eye.

Bingo.

I picked it up. It was in fact a photograph, a small black and white snap of a soldier in uniform. He was light-skinned, maybe mixed race. But whether half black and half white, or something else, I couldn't really tell. He was very good-looking.

On the back, somebody had written, '*To the cutest little kitten. Yours. S.*'

A boyfriend, surely? Was 'S' the owner of the lighter? But how recently had he given it to Dolly? Was it Sol, whom Dolly was sweet on? If it was, and his feelings weren't mutual, why lead Dolly on like this?

I slipped the portrait into my purse, grabbed the dress. Wait, the lighter. I'd take that, too. If anyone else searched the room, it wasn't a great idea for Dolly to look like she had another boyfriend.

I plucked out a frilly pink formal gown. Cheap rose fragrance lingered on the dress.

Out of curiosity, and wanting to get a better idea of Willa, I peered inside the other closet.

Three suits in somber colors and five ironed shirts. A couple of dresses, in a large size. So Willa wasn't a stick. A few pairs of good quality sensible shoes were neatly stacked up, in one corner. A practical girl, organized; one of the many ordinary girls who just wanted to make enough to enable them to live in Los Angeles.

Before I left, I did a final sweep of the drawers of the dressing table. A few bottles of painkilling tablets, nail lacquer, old restaurant bills and more jewelry.

I left the room and slipped back down the corridor.

Outside, Mrs. Olsen was waiting on the other side of the door, hands on hips. She was calling out to somebody, shaking her head.

She stood by to let me pass her. I followed her eyes; she was watching the back of stocky man in a dark gray suit and blue derby hat. He had almost reached the sidewalk.

'Huh. Someone's fella, trying to get past you?' I asked, joking.

'No. He ask for Willa.' She said, not taking her eyes from him. 'Strange.'

'Why?' My voice did its best to sound casual. She was holding the man's card in her hand. 'Not her boyfriend?'

'No. He was a private detective.'

What?

I recalled Dolly's fat guy, with eyes on the boarding house.

'And he left his card?' I asked, trying to sound as casual as possible.

Mrs. Olsen nodded. It was in her hand. 'He said he would come back later.'

'Seen him before?' I asked.

'Never. Why?'

'Maybe Willa's in trouble? I hope not.'

'Willa is a good girl,' snapped Mrs. Olsen.

Worry flashed across her face. I got a sense she was the maternal type. She turned to me. 'You have what you came for? This one?'

She glanced at the dress, and then me. There was no avoiding the fact I was at least one size bigger than Dolly. 'It must be hard to play the drums in a tight dress,' she observed.

'If need be, I can let it out a little. I'll fix it back up for Dolly.'

Her eyes swiveled to the man, who was now getting into a dark green sedan.

Fat guy, green car.

'Well, so long. Thanks.' I said. I didn't really mean it and she wasn't really listening.

The green sedan headed back towards the city, taking a more direct route than I'd used to come out. He knew his way around better than I did.

He knew about Willa. What else did he know? And what did he want? This couldn't be co-incidence.

Did Willa even know about Dolly's affair with Ronald Hunter? How friendly were they? Dolly was such a chatterbox, it was hard to imagine she wouldn't blab to her roomie, but maybe loyalty to her man had kept her mouth shut.

I kept my distance in Mabel, but the traffic was relatively sparse.

We were in the vicinity of Culver City, an area I didn't know so well. Lauder and I occasionally met in a cocktail bar there, the Rouge d'Or.

Suddenly the green car signaled right, pulling into an underground parking lot of an office block. It was a shabby 1920s affair, covered in gray concrete. I shot past, glancing right. The car was already down the ramp. I made my way around the block. It took about five minutes. I found a space on the street and parked.

I got out and walked towards the building. The windows were shaded by venetians, some broken. In one window, a sign declared office space was available to lease.

I pushed the front door open. The lobby was paneled redwood, with a gray tiled floor. Not a dump, definitely deserted. The companies were listed in gold lettering behind the front desk. On the first floor, three doctors were listed. The second floor was taken up by Anville Insurance, Inc. The third floor had quite a few names, but one stood out: *Todd F. Minski, Private Investigator.*

My guy.

The elevator light was stuck on the third floor.

An elderly guy, the concierge, shuffled out of a side door. In a flash, I dived into the stairway before he could see me. I darted up the stairs, all the way to the third floor.

I crept along the deserted corridor. Todd Minski's office was the first door of three. I pressed my ear to it. A man's voice was just about audible. 'No. She wasn't. No. I'll try again. Sure, I'll get to her.' He listened for a while. 'Yeah, that's Flannery's style. Smarty-pants tactic. She didn't say nothing to nobody? You sure about that? Good... No, I got it. Keep it nice and quiet. I'll tie up the loose ends...Sure, that's what you pay me for. Nothing to worry about.'

Flannery? Loose Ends? The PI was definitely talking to someone about the case.

I had no readymade excuse to knock on the door, nothing that could help me get anything out of him. It would have to wait. He was listening to the other person at the end of the line for a while, probably pacing the floor, since the grunts and 'uh-huh's changed direction.

I could hear the click of a lighter. He inhaled and then coughed. 'The band? A whole bunch of them. Relax, they'll be easier to deal with. No... If they know, we don't have to shell out as much as to the roommate.'

What?! He must be talking about The Charmettes. Paying them off? Buying their silence? And Willa's?

Tying up loose ends?

Seconds later, Minski hung up. The door handled twisted. I didn't hang around.

'Hey!' *Damn!* He saw me. 'Looking for somebody?'

133

I spun around, acting innocent.

So here was my male equivalent in the low-rent PI department. Certainly nothing to aspire to. He was mid-forties, with a belly that comfortably sagged over his belt. His suit was baggy, but not the cheapest I'd seen. He had loosened his tie, giving the impression he didn't expect to see anyone today. On his face, there was the unmistakable booze bloat and five o'clock shadow. His jaw worked up and down, chewing gum.

If I took Lauder's advice to take on the nobodies, would I end up the female version of Minski? Overweight, unhealthy and renting out cheap office suites?

'I'm temping for Anville. Covering the telephone lines. I got lost!' I pulled a pathetic, helpless grin.

'Anville? Wrong floor, doll. Down one.'

'Oh, thank you so much! Happy holidays!'

I bolted back down the stairs. 'Doll', indeed! The cheek!

This time the man at the front desk saw me. He looked quite frail and lost, with watery eyes and slow movements, in no shape to get heavy.

I gave him the quickest of waves. He blinked slowly; by the time he realized something was up, I was already out of the door.

I jumped in the car and took off, driving aimlessly for a while. I could have just winged it, told Minski I was in need of a PI. But I hadn't. Hopefully, he would forget my face as quickly as he saw it.

It was perturbing. Someone had paid Todd F. Minski, Private Investigator, to visit Willa. And that somebody had been upset somehow by Detective Flannery, who had done something. Some 'smarty-pants tactic'. And Dolly had seen him. Twice.

The same person had concerns about The Charmettes.

Willa and The Charmettes were going to be paid off for something. But for what?

My chief suspect for this concerned person? Linda Hunter, surely. Dolly would have told the cops her side of things, all about the affair, it was central to her statement. But maybe Linda didn't want the whole world to know. Maybe Flannery didn't want anyone to know.

Alternatively, the person instructing Minski could belong to Hunter's business.

A lot of unanswered questions, but at least I had a lead.

21

It had been a long day and it felt good to get back in the office. I had a lot to process and where better than in the bath?

I flung some more violet bath salts in the running water and watched them slowly descend, settling at the bottom like tiny pieces of blue coral.

While the water was flowing, I flicked aimlessly through one of Barney's celebrity magazines. A hairdo like Betty Grable's poodle would be fun, but I would never have the time or occasion. Too eye-catching.

Enough with the pessimism!

I would be sure to find an occasion and I would wear June's dress. It would look good with a poodle coiffure and diamond earrings. There would be some bash I could go to. There had to be.

My thoughts soon turned back to the case. Should I warn Alberta about Todd Minski heading the band's way? That was something I should run past Sonia when I next saw her.

Now relax!

I flung off my clothes and threw on my Chinese silk dressing gown. I tied my hair up in a red toweling turban. My face looked puffy and sallow.

Wait! I had just the thing. I rifled through the cabinet drawer and found a jar. The label read *Oliverelle. Eternal Elixir of Youth Beauty Mask*. It had been a gift from a client whose line of business was beauty products. The design had sprigs of olive leaves and a swan-necked woman's profile, applying something to her face with long fingers.

I twisted off the lid and smeared a load of green goo all over my face. The mask reacted with the air quickly and in seconds it started to feel tight. It tingled, but not unpleasantly, and then seemed to soften again and go warm.

I stared back at myself in the foggy glass.

A green ghoul stared back through the steam.

I turned off the faucet. As soon as I did, the bell to the main office door rang.

Sonia?

Who else? She must have fed the caretaker some story that I was expecting her. While the receptionist, Mrs. Loeb, was away, the front doors were locked and callers had to ring the bell. But it wasn't like Nathaniel not to check first, even if Sonia was at her highest and mightiest. Or maybe she slipped through the front door as some other resident had left the building.

I wanted to be alone, not see her critical expression again. I hadn't seen anyone's face so regularly since I roomed with June for three days when I first arrived in LA. Back then, June had driven me nuts. Now, what I'd give to switch Sonia for June.

This is what marriage has to feel like. Stuck, staring at the same old face. No wonder men went to bars. But what did women have? The kitchen? Brats? And we were supposed to love it?

I opened the door. There she was, pale and drawn, the stunning sable coat from earlier now draped over her shoulders. Sonia's eyes fixed on me, coldly. 'That's quite a look.'

My hands flew to my face. The mask!

She said, 'Sorry to interrupt your beauty regime, but I want to talk to you.'

'Of course,' I mumbled, hardly able to move my lips. 'Did they charge Dolly?'

Sonia looked up and down the corridor. She gave a *'Not here'* look. I opened the door wider to let her in and stepped back. 'Don't worry. The place is practically a ghost town.'

As she passed, she shot me a withering look. 'I can see that. Is that *Oliverelle*?'

I nodded. Clearly, any woman who was anybody in this town bought *Oliverelle*.

As soon as she walked in, Sonia's eyes leapt to the open magazine. 'You look done for the day.'

What did she expect? Was she insinuating she would never find a male PI in such a condition? I wouldn't rise to the bait. 'No, in fact I've got a lot to report back. But what happened with Dolly?'

'Charged, of course. Homicide.'

She explained how Dolly had got hysterical and they dragged her back to the cells. If she was protesting, it sounded as if Dolly was out of her suicidal funk.

Sonia explained that after the arraignment she would be held in the County Jail to await trial. She wouldn't get bail.

I gulped. 'That's terrible.'

'Why? We knew it was coming. She'll be in the papers tomorrow. Mugshot, and whatever dirt they can dredge up. I'll be interested in the angle they take.'

Unreadable as ever. I wouldn't push her. 'Drink?'

'Sure. Scotch, neat.'

'Er...is coffee okay?' I was pretty sure the brandy had been drunk.

'Whatever. I'm not fussy.' She sounded exhausted.

I put the kettle on. Then I slipped into the bathroom and peeled off the mask. It came off in one piece and I left it on the sink, an eyeless monster.

When I came back in with the coffees, Sonia was admiring Barney's office. 'Nice tree,' she observed. I laughed inwardly. Barney had at least achieved his Christmas decorating aim, to please clients.

'Please make yourself comfortable.'

Sonia sat down in one of the two plush leather chairs. She noticed my fresh face. 'Look at you. Positively glowing.'

It was the nicest thing she had said, yet it was faintly mocking. I sat down on the other client chair and told her I would definitely be going to the funeral, thanks to Martell Grainger.

'You haven't revealed too much, I hope? No point you going if she blabs.'

'She knows nothing. We have an understanding. Anyway, I can trust her to be discreet about who I am. I have a certain leverage.'

Sonia grunted. I felt a knot in my stomach. Being with Sonia reminded me of standing in front of the teachers who, no matter what I did, would never approve of or compliment my efforts.

Hard bitches, in other words.

You're a professional now. Suck it up!

'Maybe I can approach the secretary there, try to bond with her. Then I can find out more about Hunter and any problems he might have. Did you manage to talk to Dolly?'

Sonia nodded. She said that Dolly swore blind the lipstick wasn't hers, and she never bought *Mayberry* cosmetics. An

139

expensive brand, up there in the *Oliverelle* league, and totally out of her price range. 'It's just the same color that she wears, so anyone who wanted to frame Dolly just had to see her and memorize it. It would be great to find out who wears this lipstick, but that's like trying to find a needle in a haystack. A waste of time and money.'

'Linda Hunter might use *Mayberry* lipstick.' To me, Linda Hunter was Suspect Number One, and I still had to tell Sonia about Todd Minski.

Sonia shrugged. 'Of course she might, as well as countless others who knew Hunter. First wife, daughters. Secretaries. Well, maybe the funeral will lead somewhere but I very much doubt it will shed any light on the lipstick question. Drop it for now.'

She went on to explain that Dolly had told her that she and Willa were pals, but she swore blind she had said nothing about the affair to her. She also worked with her at Tilsons Department Store. 'So, did you see this Willa?'

'No, she's away. And the landlady hasn't got a clue about Dolly's arrest.' I showed Parker the lighter and the photograph of the musician. 'I found these in Dolly's clothes. Thought it best they disappeared.' Sonia studied the man's face for some time. 'Quite a dish,' she said finally. She told me to look after them. Then she sighed, almost to herself, 'Oh, Dolly.'

It was the first time I felt genuine concern from her for her client. An innocent woman's life in jeopardy. I doubted Parker was the type to ever blame herself if she lost a case, but a life was a life.

I said, 'But there's something else.'

Now for the big one.

Sonia frowned, wrinkles forming an eleven between her eyebrows, while I explained about Todd Minski showing up and asking Mrs. Olsen for Willa, the roommate. That he could match Dolly's mystery snooper. Sonia scrawled down a few notes. I recounted what I'd heard outside his office about Willa, and the band. I offered my theory that maybe Linda Hunter was buying people's silence about Dolly. 'After all, it's a terrible embarrassment for her.'

Sonia shrugged this off. 'Never heard of Todd Minski. Anybody could have hired him, for any reason.'

I also had to admit to Sonia that Minski saw me after I tailed him to his office. 'What?' Disdain spread over her face at my incompetence.

'It's okay. He thinks I'm an office temporary. I could use that angle on him again if I need to try and get any information out of him. Sure helps to be a woman investigator at a time like this!' I quipped, but she still didn't smile.

A long silence followed. I shuffled in my seat.

'Can you break into his office?'

Was she joking? My mouth fell open. 'You want me to rob him?'

'Your hunch about Linda Hunter hiring him might be wrong. I need to know what this creep's up to, if it concerns Dolly.'

'But assuming I'm right about who's hiring him, Minski won't need to pay Willa off if she didn't even know about Dolly and Hunter.' I observed. 'Should I warn Alberta he might come snooping around Joyce's?'

'Don't interfere. One, you could be wrong. Two, it might take him a while to find the band. Dolly only said in her

141

statement to the police she sings for a band. She didn't give Flannery the name even today. So even if Minski's got an insider contact, he won't get much. Not unless Flannery questions Dolly again and wants to know more about her associates. And in that eventuality, I'll be there and can alert you after.'

The thought of seedy Minski waddling into a crowded club of lesbians would be funny in any other situation. But I felt tense. Sonia mentioning cop insiders bothered me. I had to change the subject before she remembered I was supposed to look into Lauder, using my own 'insider'. So I returned to my suggestion of warning Alberta.

I coughed. 'But what if he does find any of them? I'm sure the band know she was with her as well.' Not only did Dolly call the club, Alberta went back to Joyce's after she brought Dolly to Sonia.

Sonia sipped from her cup and lit a cigarette. 'Correct. I wasn't thinking straight. It's been a long day.'

It was a surprising admission of weakness. Sonia was definitely not herself tonight.

'Okay. Tell Alberta, if Minski or anyone else approaches her, to say nothing except Dolly didn't show up. And she should warn the other and members to do the same.'

'What if Detective Flannery uses dirty tactics to get them to throw Dolly under the bus in court? Wouldn't be the first corrupt cop in town to do it.'

If any of the band members had family or friends in jail, which was quite likely, considering most of the prison population was black or Hispanic, Flannery could easily put the squeeze on them.

Sonia said, 'Flannery's a squeaky-clean type. Personally, I don't think he'll bother. In his eyes, she's practically convicted already.'

Convicted. Like me.

If I was caught and sent back to England, I'd face the hangman.

My hand instinctively went to my neck.

Sonia was puzzled at my discomfort. 'What? Is there something else?'

'Just...just the thought she could be executed.'

'Pull yourself together. We've got a job to do. And it gets worse. Of course, Dolly's got a prior. As I predicted.'

'What?'

'Stole candy from a store, aged fifteen. A juvenile offense that Dolly claimed she'd forgotten all about. Thank goodness you got the wristwatch back on Hunter. One less strike against her.'

'Could any of The Charmettes be character witnesses for Dolly?'

'You just can't resist strategizing, can you?'

The mocking glint in her eye belied her gentler tone. 'Look, presumably Willa likes Dolly well enough if they're roomies. She can be prepped. Flirtatious can be described as 'friendly', that kind of thing. But I won't call Alberta to the stand, anyway. Or any of the band, for that matter.'

'Why not?'

'Why do you think? The jury will be white.' Irritable Sonia was back, rolling her eyes at my stupidity.

She put her cup down, stood up and threw her coat back on, looking revived.

'Oh, yes, a little bird in the Coroner's office told me Hunter's body will be released to the family tomorrow, so the funeral should be soon. Let's hope you glean something useful.' Then she glanced at the magazine with a sarcastic smile. 'You can get back to your reading.'

I followed her to the door. Suddenly Sonia spun around, her hand extended. I guessed she meant for me to shake it. Maybe she wasn't totally unimpressed.

'Oh, and what progress have you made on that vice cop who was visiting Linda Hunter? We've got a sleazy PI and an LAPD vice dick sniffing around the same case. Now these are leads I am interested in. Linda Hunter can wait. I just don't like her for it.'

'Okay.' My voice came out like a squeak, as I gave a thin smile.

When I got back into the bath, it was tepid and the unstirred bath salts had formed a violet puddle at the bottom like a large bruise.

I turned on the faucet and swirled the water around till it was a welcoming translucent lilac and sweetly scented. But just like me trying to warm up Sonia, the hot water just couldn't beat the lukewarm.

I leaned back and thought of Lauder. Could he be involved somehow in framing Dolly?

He wasn't exactly clean in his methods, but surely he was a good guy? But did I really know him? What was had he been doing at the Hunter residence? And he had been so quick to blame Dolly.

I couldn't forget that.

He'd given me a chance, so why not her? But the best thing I could do was forget all about him being there. I'd never get a thing out of him.

Don't kid yourself you know him!

I ran my hand over my body and between my legs, turned on by the thought of him.

What we had, other than a need to keep each other safe, was nothing more than a perverted mutual lust. It wasn't born out of anything decent or respectable, not by society's standards. I wasn't sure if we even liked each other. We couldn't get to know each other in any normal way, like going for a walk, to movie and then dinner to discuss it after.

We just had sex and secrets.

But our affair aside, I just couldn't investigate him. One door that could not be opened, period.

I'd have to concoct some story to get Parker off his scent for now.

Why did you open your big mouth?

The task ahead was to go back and work on Minski. Talk about a tough sell. It was already a dicey move in case he rumbled my lie about being a temp.

Got it! I could say I was really looking for him, but got cold feet and so made the Anville excuse.

He would buy that. I bet he was used to it. I bet a lot of people called him up about using a private investigator, but when crunch time came, they bailed. Many spouses thought they were desperate to know the truth, but in reality, they weren't.

Ignorance is bliss.

Lauder and The Fiancée dancing the night away flashed

across my mind. She would be in a frothy white gown that bared her shoulders, with her expensive diamond necklace twinkling around her long neck, and he would be in his sleek black tux, matching his jet-black hair and cold turquoise eyes.

I shut the image out of my mind.

Joyce's cocktail. I craved one of them right now.

Joyce's Bliss wasn't just ignorance in a glass.

It was getting smashed out of your brains till you forgot your woes, your pain, your loss, your hate, and your fears.

22

Alberta came in with a tray loaded with two cups of coffee and a glossy, dark fruitcake on small plates. The cake burst with red and gold fruits, made all the more vivid by the sunshine pouring into her apartment.

She put the tray down on the glass coffee table. 'Old Jamaican recipe, passed down through the family. I load it with rum, far more than the recipe says. I figure my slave relatives couldn't get their hands on too much of the stuff, so I do it for them.'

I met her eyes, not knowing quite what to say. She spoke for me. 'But you don't know anything about that.'

It was a statement not a question.

'Where did they come from?'

'You mean, after Africa? Well, originally, my great grandparents were sold to a Louisiana family.' She took a piece of cake herself. 'I hate that state, but I love it, too.'

'Do you go back much?'

'No. My mama died a few years back, my pops is still there. Married a woman my age.' She laughed, wryly. 'They got kids now. I don't know them so well. I'm the mystery aunt in the big city.'

I bit into the cake. It was moist, full of orange, spice, treacle and vanilla flavors. 'Delicious.'

Alberta, leaning over the back of a chair, gave me a funny smile.

'How about you? Where are your people from?'

'My mom was a Londoner, but she died when I was little. I can't really remember her.'

That was a lie.

'That's sad.'

What was sadder was that I didn't even know if Violet was actually dead. Dead to me, at least.

'So you grew up in England?'

'No. I lived here till I was six. My father was a GI. My mom moved here after the war, to look for him.'

'GI? So that makes you really American?'

I nodded. 'Guess so. At least half.'

Was I? Elvira Slate and her fake papers were one hundred per cent American.

Jemima Day, the child I was born, was a mongrel.

'He was passing through London, end of the war. Turns out he gave my mother a false name and address. If he's alive, I don't think he'd be desperate for his long-lost child to show up.' I took another bite. 'I have no intention of looking for him, anyway.'

Alberta nodded, studying me. 'So you're just like Dolly. All alone in the world.'

I met her eyes. 'Dolly could be named in the papers today.'

'Charged?'

I nodded. I wished I could just tell Alberta everything, all the progress—or lack of it—I'd made, but Sonia had cautioned silence. I felt very torn. But if Sonia was reporting back to Dede, then maybe Alberta would find out more anyway.

I put my cup on the coffee table and explained that she should be on guard in case anyone started asking questions about Dolly and her personal life. I told her some shady guy with a beer belly could show up, by the name of Todd Minski.

'Todd Minski? You're telling me I shouldn't talk to a fat guy called Todd Minski. You really think I'm that dumb?'

I was shocked I'd annoyed her and I felt my cheeks flush. I'd probably sounded really patronizing. 'No, of course not. Try and see it my way. The band know you were with her after she discovered Hunter's body, right? That goes against Dolly's statement. It's just better if nobody says anything to anybody who's snooping around. That includes the band. They can't say anything. Dolly didn't show, period.'

'Jeez, girl. You're too much.'

'What? Why? This is important.' I didn't understand her reaction. I explained again how Minski could be a major problem. We didn't know who he was working for, but he definitely wasn't a cop.

Alberta listened, crossing her arms. Looking more annoyed as I went on, not less.

When she spoke, her voice was loaded with as much sarcasm as her cake was laced with rum.

'I get it. You think you gotta look out for us, don't you? To explain what to think and how to be careful? You don't think we know how to do that already? That we haven't needed to before you came on the scene? That we don't, every day of our lives?' She guffawed, shaking her head.

'No...'

Her eyes flashed in anger. 'No? And why can't you just trust me when I say that I *know* those girls? You think I don't know my own people? Or is it, because you ain't got no folks of your own, you don't even know how to trust? I wonder which.'

I swallowed the cake. Alberta was the last person I wanted to annoy.

149

'Nobody in the band's gonna say a thing about Dolly. Nobody's that stupid.' Alberta shot me a pointed look. 'You hear me?'

I looked down, ashamed. 'I'm sorry. And you're right. I don't trust anybody...easily. So if I sounded like I was insulting you somehow, and your friends, I'm just trying to cover all bases. But you know them best.'

'I do.'

There was an awkward silence.

Alberta finished her coffee, not taking her eyes from me. Then she let out a sigh. 'I get you are trying to do your job and all. But listen up. We are smart women. Wanda, Jewel, Carmen, Bertha. I trust them with my life. Zetty, I gotta be honest, I don't know her so well. She's seems okay. Dolly and Zetty, they're good buddies. Zetty's always running errands for Dolly. Zetty don't show it but she's real upset.'

'Yes, she sounded sad Dolly wasn't going to sing at the party.'

'Yeah. It's on New Year's Eve, right around the corner.'

'Oh, that soon?'

'Uh-huh. So we got to get to practicing all Wanda's new songs. There's a whole bunch of stuff to do. It's in Santa Barbara. We can stay on for a while. It'll be nice to get out of the city.'

Santa Barbara. I'd heard about it but never been there. I felt a twinge of envy.

'Now, tell me what you've got on that wife of Ronald Hunter? Anything?'

I hesitated. Screw Sonia Parker! I really wanted to talk openly to Alberta. Dede was paying my fees anyway, and so far, Alberta wasn't that impressed by me.

150

'Nothing, so far. Parker doesn't think she's in the frame.'

'What? Seems like the prime suspect to me. But what do I know? I'm just a housekeeper and a sax player.'

'I feel the same, if you must know, but I've got to do what Sonia tells me to. To the letter.'

Alberta looked skeptical. 'Let's hope Sonia Parker is as good as her reputation.' Then she stood up. 'We done? I'm real busy.'

I stood up. She said, 'You wanna take home some cake? I'm just going toss it in the trash. Got a dress to squeeze into.'

I nodded. Alberta went to the kitchen and came back with a large cube of cake, wrapped in parchment.

'Thank you,' I said, meeting her eye. She nodded.

Alberta was building a bridge in a way. I'd annoyed her and she'd let me know about it. She was also letting me know she'd forgiven me.

23

Time for another act, one Todd Minski would buy.

After saying bye to Alberta I went back upstairs to dress for the part. I put on a navy suit and a turquoise cotton blouse covered in white and blue flowers, with little white covered buttons that looked like my morphine tablets.

I could always lose myself in clothes. The choosing, the pressing, the accessorizing. Nobody could ever take that pleasure away from me.

Being practical was the best antidote to brooding.

The telephone rang. Martell, with the news the funeral would be on 30th December. There would be a private family service followed by a larger reception at the house. 'How they'll keep the vultures away, God only knows.'

She said I should come to her house first, to get the hat with a veil, and then we'd set off together to the reception.

The 30th was soon, unseemly so. Linda Hunter couldn't get 1946 off to a fresher start.

After the call, I finished off my look. I put on a jaunty tilt hat in a blue woven straw, with thin white edging and a white band. I powdered my eyes with pale blue shadow and loaded on the mascara. Then I smeared on pink lipstick, before drenching myself in perfume. Not my favorite French perfume. I wouldn't waste that on a slob like Todd Minski.

The finishing touches, a brand-new pair of white kid gloves and horn-rimmed glasses. No longer the gormless office girl, now I was a woman with a few personal problems who had finally summoned up the courage to get what she needed. She looked respectable enough to compensate for the seedy task she was about to give a slimeball private investigator.

I admired myself in the mirror. Fresh as a daisy. On the inside, a trampled one.

I drove towards Minski's office in Culver City, stopping at a drugstore to down a cherry soda. Something was bugging me and I didn't know what. As I paid for the drink, I noticed a newspaper on the counter. I should read it, but I didn't want to. I didn't want to see Dolly's mugshot.

Not yet.

I wasn't sure why. Because I was worried I would fail her?

There were a few tables against the wall, so I sat down to think. Think? Brood, more like.

You're just like Dolly. All alone in the world.

Alberta's words. Those were the ones that stung the most.

Only a few days ago, I was happy to ally myself with Dolly. So why was being like her, being seen to be like her, now eating at me? What unhealed scar had Alberta prodded, even unwittingly?

Alberta had made a casual observation. No way was it a dig. But the implication, however nicely meant, was that we were both pathetic, somehow.

Unwanted, alone and in trouble.

Was I, too, only headed for disaster? Had Alberta uncovered a secret dread? That maybe there was no cure for me after all.

Were Dolly and me doomed, like the bad girls, damaged girls, lost girls in all those moralizing motion pictures? Were we supposed to become nuns, forever paying penance? Or

153

assume an identity of the nice girl with the stable loving family just to dupe some guy, pump out the brats and hope to God he never found out?

Try our best to fit into a society that condemns our truth, by living a lie?

Was that life worth it? Was what I was doing going to get me somewhere better? Was I already on my way, or was it all a big con? I was sick and tired of not knowing.

Alberta knew who she was. She had made a life. Her band, good friends, a musical passion. She knew who her family were, whatever she thought of her father. Her history was scarred by slavery; she had referred to it to me for a reason. To remind me even if we shared untold secrets—her forbidden love, my criminal past—that was the extent of our similarities?

To warn me not to make any assumptions that I could ever really understand her, or her friends in the band?

Maybe she was just telling me I should open my eyes and find out who I was.

Whatever she had meant, she would be right, on any of those counts.

If I didn't want to be tragic and alone, I needed to do something different. But how were girls like me and Dolly supposed to change, to pretend certain things hadn't happened to them?

A scar is there for a purpose. You can try to hide it, it can fade, but it's always going to be there.

In mine and Dolly's case, the deepest scar was loneliness.

I didn't choose for Violet to disappear and leave me with the nuns. I didn't choose to get beaten by bitches. I didn't choose to be raised on the street by a no-good drunken cow whose betrayal landed me in reform school. I didn't choose to be fostered by someone who spoiled me and then went and died on me.

I didn't choose any of it.

But each loss tore open the original wound.

I never trusted a soul, and I never felt I belonged.

Everything after that, going with Billy, joining his underground world, those things I had chosen.

Because that life made sense. I was just as lonely but, surrounded by people and a world that was noisy and colorful, I could ignore my loneliness.

And whatever cards Dolly had been dealt, she didn't choose her lonely fate, either. She was orphaned and she'd survived somehow and discovered her talent. She wanted to love, to be loved. She was desperate to be loved. She made up lies and promises to get love.

Nobody really did love her, though. Except maybe Zetty. People pitied her. Alberta looked out for her, but that wasn't love.

Hot tears pricked my eyes.

Jeez! Get a grip!

I grabbed a napkin and turned to the wall. My cheeks felt hot. I had an overwhelming urge to call Beatty Falaise, to hear her voice. I could find some pretext to see her.

But she was sailing, having fun, or by now moored in some harbor having the time of her life. She deserved her vacation, free of worrying about her useless charge. I wouldn't interrupt.

And what could I say to her, really? I didn't even know what I wanted from her myself.

I blew my nose and slurped the rest of the soda.

Stop feeling sorry for yourself!

Alberta was right. Dolly and I were similar, as far as loneliness went. But Dolly depended on Elvira Slate pulling herself together and doing her best to save her.

I got up, feeling drained. The druggist watched me without smiling. Perhaps I'd looked a little deranged for a minute and he wanted me off the premises.

So long, Mister.

Out in the sunshine, I headed over to Mabel. Before I opened the door, I stopped, a thought striking me.

Becoming Elvira Slate had been my choice. I was trying to live my best life now, in a way that made sense to me. But was she just another survival tactic? Or was she a mask?

I had absolutely no idea.

And if she was a mask, she was the one that so far fit the best. But she got so heavy at times.

Sometimes I just wanted to lift her off, and see who was really underneath now.

24

'Hello? Mr. Minski?'

My outfit worked its magic, imbuing me with oodles of confidence to bluff my way into Todd Minski's affections. And I'd come up with the perfect scenario on the drive over.

A tearjerker fit for one of Martell's slushy movies.

My boyfriend Bill had proposed to me, but paranoia was raging. I was convinced he was actually married with kids! I just needed proof he was a good guy.

And when Minski asked if I had any evidence that might lead me to suspect poor old Bill, I'd burst into tears and say, dramatically, that I smelt perfume on his jacket!

By winning Minski's trust with my plight, I'd then ask him if he had any people who would vouch for him and the kinds of work he did.

And my name? Harriet Olsen.

I wanted to test his reaction to the surname and watch for a reaction. And should he ask if a relative happened to run a boarding house in Compton, well, yes sir, that's my mother. What a coincidence. Why? Sure, I knew Willa and Dolly. Why ask?

How nice it would be for the scene to unfold like this.

Silence. I rapped again on the door. The buzzer didn't seem to work.

Damn!

I called louder. 'Mr. Minski? Mr. Todd Minski?'

I put my white-gloved hand over the doorknob and turned.

Just in case it was open, and he was somehow out of earshot in a back office.

Locked, I'd have no choice but to come back another time.

But the door did open. It was dark inside. I stepped over the threshold. The venetians were pulled down, and flat.

'Mr. Minski? Hello?' I coughed to announce myself. There was a smell—old sweat and cheap aftershave clashing with floral notes. He was here, somewhere.

My eyes adjusted to the gloom, searching for the inner door. Maybe he was dozing. My hand groped around the doorway for a light switch. I found it and switched it on.

The front office had a two-person couch covered in a thick zigzag-patterned fabric, a low marble coffee table, and a pile of magazines in a holder. On the walls, a few prints of early light aircraft models.

At the far end, a door to another room, and a thin streak of daylight bursting through the bottom.

So Minski was in, all right. Maybe just hoping whoever it was would just go away.

I needed results. He *would* see me.

'Mr. Minski?' I called out.

I marched over and rapped on the door. 'Sir? May I come in?'

Silence. A creak. What was it with this guy? There was nothing for it but to bluster my way in. I turned the handle. 'Sorry for busting in, but...'

Mr. Todd Minski was right in front of me. He stared down at me coldly, in the same disheveled suit. His white belly hung over his belt. His greasy hair flopped over his brow. His brown and white brogues, scuffed.

He would only ever look at me coldly. His shoes would only ever be scuffed.

He was hanging from the ceiling light.

Dead.

I reeled, hitting the wall. I grasped for my own neck, cold sweat breaking out, my heart racing a thousand a minute. I felt dizzy, everything went black.

I panted heavily.

It's not you there, it's somebody else, dummy.

My hanging nightmare was somebody else's reality.

Wait, was I even alone? My hand instantly leapt to my purse for my pistol. I should get the hell out.

Stop! Think it through. Nobody saw you. Find out what you can. For Dolly!

I could do it. I could look through his papers. I was here for a reason and I had to do my job. I straightened up, wiping my brow. There was a low, two-door filing cabinet behind the metal desk.

I stepped back, noticing his feet were swaying a little. If he had committed suicide in a fit of despair, rage even, maybe Todd Minski wouldn't care about his files being exposed to the world. If you're dead, you're dead. Ultimate acts of defiance didn't care about consequences.

I kicked the door closed and locked it from the inside. If anyone came into the main office, there would be a chance they would just leave.

Now I was locked in a room with a corpse. A hanged man.

Today was getting better and better.

With a deep breath, I edged around the body and a discarded chair to the filing cabinet. Locked, predictably.

I checked the drawers of the desk. No keys, just a packet of gum, a lighter and a packet of French letters. Did Minski like to have fun in working hours? Did he offer 'sympathy' to some of the wives who came to complain about their husbands?

Surely the keys to the cabinet weren't in his pockets?

I looked up at the body and shuddered. At some point, he had pissed himself. The stain was obvious.

He had been knocked off. I just knew it.

Faked suicide, the ultimate frame-up.

I picked up the chair and took a deep breath. What was it with this case? What felony was it called, anyway, rifling through a dead man's body? Thieving from a corpse?

I stood on the chair. Carefully, I shook his jacket pockets and felt his pants. No jangle, no hard lumps.

The keys weren't on him! The body wasn't even stiff. In fact, it felt warm, or was I imagining it? I got a whiff of something rancid and foul. I felt an urge to heave and jumped off the chair.

Now what?

Pick the lock.

It would be slower and might not work. I removed a hatpin and went back to the cabinet and knelt down.

After a couple of minutes, it finally gave. I pulled open the first drawer and rifled through it. Nothing labeled. Bills, lease agreements, all had been stuffed in willy-nilly.

Nothing remotely like paperwork for a case.

The bottom drawer was a different story. A few hanging folders, with labels handwritten in dark ink, surnames in alphabetical order. Many were empty. Empty or *emptied*?

My hand instinctively went to the H section. Hunter. Nothing. Then onto P. No Perkins either.

My eyes scanned the other cases. Under one called Brown, there were some scrawled notes about what looked like a blackmail job with dates.

Phrases jumped out at me. *Wife doesn't know. Three hundred bucks per month.*

Funny, low-key work with nobodies. Exactly the kind of case Lauder wanted me to take.

The click of a door. Voices. Men's voices.

'Buddy, you coming?'

My heart pounded as footsteps approached the internal door. 'Hey, Todd, let's roll.'

The handle twisted. I aimed my pistol at the door.

'Bet he's at the bar already, leaving his place wide open. What a dope. Better tell the old boy to lock up. Let's split.'

The outer door slammed shut, leaving me and Minski alone again.

My heart slowed a little. I remained motionless. How long would it take the doorman to get upstairs and lock me in?

I scooped up the hanging folders, shoved them under my arm and crept out.

25

Sonia's voice was impatient. 'It can't wait?'

'No.'

She paused, thought about it, then told me to go straight to her office. I hung up, and left the gloomy dive. Three guys playing pool made a point of ogling me. I would have had a drink to knock the edges off my shock but was in no mood to be an exhibit for creeps.

By the time I reached the office, Sonia was already in the lobby, puffing on a cigarette. She glanced at my outfit, crushed her cigarette butt in a tall chrome ashtray, and ushered me through into a long leading to a large main office. Tidy dark oak desks topped with dark blue leather were devoid of the underlings who would normally sit here.

A young man was bent over a large file of papers. He had a heavy brow that gave him something of a permanent scowl. Or maybe he was just in a bad mood as the only person summoned in for work.

Sonia introduced him as Joseph Bergman, a junior attorney who had kindly volunteered to come in during the holiday to help her on the case. The rest of the staff and partners would be back in the New Year.

Joseph Bergman came over, with a smile that changed his expression from grumpy to cheerful. His thick bottle glasses made him look older than he was.

'Joseph, this is Elvira Slate. The PI. She's been doing a few things on the case.'

So he hadn't been fully briefed about me.

Joseph smiled. 'Good to meet you.' His handshake was strong and warm. It was unexpectedly soothing, after the horror I'd witnessed.

I met his eyes, mentally thanking him for something he didn't even know he'd done.

Sonia looked at me, eyes narrowing. Maybe she could tell I was in shock. 'Have you seen the papers yet?'

I told her I hadn't.

'As I thought, they're presenting Dolly as an obsessed stranger. No mention of the affair.'

'They can do that?'

'Her word against theirs. Hunter's people will pull strings. The fact nobody knew about the affair could play nicely into Flannery's prosecution.'

'What about the doorman? He knows the truth.'

'He'll have been paid off by now.'

'What about the writing in lipstick? How does that fit with the obsessed stranger theory? Why would a stranger do that?'

Sonia shrugged. 'Like I said. Crazy people do crazy things.'

I gulped, looking from Joseph to Sonia. 'This is really bad for Dolly, isn't it?'

They both just stared at me. I felt annoyed. Didn't my question warrant some kind of reaction?

I still had to break the news about Minski. Could I speak in front of Joseph?

Sonia read my mind. 'Don't know about you, but I could do with a drink. Joseph, do you mind closing up today?'

'Hung himself?'

I knocked back the excellent gimlet. 'Supposedly.'

Sonia and I were now sitting face-to-face in the swanky bar of the Roselton Hotel, with its mirrored walls and low, fan-shaped suede chairs and sofas around glass tables.

Genteel, discreet waiters with starched shirtfronts swanned around, holding trays high. The clientele was middle-aged and upwards. A rich, polished set. Parker was in her natural habitat. Elegant, expensive and superior.

'And you are sure nobody saw you?'

I shook my head.

Sonia puffed on her cigarette. 'Maybe somebody's tying up loose ends. The person that instructed Minski could have had him killed.'

Somebody like Linda Hunter, I thought, but didn't say.

The tinkling of a piano, a romantic classical-sounding melody, interrupted our thoughts.

A female pianist in a lemon chiffon dress with puffed sleeves sat at an ivory grand piano. She was in her forties, her dark hair piled up, wearing too much makeup for daytime. Her bright blue eyes twinkled, but at no one in particular. Her long, slender upper body swayed over-dramatically and her long fingers danced over the keys. Lemon and white paper flowers were pinned to her swaying head. She reminded me of a daffodil, blowing in the breeze.

Minski's swaying shoes. I tried to shut out the image.

The Roselton was probably a pretty good gig for a forty-something hotel crooner, but I bet she hadn't intended ending up here. She had the looks and voice to star in a musical. But something, somehow, hadn't worked out. She came nowhere near close to Wanda's verve. But she blended well with the fine and polite society at the Roselton.

She sang softly of love and regret. I tried to shut her voice out.

Sonia mused, 'If somebody strangled Minski first, the coroner should be able to tell. Depends on the…skill of the killer in disguising strangulation with the rope.' She leaned in, her voice lowered. 'You've seen a corpse before?'

'Put it this way, they're stacking up.'

She nodded, relieved she didn't have to offer any moral support.

'Well, the Todd Minski connection is a bust. Somebody could have killed him, or else he was a depressive and things suddenly got to him.' She let out a sigh and lit a cigarette.

'I got the client files.'

Sonia's brows jumped up.

'There aren't so many. Maybe the killer took others.'

A moment while Sonia pondered this. 'Missing client files in his cabinet looks suspicious.'

'If he took his own life, he could have burnt or dumped his files to protect his clients' interests?'

She sipped her martini, eyeballing me.

'Do you want them? Should I keep them or burn them?'

'You keep them, of course,' she tutted, rolling her eyes. 'I can't have anything like that in the office. Take a look, see if there's anything in there. Actually, I might send Joseph over to go through them. I assume that's okay?'

I nodded. 'Sure.'

Anyone would be a refreshing change from Sonia. I said, 'Well, whatever Minski was asked to do, I doubt he got to

165

finish it. Alberta hadn't met him yet. I saw her this morning. So it's likely he didn't get to any of the bandmates.'

'All right, go talk to Willa. See if you can get anything out of her, her opinion of Dolly, and judge if she'll be any good on the stand. Dolly said she didn't know about the affair, so we can't get her to testify that she did. But if she liked Dolly, it's a start.'

'I'll go back to the boarding house tonight. The trick will be avoiding the landlady again, but I've got the lie of the land.'

This would enable me to go home, take a shower, and rinse off dead man's odor.

'Why wait? The Tilsons Department store is just a few blocks away. Glove department. She might be there now.'

It sounded like an order. I inwardly cursed. It could be a wasted journey and my skin still felt yucky.

I stood up. 'All right. Then I'll go home to check the files. If Joseph wants to come over, I should back in a few hours. Then, I guess, next in line is the funeral reception?'

Sonia looked me up and down. 'You got something to wear? You have to blend in. Nothing like that outfit, obviously.'

I nodded, biting my tongue.

Sonia was clearly in no hurry to leave the ambience of the hotel lounge. She lit another cigarette and waved at the waiter, pointing at her empty glass. He swooped in with a silver tray, whisking the glass away, and giving Sonia a fetching smile. As he retreated, Sonia said, 'Oh, get anything on that vice cop? Maybe he's our killer!'

My stomach flipped. I came closer. 'What?'

She shrugged. 'If anyone knows how to make a strangulation look like suicide, it's a cop. Why are you so horrified?'

166

I tried to adopt a more blasé expression. 'Well, I'm just surprised you suspect the cop. All because he was at Linda Hunter's? Kinda long shot?'

She studied me. 'I'll know when you get me answers, won't I? Let's see what you can dig up. Anyway, if they suspect foul play in Minski's death, the murder squad will be busy over the holiday. Ironic if the killer's one of their own.'

I told her, cool as a cucumber, that my cop contact wasn't in town, so that whole line of enquiry would have to wait.

She managed to hide her irritation. Just. 'Well, see Willa and then report back later. Actually, report to Joseph. He's pretty much up to speed on the case.'

She said I could tell him everything. Then she crossed her legs. 'Oh, maybe don't mention the blood-stained hankie. That can stay our little secret, for now.'

Then she grinned at me. The grin of someone holding all the cards.

26

Tilsons Department Store occupied a large corner block on South Broadway. I'd driven past it countless times and regularly glanced over its many advertisements in the paper, whole pages offering discounts on furnishings, toys, children's clothes and anything for the growing household.

I'd never ventured in. My aspirations in life were more Bullocks Wilshire than Tilsons on Broadway.

It was the kind of place a woman office worker could dash to in her lunch hour to pick up lining for the drapes, or something cute to shut her brats up.

Now came the inevitable lull after Christmas and before New Year. The store was practically deserted apart from shop girls in black dresses. The shopping had been done, gifts had been given, and the city hadn't quite woken up.

I cruised down the empty aisles on the ground floor, looking for the ladies' glove section. The gimlet had calmed me down and it was therapeutic to gaze at glittering brooches, perfect square handkerchiefs and perfume.

I could make out the display of colorful arms and hands on top of cabinets in the far corner. With the help of the alcohol in my system, it wasn't too much a stretch to imagine they were waving me over.

A young woman was bending down behind the counter, busy putting new stock into the drawers. I swallowed an unexpected hiccup. 'I'm looking for Willa.'

She stood up. 'That's me?'

Her pale blue eyes narrowed. Flawless blue, no flecks, no cloudiness, like a pale English sky in summer. She had natural baby blonde hair in an immaculate hairdo, coiled into elegant rolls on each side of her face, and up and over her wide forehead. Her hair was tied back with a black bow. The blonde curls rolled down her back like soft sponge fingers. A dusting of freckles darkened her thin nose. She wore a starched white shirt, buttoned up to the top, a sleeveless black cardigan, and a pleated mid-length black skirt.

She looked me up and down. What would have worked for Minski might work for Willa, too. I looked nice enough not to scare anybody.

'I know Dolly. She told me about you.'

Willa froze, a glove mid-air. 'I can't talk. Please leave.'

It was a bizarre reaction. Sheer fear. I knew then and there Flannery had got to her. Not Minski. But when?

I said, 'I just want to help her, don't you? Cops sure as hell don't. I know you live with her, Willa.'

'Well, I don't know who you are, and I don't know anything about what she's done.' When she saw I wasn't moving, she hissed, 'Go away, will you? I just can't talk to you! They told me not to!'

'Who? The cops? Detective Flannery?'

Panicking, she glanced from side to side, wary of eavesdropping colleagues. I followed her eyes. A shop girl at the scarves counter was looking in our direction, curious. We didn't exactly look like we were discussing gloves.

'Smile,' I ordered.

'What?'

'They're only looking because you are being over-dramatic. Look friendly.'

Willa tried to look relaxed. She might have been having her nails pulled out.

Did the other girls know that Dolly was Willa's roommate? It made sense Willa didn't want to be tarred by the same criminal brush if the murder was now a Tilsons Department Store scandal.

'If Dolly's got herself in trouble, it's nothing to do with me.'

'If nobody helps her, the trouble she's in could be the gas chamber. And she's innocent.'

Willa's face changed. She looked faintly nauseous.

Glancing at her watch, she said, 'It's my lunch break soon. I can see you out on the street. Just wait outside the store.'

I nodded and left.

Outside, I turned to window-shopping. Three mannequins were wearing winter coats, hats and ankle snow boots lined with fur, with cute little zippers.

'You really think she'll get the death penalty?'

I turned. Willa now had on a simple checked wool jacket and a light blue bonnet hat. Her expression was pained, her face pale.

I tried to give a reassuring smile. 'We know Dolly didn't do it and we want to help her.'

She glanced at me. 'Who's "we"? You her lawyer?'

'No. Just a pal trying to help.'

'The detective didn't say nothing about the gas chamber.'

'Well, he wouldn't. What do you say we take a stroll? I can buy you a sandwich, if you're hungry.'

'I'm not.' Willa reluctantly started to walk. 'Are you the lady who came to Mrs. Olsen's yesterday?' Her eyes were still suspicious, but less so.

'What? No, I don't even know where you live,' I lied. 'When did the cop come by?'

'This morning. Before work. Mrs. Olsen wasn't there. I didn't know what to do.'

'And who's this woman who came by?' I acted innocent.

'Apparently a friend of Dolly's.'

I asked her if she'd told the cop about her. She said she hadn't.

'What's your name?' She suddenly asked.

'Patricia. Patricia Hughes.'

'Dolly never mentioned you. Not that she would.'

'You weren't close?'

'Sure, we're friendly. We just don't socialize together.'

I wanted to get straight to the point and ask about Minski, see if he'd made it back again, but decided against it for now. Flannery would have warned her off talking, so she needed to be eased into it.

Willa blurted out. 'I just don't think she's a killer. Not Dolly.'

I nodded. 'She a good roommate?'

Willa nodded. 'We get along fine.'

I asked how long she'd known her and what she knew about her. Willa said they met working at the store. They'd shared a room for some months without a hitch. 'She's just untidy. But she does something odd in the night. She shouts out in her sleep. A lot. It sounds awful, but when I ask her, she doesn't remember a thing.'

'Well, she's had a troubled life.'

'I know. Orphan, and...' Her voice tailed off. Did she know about the thrashings?

'Was your room ever broken into?'

'No, why?'

'Ever see anyone, hanging around?'

She looked blank.

'Doesn't matter. So know who Dolly's pals are?'

'No. But she sings in a band sometimes. The Charmettes. A wild bunch, if you ask me.'

'Why? You know them?'

'No! ' she looked around to check if any passersby were listening. They weren't. She whispered anyway, 'They play in a...a girls-only club.' Accompanied by a meaningful look. 'One of them comes around a lot, for Dolly.' This had to be Zetty.

'Did you tell the detective about her?'

'Oh, no!'

'Why not?'

Willa glanced down. 'I didn't want them to give the wrong impression about Dolly.'

Loyal. She was protecting Dolly's reputation.

I didn't get any sense Willa would want to frame Dolly. She would make a decent character witness for Dolly, if she could be persuaded.

But the District Attorney's people once they got digging might pressure her otherwise.

'What did you talk about with the detective?'

Willa hesitated. She said, almost reluctantly, 'How she met Mr. Hunter.'

We stopped at a traffic light, watching cars. 'So what did you tell him?'

Willa flushed. She was in too deep, conflicted between obeying the law and wanting to save her friend's life. 'That he came to the department store. With his wife. She was buying makeup.'

'What makeup?'

'I have no idea. Cosmetics are on the other side of the store. Anyway, he wandered over to us. He took a shine to Dolly, they were laughing together. I could see she liked him, even if he was old enough to be her granddaddy.'

'Was she flirtatious?'

The lights changed and we started crossing.

Willa nodded. 'Dolly likes attention. You know, from men. All men. I always thought it could get her in trouble one day, but I don't think she can help herself.'

That fitted with what Alberta had said.

'Do you know if Dolly met up with Hunter again?'

She shook her head. 'She never told me if she did.'

'Do you know anyone who might want to hurt Dolly?'

'No. Look, I've told you more than I told Detective Flannery and the other cop when they came. You know they searched the room. Mrs. Olsen won't like it.'

'Well, they had a warrant, right?'

'I don't know. Should I have asked?' Her eyes widened, alarmed.

'Probably. Did they take anything?'

'I don't know.' She was a clueless girl who would dance a jig nude if a cop told her to.

At least I'd got pictures of the handsome 'S' and his lighter out of the room.

27

By late afternoon, I got back to the hotel and finally was able to take a long hot shower.

Joseph showed up soon after, while my hair was in a towel and I only had my dressing gown on.

He stood at the door, awkward. He didn't know where to look. 'Oh, Sonia said...'

'It's fine. I'll get dressed. Just felt really grubby.'

He said, 'Sure. I don't blame you.' Sonia must have told him about the corpse.

He couldn't look at me as I held the door open. His neck was scarlet at the collar. Was he a tiny bit attracted to me?

I pointed him to Barney's desk and Minski's client files, then I went through my office to my bedroom leaving the doors open. I threw on pants and a blouse, and softened my face with some red lipstick.

I could hear him coughing nervously. I called out, telling Joseph about Flannery's visit to Willa and that he had searched the room but she wasn't sure if he had found anything. That Willa had witnessed Dolly and Hunter's first flirtatious encounter, but nothing after that.

I was secretly glad Joseph could relay all this to Sonia rather than me doing it.

When I came back in the office, he said, 'Sonia won't like any of it. Willa's testimony is useless to us.'

I told him that Mrs. Olsen had been out when Flannery came. So the odds were good Flannery didn't yet know about Minski's visit, and mine, for that matter.

He said, 'Finding out who instructed him is the key.'

'Surely it has to be Linda Hunter?' Maybe if I repeated it enough, somebody other than Alberta would agree with me.

'Or someone else who didn't want Hunter's reputation in tatters. Even after his death.'

'Like the brother? Rufus? Trying to keep the family name respectable?'

Joseph thought about this. 'Someone who wanted Minski silent badly enough to kill him.'

He was noncommittal, just like Sonia. That or he was under strict instructions not to get into things with me. I wondered now if they thought Minski was the killer. Maybe he was really seedy. Maybe guilt had got to him. No point in hypothesizing now.

These attorneys were unlike any people I'd met before. No emotion. No need to confide, to discuss. And zero sentimentality.

A case to these people was just like a game of chess. Silence, strategizing, observing the opposition. Countering, blocking and concealing, as the need arose.

I'd make a useless lawyer, blurting out whatever, getting over-involved and taking wild risks.

Joseph wanted to get down to work, so I offered him a drink. He wanted tea. I fumbled in the ceramic jars in the kitchenette. Bingo! I found a box of English Earl Grey. I also found some cookies. Barney must have stocked up.

I sat back down, suddenly feeling quite drained. I flung myself on one of the client armchairs, swinging my legs over one of the sides. Joseph glanced at me, then as quickly looked away.

After a while, Joseph tapped his finger on some files he had separated from the rest. 'Minski had three petty blackmail cases active. Unless it's coded, I can't find anything that obviously links to Hunter or Dolly.'

'Maybe he's taken his secrets to the grave.' I offered, unhelpfully.

'Could be. Or somebody got there before you did.'

What? That felt like a dig, Sonia style.

'Maybe if I had more of a free reign I'd get results quicker.'

Joseph leaned back in the chair, awkward. He sighed. 'You're on a tight leash because you're new. Don't take it personally. My advice? If you like this kind of work, stick to the brief. If you get another job, it means you passed the test.' He sounded honest, at last.

'So why won't Sonia entertain the idea of Linda Hunter as a suspect? She totally ruled it out right off the bat.'

Joseph looked bland. 'Alibi probably. And Linda could just divorce.' He looked back down, flicking through a few papers, a cue for me to not go there.

I sighed, watching him for a while.

'Did you always want to be a lawyer?'

'In my family, Bergman sons have a couple of options. Being a lawyer...or being a lawyer.'

I laughed. I hadn't expected a joke from him, let alone candor.

'Plus, my younger brother is the rebel, so that spot's taken.' He sipped some tea.

'How did he rebel?' I asked, very curious.

'Oh, it's complicated.' Joseph was already standing up. He had said too much and held the files like a fence going up. 'Your turn.'

He slipped on his jacket and picked up his lawyer's briefcase. 'Oh, and Sonia wants you to talk to Hunter's secretary. The office is no longer a crime scene. Her name's Pauline Dobson.'

He had mentioned Linda having an alibi. Now the fact the office was no longer a crime scene. Sonia had her own cop insiders, obviously.

I said, 'The secretary? Getting her to open up is gonna take some figuring out.'

'You can report back after the funeral, unless something urgent crops up.'

'Why don't I make friends with her there? Then follow up? It might be more natural.'

'You might have other fish to fry there.'

We shook hands and the cool but amiable Joseph left.

I sat at Barney's desk and took a look for myself. The handwriting of the late Mr. Minski was barely legible. Three blackmail cases? Whoever was being squeezed out there in the big city no longer had Todd Minski to depend on.

Maybe I should contact them and offer my services?

I checked the clock. Almost four thirty. If I hurried, I could drive to Hunter's apartment and see if Pauline Dobson was still there.

I didn't relish going back to the scene of the crime. But my mission now, beyond helping Dolly, was to impress Sonia. Me and Barney needed the work.

My hair now was practically dry. I shoved it in a hairnet and pulled a beret over it.

I went down by the stairs, slipped out of the side entrance and jumped into Mabel. Funny how just a few steps out of the office can give you an idea. I looked in the mirror to redo my lipstick. I didn't need to persuade Pauline Dobson.

I just needed to bribe her.

28

'Oh, gimme a break! I'm her pal!' I growled.

Under the uniform, Bogdan was an artist earning a crust as a doorman. He had hidden his sketchbook as soon as I entered. But not in time to prevent me seeing his muse—a girl with a turned-up nose and soft eyes, in the pose of one of those religious icons.

I'd come prepared. In my arms, a big white cake box tied up with a pink ribbon. All part of the ruse.

'Serena who?'

'Serena Jenkins.'

'You look like reporter.' His eyes narrowed with suspicion. At my pants, the hairnet, the bare face, the whole working girl demeanor.

'No! I'm her friend. Why the hell would I be a reporter anyway? What reporter lugs something like this around? Take a look!'

I put the cake box down and began to untie the ribbon. 'It's her birthday. She's had a real tough time, lately, so I wanted to surprise her at work.'

'Her birthday?'

'Yes! She's a Capricorn. Hard working, loyal. Very upset by everything that happened. You know she could lose her job now? Would you just let me surprise her? Perk her up.'

I opened the lid, and Bogdan peered inside. His eyes widened.

I'd stopped at a French patisserie in Larchmont Village on

the way here and picked up a cake. The hearts and flowers in pink, yellow and gold reminded me of one of those mesmerizing antique porcelain clocks covered in ceramic flowers and gilt.

'I didn't know it was Pauline's birthday.' Bogdan was clearly soft on her, his voice a little remorseful.

'Let me give it to her, maybe she'll cut you a slice. How about that?'

'All right. Go. As it is her birthday.' He nodded to the elevator. I smiled. 'Thanks.'

It was eerie walking along the same corridor, strange knowing exactly what door to knock on. Last time, I had come at great risk to myself. This time was down a few notches on the danger scale, though not exactly a breeze.

I rang the bell and waited.

I hoped the clean-up team had done a good job. Heaving over the cake would sure mess the plan up.

Nobody answered. Strange, Bogdan sounded like he knew she was up here. I rang again.

Finally, the door opened a crack. Pauline Dobson was about eighteen. She had a round face and soft brown curls flecked with gold. A little snub nose and a cupid's mouth, which I'd only seen on paper downstairs.

Bogdan's muse.

'Wrong place. I'm not expecting anything.'

'You ain't Pauline Dobson? Delivery from a Brad…. Oh, shoot. I left his details in the truck. Know a Brad, ma'am?'

Pauline looked a little hassled. 'Brad?'

'Want me to bring it in for ya?'

Pauline hesitated, but I barged through. She closed the door behind me. 'I only saw Brad an hour ago. He never said anything about this.'

I was back in the same lobby. The same hallway. Paintings, heavy oil landscapes of harbors and countryside, had been taken down and were now propped up against the plinth. I could only smell lemon and pine. Good.

'Guess he wanted to surprise you. Is it your birthday, or something?'

'No. It's not. This way, please.'

I followed her down to the far end, past doors to the other rooms, all shut. I hadn't got this far last time. I passed the bedroom where Hunter had been slain. I shuddered slightly, remembering the corpse.

'Coming or going?'

'Excuse me?'

'Looks like you're moving. In or out?'

'Oh, out.' She opened a far door into a luxurious kitchen, wall-to-wall apricot and black tiles. Chrome handles adorned the cupboards. The worktops were a pale peach marble. They had never been used. Barney would approve of a makeover like this for our kitchenette.

Pauline stood against the door. 'Set it down there.'

'Nice pad.' I whistled, lowering the cake.

'It's my boss's place. He died.' She was young enough to want to get it off her chest. 'I've got to pack it all up.'

'You quittin'?'

She nodded. 'End of this week.' Then she flushed, unable to contain herself. 'They didn't even pay me for the whole month.'

'That's too bad. Maybe that's why this Brad's giving you a cake, huh? Want to take a look?'

She shrugged. I untied the bow and took off the lid.

'Take a look at that! He must sure have the hots for you.'

Pauline didn't look thrilled.

'What's the problem? Watching your figure?'

She squirmed. 'I just don't get it.'

I pulled out the twenty dollars rolled in my pocket. 'Then maybe you can get this.' I slapped it on the marble worktop.

Pauline looked at the money. 'What's that?'

'Look, I know who you worked for and I know he was bumped off. I need information, you're gonna need some bucks.'

Terror spread over her face. 'Is this a trick?'

'C'mon, Pauline. You can't get in any more trouble. They already fired you, right?'

'Who are you?'

'Just a friend helping the innocent.'

'You mean the crazy girl who did this?'

'I thought in America you were innocent until found guilty. Or am I in a different country?'

'I can't say anything to anyone. The cops said I shouldn't. They warned me people might come here. We aren't supposed to let anyone in.' Her eyes filled with tears of rage. 'This is the most horrible time of my life!'

I was still chasing Flannery's shadow.

Pauline's dam suddenly burst. Fat tears rolled down her cheeks, and she shook, arms crossed, clutching her elbows.

'Hey, hey, calm down. Take a deep breath. Nobody's getting you in trouble. I don't want anyone to know about us talking any more than you do.' My voice was soothing, convincingly caring.

Pauline sniffed, gulping her tears back. I was on the right track with the big sister act.

'Look. I'm helping Dolly Perkins because she deserves a shot at real justice. Us talking doesn't change anything you said to the detectives. You're a truthful person and that's good. I really don't want to get you in trouble. It's just maybe you can tell me some other things, things you may have forgotten about. Something that could help Dolly Perkins.' I saw a box of tissues on a tiled shelf above the stove and handed her one.

'Bogdan saw you. He can tell the cops, then they'll ask me about you!' She blew her nose, noisily.

'Relax. Bogdan thinks I'm delivering a cake for your birthday and I'm your pal Serena. Just remember to give him a piece of cake. Keep him sweet.'

Her eyes widened. 'My birthday's not till next week.'

I put another ten bucks on the counter. 'A gift. From me.'

She glanced at the notes, then back to me. I said, 'Let me ask you something easy. Did you know Hunter was having an affair?'

She shook her head but there was something else. Something off.

'So, he loved his wife? Guess she's the one firing you?'

She shook her head. 'No. His brother came to see me. But she doesn't like me anyway. I only met her a couple of times.'

'How long have you been working for Hunter?'

'Two months.'

'Oh, not long at all!'

That was a surprise. But it also explained why Pauline had been so desperate to knock on the door when Linda Hunter sent her here on Christmas Eve. To impress, be dutiful to the boss's cold wife.

But it also meant maybe she didn't know a thing about his sideshow with Dolly, and I'd just wasted money on Pauline's birthday. 'Who was his secretary before you?'

'I never met her. Agnes something.'

'So there was a gap between his secretaries?'

Pauline shrugged.

'How did you get this job, anyway?'

'Through an advertisement in the paper. I called a lady. Tells me to come here.'

'A lady? You know her name?'

She shook her head.

'I don't remember. I never met her. She sounded real nice, said she'd meet me here. I came here, but it was just Mr. Hunter. Alone. He offered me the job on the spot.'

I bet he did. I was beginning to guess Hunter liked them young and cute and he had someone procuring them for him.

'Was he a good boss?'

She avoided my eye.

'What is it?'

'Sure. He liked me.'

That wasn't what I'd asked.

'But what was he like to work for?' I had no measure of Hunter whatsoever. Did he laugh? Was he witty? Was he caring? Who was he, as a man?

She shifted from one foot to the other. 'He was...fine.'

'Fine?' I sensed she wanted to say more but didn't know how to go about it.

I sighed. My hip was sore. 'Can we sit down anywhere? I got a bad leg.'

Her eyes gleamed with sympathy. 'Sure. My office.'

We left the kitchen and she opened the door on the left. It was a small room, with a desk and chair. Files had been piled into boxes. More framed prints against the walls. A filing cabinet stood in the corner. Another chair was pushed against the window. I sat down on that. Pauline didn't go behind the desk but hovered in the doorway.

'Did Mr. Hunter have any business troubles?'

'I don't think so. He was real busy setting up a foundation. The Ronald Hunter Foundation.'

'To do what?' Her angle on this might be useful.

'Help veterans. Build retirement homes, clinics. That kind of thing. I liked that part of the job. My brother was injured real bad in the war. He's never gonna be the same again.'

'Sorry about that. So sounds like this was a good job?'

Pauline averted her eyes again. 'He dictated letters, got me to run errands...'

And? What isn't she telling you?

'But what?'

She met my eyes. 'A week before he died, he did something.'

'What did he do?'

She let out a long sigh. 'You promise you won't say? I didn't tell anybody this.' She was desperate to get it out. I was encouraging. 'I won't say a word.'

'You just can't. Promise me?'

'Of course.'

'I thought it was a mistake at first. I was filing documents away in the filing cabinet. He was behind me. He touched me. Apologized. But then it happened again, the same day. And the way he looked, I knew something wasn't right.'

'He touched you where? On your ass?'

She nodded.

'He do anything else?'

'No. But I didn't want to work in case he did it again. The terrible thing is that when he died, I was so relieved! It's awful, but I was!'

'You sure you didn't say any of this to the detective?'

'Not a word! I'm so ashamed. I wanted to pretend it never happened. I shouldn't even be telling you. I don't know who you are!' She started to cry again. I should be big sisterly now but I wanted facts.

'So you had no idea about Dolly Perkins being his girlfriend?'

She shook her head, wiping her eyes with her sleeve. 'When I read about her, I figured maybe he'd done the same thing to her that he did to me. And maybe she got mad.'

Kill a guy because he forced you into something? Some women would. And they'd go to jail forever.

I wanted to know more about the previous secretary. Pauline said she didn't know how long she was with him. She only found out her name by accident—Hunter had called her "Agnes" one day. 'He apologized for it. Said she was the girl before me.'

'I wish I could talk to her,' I said, thinking aloud.

Pauline went over to the filing cabinet. She pulled out a piece of paper and handed it to me. 'I found this at the back. It could be where she lives.'

It had a handwritten name and address on. Distinctive loopy writing. But that wasn't what stood out. I read, and I blinked. I read it again.

Agnes Hunniford, The Miracle Mile Hotel.

Someone who worked for Hunter lived at my place of residence! Was she one of the career girls who would return after the holiday?

'You can keep it. I was just gonna toss it.'

'Did Flannery ask about the other secretaries?'

I knew the answer. He wouldn't bother. Pauline shook her head.

I slipped the paper in my purse. 'Listen, you've been real helpful. You're better off out of this situation anyway.'

Pauline nodded.

'If I need to see you again, where can I find you?'

She wrote something down and gave it to me with doe eyes, like I really was her big sister.

When I re-entered the lobby, Bogdan was bent over his sketch. He didn't even hear me. Was it bad for Pauline that she now had to give him some cake? Would he get the wrong idea, or was he just a nice guy with a crush?

Who the hell knew?

I drove away. I felt sickened—by fragile girls who were trapped in jobs, by guys who had it all, expected it all. A guy who groped his secretary wouldn't stay satisfied with that for long. Soon he'd have wanted more.

Soon she'd have had to give it to him or run.

And there were enough desperadoes like Dolly to stroke these guys' egos in the hope they'd get a better life.

Rich men and pretty girls. All those marriages in which the ugly old rich guy marries the young pretty thing. It's his right.

The rules of the game—he stays rich, she stays young and pretty.

Everybody's happy. Or pretends to be.

Linda Hunter came from money, so it was only right she wouldn't marry a pauper. But she wasn't so young and maybe that was eating her up.

Or could it be Hunter had another mistress who had gotten jealous?

Alternatively, Pauline Dobson might just be a great actress and I'd just been reeled in. Her expressions of concern outside the block that night could have been totally fake. And now she was feeding me this line about groping. Maybe she was the wacko who resented Dolly?

What about Agnes Hunniford? Was she another one he had groped and then taken to bed? Or had she wanted to play the game?

I drove fast, winding down the window.

I was suddenly glad my job was only to report to Sonia. Glad it wasn't my job to build the case, to work anything out. Glad it was Sonia's job to save Dolly.

Not mine.

29

Early evening, I raced upstairs to the fourth floor and pounded on Alberta's door. She answered, in a housecoat and rubber gloves. 'What is it?'

'Agnes Hunniford. She worked for Ronald Hunter.' I explained she was his secretary. 'Does she live here?'

Alberta thought about it. Recognition slowly dawned in her eyes. She said Agnes was a quiet girl, who rented a single room and kept herself to herself. She wasn't one of the party girls. She was sure Agnes had left. 'You want to come in?'

I said no. She was being polite. It was obvious she was busy with chores.

'Mrs. Loeb will know more. She might even know where she lives now. She stays in touch with some of the girls after they leave.'

She said the receptionist would be back in early January.

'Can't we call her?' I asked. 'It's kind of important.'

'Mrs. Loeb? Hell, no.' Alberta raised her brows. 'She's at her sister's in Miami. I don't have the address. But, you know, June might know where Agnes went. She's always friendly with everyone who stays here. Come with me tomorrow.'

'Tomorrow?'

'Oh, you don't know! June's back in town. She's rustling up our formals for the party. She's got six dresses to make in three days so she's sleeping over at her shop!'

'June is making the dresses?'

'She sure is. My idea. Zetty's boss is in the big money and

189

June needs the business. I'm going there tomorrow for a fitting. I know she'd love to see you.'

June threw her arms around me. The job of running up six frocks as a rush order was obviously taking its toll. A needle and thread pinned to her housecoat, her ginger hair falling out of a messy bun and fabric cuttings stuck to her legs. A trundle bed was pulled out.

'Oh, I've missed you so, so much! Did you have a wonderful holiday?' She gushed.

'It's been fine,' I said, embarrassed, pulling away slightly. 'I'm not such a big fan of Christmas. Thanks for the dress. You shouldn't have.'

I tried to sound animated, to convey to her how touched I was, but my voice came out flat and strained.

Will you always be so awkward?

'Oh, it's nothing. You'll look wonderful in red velvet with that hair. And I had this idea for that design, so....' June widened her eyes and lifted her shoulders in a *Why wouldn't I?* shrug.

It was good to see her. She was frazzled but happy, in a uniquely June kind of way. She always tried to present an upbeat veneer, no matter what. June really did see the world through rose-colored spectacles.

'I got you something, too. Here.' I opened my purse and handed her a small box prettily wrapped with a blue satin ribbon.

I had dashed out early and hit various departments of Bullocks Wilshire for three gifts.

For June, I bought a pair of gold hair clips with pale pink stones.

For Barney, a box of three hand-rolled silk handkerchiefs with orange edges. The print was of toucans sitting amid tropical leaves.

For Beatty, nothing. It was impossible. Nothing seemed right. I had no idea when she would be back anyway, so I had time to figure something out.

June loved her hair clips, and immediately put them to use in her hair. 'They're just so beautiful! I'll treasure them forever.'

'Nothing on a velvet dress,' I said, gruffly.

We stood on the bare wooden floor of the workshop. It was on the first floor of a two-story building. Downstairs, the dress shop itself was in a better state with a tiled floor, mirrors with brass surrounds lining the walls, and a comfortable changing area behind a satin curtain.

The storefront had mannequins in the windows, showing off June's new line of winter frocks and ladies' suits.

The only areas downstairs that clients didn't go into were the small kitchen and another workroom at the back. It didn't get much light, so just was used for storage.

June preferred the upstairs room to work. It was airy and looked out over a bustling street. From the open balcony, sounds of the street wafted in. Just inside the door, an array of succulents in Mexican painted pots covered a mosaic table while outside, the dark glossy leaves of a magnolia tree provided some privacy and dappled shade.

The workshop had a long wooden bench, with three heavy duty sewing machines. Rolls of fabric were stacked on shelves along the walls.

Several rolls, featuring shades of green and gold, were lying on the workbench.

'Next year, we'll spend it together,' she was saying. 'We'll go somewhere fun.'

You and June on a trip? Why not?

'Sounds good.'

She lowered her voice. 'I couldn't wait to get back to the city. My family drove me crazy. Hey, you realize we're both businesswomen now, aren't we? '46 is going to be our year!'

'Well, I could handle a few more rush orders.'

'Oh, you've just gotten started. You'll be fine! I'm so grateful to Alberta for suggesting me.'

'You're gonna make the dresses in time?'

June gave me a pointed look. 'At the studio, I made forty crinolines for forty dancing Southern belles in one week, and with no help! I can manage six dresses in half that time. And I've got Sarah and Maria to help. I don't think I could pull it off without them. I have a couple of other commissions.'

'I know Maria, is Sarah new?'

June's eyes rolled towards a door. Her voice was hushed. 'She doesn't like meeting new people.'

'Okay.'

'She's Polish. She was in a camp. She got here a month ago.'

I stared at the door. 'A concentration camp?'

June nodded. 'She's working on another job in there. It's okay. She just wants to be left alone.'

We had all read about the camps and heard the reports on the wireless. We saw the terrible pictures of Nazi horrors: the starving people, the bodies, the gas chambers. From our sunny LA, we were at a safe distance.

When Barney told me about the devastation inflicted by the Nazis on his family—his cousins, uncles and aunts, both kids and adults—it made the atrocity more real. In the same room as him, I could sense his anguish. His revulsion. He shook when he talked about it. 'How could Nazis kill all those people? How could they invent that killing machine?' He just couldn't believe it.

The undeniable fact was that if he'd been in the wrong place at the wrong time, he could have been gassed alive as well. A Jew *and* a homosexual. Odds were not good he'd have got out.

And here, within five yards, divided by a thin wall, I stood near a woman who had somehow survived that hell.

A woman who couldn't face people yet, who wasn't ready to pretend everything was normal. Would this sunshine ever heal her? Make her forget?

No. Nothing could. My traumas were nothing compared to this woman's. With so many dead, was she thinking, *Why me? Why did I survive?*

Alberta emerged from the changing cubicle, a ravishing sight in long swathes of the dark green and gold fabric against her dark honey skin.

'Feel like a green goddess,' she grinned.

'Wow,' I said. 'You look fabulous.'

The shape of the gown was taking place, even if it was loosely tacked together.

I'd driven Alberta down in Mabel. On the way down, we agreed June didn't need to know anything about Dolly. She didn't know her anyway and the case was confidential.

But really, I was protecting her, in a way. June didn't need to hear other people's bad news. Things were going well for her now. I just needed to find out about Agnes.

But was I under-estimating June? She had just given a job to a refugee, after all.

June sighed, studying the dress. 'I think it's too loose on the hips, isn't it?'

Alberta and I looked at each other. It looked pretty good to us. Alberta said, 'Remember we gonna be playing. We don't stand like statues.'

June looked up at Alberta. 'You're right. Just a few adjustments.'

I sat on a high wooden stool, watching as June got down on her knees next to Alberta's legs. She was feeling the fabric, pinching it up and down from the hem to the hip, marking it with little dashes in tailor's chalk, then putting a few stitches in. 'How does it feel? Can you give it a try?'

Alberta played an invisible sax, arms raised, fingers bent. She moved it up and down, swung and twirled the imaginary instrument.

She finished with a flourish and bobbed a comical curtsy at us. 'So far nothing's ripped or bust out.' She winked. 'I can give the horn section's approval.'

June was delighted.

'Will you get to keep them?' I asked Alberta.

'I sure as hell hope so. Don't want to dress up as an olive tree only once in my life, do I?'

'Olive tree? Why do you have to look like olive trees?'

'The boss makes beauty products. Out of olive oil.'

I jumped and then looked at them both. '*Oliverelle*? You're not playing for Floriana Luciano?'

Alberta nodded. 'Mrs. Luciano is Zetty's boss.'

Zetty! Of course. Now I knew why I'd recognized her at

Joyce's on Christmas Eve. She was Floriana Luciano's driver. I'd once seen her in the driver's seat of an enormous car, with a uniform and cap on.

Floriana Luciano was the dynamic Italian entrepreneur who had given me the *Oliverelle* face mask. Her family business produced a bestselling range of luxury beauty care products made from Italian olive oil imported from the family estate. Or so she claimed. I'd done a small assignment for her, helping with a little corporate espionage.

'She's moved to Santa Barbara?' I asked.

'Yeah. Set up some kind of beauty resort. She's been restoring a rundown estate, set in thousands of acres. Got its own lake, private beach, the whole deal.'

June got up, went over to the worktop and opened a large square wooden box. She held the lid open, revealing six flower corsages—fake silk olive sprigs and yellow daisies—works in progress. She handed me one.

'Aren't they beautiful? Maria is making them for the band. They'll go just here.' She pointed at her bust. 'And we're doing matching little hair pieces.'

Alberta smiled. 'You're gonna do us proud.'

I swiveled on the stool, trying to sound as casual as possible. 'June, do you remember an Agnes Hunniford? She lived in the hotel.'

'Sure. Why?' It was a reasonable question, but Alberta and I exchanged a glance.

'Some mail arrived for her. Do you know where she lives now?'

June didn't answer. She had a pin in her mouth. She 'mm'-ed in answer.

'So you do?'

June pulled the pin out of her mouth, looking uncomfortable. She knew something. And I knew this wasn't going to be easy.

June said, 'You got it with you? I'll drop it off later today. I owe her a visit.'

'You've got enough to do. All these formals! Just tell me where.'

'No!' June blurted out. 'Just give it to me, okay! That's what Agnes wants.'

Alberta and I looked startled.

'What's the matter?' I asked.

June's cheeks were red. She couldn't lie. A penny was dropping in my own mind. It was spinning. Maybe it would land where I thought it would. 'Is something wrong with Agnes?'

'It's a private matter.'

Was it a private matter for Agnes and Ronald Hunter?

Alberta gave me a *You better tell her* nod.

I let out a sigh. 'June. I wasn't straight with you. Your pal Agnes might be able to help out with a case I'm working on.'

June stood up. 'So, the thing about the mail, that's a big fat lie?'

I nodded. 'I didn't know what to say. I've got to keep things quiet for clients. Like, I guess, you are, for Agnes.'

June's eyes went from Alberta to me, pained. 'You both saved me after my bad time. And Dede. You all know what I went through. I just can't handle secrets and lies, not from my pals. Kinda hurts. If it's important for you to talk to Agnes, then sure. I don't want to know why. But I'm coming with you, to make it right with her first. Okay?'

We both looked humbled. I nodded.

June added, 'They won't let you see her, anyway, without me.'

'Where is she?'

'You can't say a word about where she is. To anyone, okay? Swear on it?'

I swore to June, with my fingers crossed under a sprig of fake olive.

30

Sonia Parker would deem this trip improvisation, or "*unauthorized activity*". But if I got results, surely she would be impressed? I'd play it safe, coax information out of Agnes Hunniford, and not do anything to endanger the case.

Far from endangering it, this could be the thing that clinched everything. I felt excited, and proud of myself.

The Pineview Clinic was a substantial house, built for a big, respectable family sometime in the 1890s.

Now it housed a big group of unrespectables, at least in their families' and society's eyes—single mothers and their babies, expectant mothers who had nowhere to go before their babies were born.

The clinic had wide stone steps, leading up to an imposing porch supported by four thick brick columns painted white. Conifers grew out of two tubs at the foot of the steps. Window boxes on the dark gray ledges were full of flowers. The windows were shaded in Venetian blinds and sheer curtains. They let light in but kept accusing gazes out.

The narrow front garden edging the sidewalk was protected by a small picket fence.

I liked the fact it wasn't hidden away. The clinic could be anything. Any passersby wouldn't have a clue.

Beyond the large double doors, June and I were greeted by a tall woman in her late forties. Mrs. Devine was every inch the pillar of the community type, someone dedicated to putting things right. She had kind eyes, papery-skinned hands, and the permanent pained smile of the do-gooder.

She was elegant too, wearing a fashionable dove gray suit with blue buttons and a cream silk blouse that just poked over the high collar. This was itself edged by two darker blue arrows, facing in opposite directions, made of curved piping.

Wasn't it *too* elegant? I bet the pregnant inmates didn't look as good.

A large Christmas tree stood behind her. On the wall, a plaster bust of a mother and child.

June's presence was completely indispensable. Mrs. Devine was very pleased to see her. I was introduced as a good friend of Agnes. Mrs. Devine studied me, pondering whether to let a stranger in. She relented.

'It's nice for the girls to have friends come by. Please take a seat.'

She showed us to a waiting room, a small salon on the side. Above the mantelpiece was a delicate oil painting of a child holding a dove. A huge vase of flowers dominated the fireplace. Tinsel hung down the walls, and chains of paper holly looped across the ceiling.

A mixed-race young woman, wearing a headscarf and checked loose smock, and pushing a small cleaning trolley, was dusting the window ledge. She was pregnant and about seventeen.

'Kitty, would you please fetch Agnes?' Mrs. Devine's voice was unexpectedly firm.

Kitty nodded and left as we came in, her eyes down. Mrs. Devine asked us to sit down, then retreated to her office, leaving us alone.

'How many live here?' I asked June, who duly sat down.

'Twenty or so. They stay, have their babies.'

'Then what happens?' Why was I asking a question to which I already knew the answer?

'Well, the babies go to their new homes, I guess. Come sit down. Could be a while.' June looked around, approvingly. 'So nice they've made it all pretty for Christmas.'

I didn't want to sit down. I wanted to ask questions, get answers, and get out.

The place was starting to make me feel uneasy. The odor was a combination of flowers, pine disinfectant and fake concern. I didn't like it one bit.

Did Violet end up in one of these places when I was born? Did they even exist, twenty-six years ago? How on earth did she manage? I had no idea about my mother's life with me as a baby when she first arrived in America. I'd never allowed myself to dwell on it and I didn't want to start now.

I looked out of the window, through the venetians. Mabel sat outside the front of the building, looking comforting.

Maybe coming here was a mistake.

'June?' A sweet, high voice. Slightly pathetic.

I turned towards the door. A young woman, her skin as white as milk, with watery eyes, stood in the doorway, wearing the obligatory headscarf and flannel smock, except hers was covered in tiny flowers. Not a scrap of makeup. There was a slight bulge to her belly, but she didn't look very pregnant. She looked drained.

The image of a very different Agnes, in Hunter's apartment, flashed across my mind. I could see her in a stylish suit, with red lipstick on, getting him coffee in the swanky kitchen and getting fondled, or worse, in return.

I blinked it away.

'How are you? How is she?' June embraced Agnes. 'I got you this for her. Thought maybe you could use it.'

'*She*'? '*Her*'? Had Agnes had already had her baby?

Agnes smiled, taking a wrapped gift that June pulled from her crocheted purse. 'Oh, you shouldn't have. She's doing so well.' She gave me an odd look.

'This is Elvira. She's my best pal. I hope you don't mind. She understands, and we were passing, so....'

Agnes gave an uncertain smile. 'It's okay. Hello.'

I arranged my expression into something more friendly. 'Hi.'

'I'd love to see her,' June said.

June had kept Agnes's secrets on the way down, said I'd find out everything when we met her. She had insisted I took it slow. 'We can't put her under any pressure to talk.'

Agnes was saying, 'Sure. She's in the nursery. You can take a peek through the window, if you want.'

June beamed. 'We sure do!'

Agnes looked at me. 'Want to come see my baby?'

'I'd like that,' I lied.

Agnes led us back into the wide corridor and through some ornate, glazed double doors. We passed a heavily pregnant Japanese girl and a skinny white girl pushing a cleaning trolley. Both were clad in the ugly smocks and scarfs. When they saw us, they stopped and hung their heads low as if they were lower class.

What was it with the hanging heads? Had I been like that in prison?

The modest decorations continued along the way. Around a corner, Agnes stopped and smiled. 'Here we are.'

To her left, there was a wall of which the top half was glazed.

We peered in. Two rows of white cribs, each one holding a tiny, squirming baby, swaddled in blankets. I was glad we could only peek.

'Which one?' June asked, eyes bulging out in joy.

Proudly, Agnes pointed to the general direction of three cots in the corner. June squealed. 'Oh, she's adorable! She looks just like you. Isn't she cute, Elvira?'

'Yes.' I couldn't bear the gushing. I wanted out of this hell.

They *oohed* and *aahed* for some time together. Agnes updated June on feeding, burping, changing diapers.

I tried to feign interest, but this was heading nowhere. Luckily, June spotted the bathroom. 'Can visitors use that?' She whispered, to Agnes.

'Sure. Just be quick.'

June slipped across the hall.

I turned to Agnes. 'So who's Daddy?'

Agnes gasped. 'Sorry?'

'That came out wrong. I don't have much time and I need your help.'

Agnes folded her arms. 'I don't understand.'

'Do they let you know what's going on in the outside world? You know your old boss is dead? Ronald Hunter?'

A cloud crossed Agnes's face. 'I heard about it. It's awful news.'

'Sure. Is he anything to do with you being in this place?'

'I don't know who you are. But you need to go.' She pursed her lips.

'Look. I'm happy for you. The baby's cute. But another girl he's got pregnant is facing death row. If he's got a habit of sowing his seed, it would be real helpful to know.'

202

'Ronald Hunter is not the father.' Agnes said, with a level voice. 'And you are way out of line!'

'So no daddy on the birth certificate?'

'Get the hell out of here, or I'll scream!'

From behind, June cried out. 'Elvira! That's enough! I'm sorry, Agnes. I thought she was going to be more delicate.' She turned on me. 'What's got into you? She just gave birth a week ago. I'm so sorry, Agnes, really I am.'

June pulled me away by the arm. I called back. 'Think about it, Agnes. Someone Hunter used just like you is gonna die. They already killed her kid!'

Agnes' expression was hard to read. June's wasn't. Horrified.

Mrs. Devine was approaching, the other side of the ornate glass doors. Concerned.

June hissed at me. 'What the hell's wrong with you? Wait for me outside! I've gotta make this right.'

In the car, I lit a cigarette and puffed on it like it was going out of fashion.

What's gotten into you?

A few minutes later, June got in beside me, slamming the door behind her. She immediately unwound the window. 'Well! You just did yourself proud. Jeez, Elvira! You upset her real bad.'

I didn't want June's moralizing. 'Forget you heard any of that stuff about the other girl.'

June gave what was, for her, a sarcastic look. 'Oh, sure. I'll just go right ahead and forget all about the fact someone's kid has been killed!'

'It died in custody. Mother had a miscarriage.'

'And you just couldn't tread gently, could you?'

She was right. I had completely lost it.

'I don't care to know a thing about your rotten case! But you had no right to treat her like that! We could have gone for a walk with her, you could have explained the situation. Made her feel comfortable. Do I really have to tell you how to do your job?'

'She wasn't going to talk anyway. I could see it in her eyes. She's cowed. They all are.'

'What do you mean?'

'Didn't you see it? The way they're all hanging their heads, the way they dress like dirt-poor farmers' wives while the staff glide around in their stylish suits. Gave me the creeps.'

But that's not all, is it? You know it's deeper than that.

'It's a good place! Those ladies are giving them a chance!'

'Yeah, a chance to feel like trash.'

'No! A roof over their heads. Security. Food. Good homes for their kids with decent, caring people who can't have children of their own.'

I snapped back. 'Please! So you can see how much she loves that baby. And she's going to just give it up to some strangers?

June shook her head. 'Agnes is keeping her baby. She's going to raise it on her own.'

'What?' I glanced at June, genuinely taken aback.

'The moms do get a choice. Sure, it's gonna be tough for Agnes on her own. And the kid. She'll get called names, you know she will.'

You've been called those names.

I exhaled. 'How many of those girls really think they have a choice? Cold water flats, no money to pay for a babysitter. She'll give it up.'

'Well, Agnes is gonna try. And I, for one, am gonna help her anyways.'

'Don't you have a dress shop to run?'

She huffed, furious. Then she grabbed my cigarette packet, with shaky hands, and pulled out a cigarette. June didn't smoke.

I'd unnerved her. June's world and entire values system had been rocked by events in her own life. She had done her best to marry the new June, who had wised up out of necessity, with the old, dewy-eyed June. Most of the time it worked.

But it was an effort for her. Just like me being Elvira Slate was an effort for me.

Feeling guilty, I prized the unlit cigarette from her fingers. 'C'mon. You don't smoke. I apologize for going...nuts. The case is getting to me. Race against time.'

'It's okay.'

We sat in silence for a while.

June finally spoke. 'Sometimes I even find myself judging her. Like, wouldn't the baby be better off anyway with a respectable family? But who's respectable anyway? How can you know? And then I just get confused.'

'So long as it's loved by somebody, that's the only thing that counts.'

She nodded.

I turned to June. 'Maybe she's got some help from somebody. To keep it?'

Maybe a rich man has paid her off, I thought, but didn't say.

'I really don't know.' June's voice was flat, and tired.

She wanted this over, so I switched on the engine, the cigarette dangling from my mouth.

31

I had one day to myself before the funeral. One day to forget what felt increasingly like a string of dead ends.

Girls who wouldn't talk. Leads I couldn't follow. Attorneys who would get mad at me if they knew what I'd tried to do, particularly about Agnes. I'd have to tread carefully if I told Sonia Parker. There was no way Agnes would testify. Ever.

But screw them all. Dolly was in line for the death penalty. How on earth was she coping?

I made myself an instant coffee and sat on the couch. I had one day to pretend to myself I was having some kind of break. I would put on a pretty frock, some makeup and take myself off to a picture house. Then supper.

I picked up the holiday survival list I'd written to myself on Christmas Eve.

I had to laugh; Christmas Eve felt a century ago.

TRING! The telephone rang. My private line. I definitely hadn't given this number to Sonia. Barney? Lauder?

'Hello?'

'Booby! How the hell are you?' Beatty's rich, booming voice.

I couldn't wipe the grin off my face. 'Oh, my God! How are you? Where are you calling from?'

'Back in the smoke. Had to cut things short. Client in a jam. No rest for the wicked, eh?'

'Tell me about it. I've got a new case, too.'

'Career girls, what can I say? Want me to buy you lunch?'

I grinned. I wanted nothing more in the world.

Beatty was in her usual corner table, a majestic sight.

She had changed her hairstyle since I last saw her. Now, her steel blue hair was in tighter curls, pinned back on the sides. On top of her head, an oval felt hat in scarlet, with a scalloped structure of lace and felt on top, tilted over her face.

She wore a harlequin wool dress with billowing puffed sleeves, drawn in by tight cuffs. The diamond weave of the fabric was an assortment of purples, yellows, mauves, turquoise and scarlet. Scarlet glass buttons went up to her neck, securing the collar which was wide and pointed. A flamboyant scarlet silk scarf was pinned around her neck by an oval amethyst brooch. This matched the chunky amethyst and gold bracelet on one wrist. The usual array of gemstone rings set in gold adorned her fingers. Her nails were varnished in a bright red.

Next to her, I was somber in my pleated black skirt suit, aqua silk blouse and black cardigan.

I wanted her to see me looking sophisticated and in control of life. I was anything but.

Sitting among the tables with their pristine red and white tablecloths, the picturesque murals of pastoral Sicily in *Luigi's*, and the noisy crowd was the lift I needed.

The restaurant was Beatty's favorite haunt. We would often meet for lunch here. I'd have pasta with a tomato sauce washed down with plenty of red wine. Beatty normally went for lasagna.

Hopefully no mafia would be paying a visit today, to gun some customer down. Poor old Luigi had been forced to close briefly for that reason.

I sipped my Chianti and looked around. The diners looked regular enough.

Luigi came over. He explained all his murals had been

repainted as they had been riddled with bullet holes. 'Terrible, terrible. I wish these animals all stay away. Why they come to Los Angeles?'

Beatty ordered a mushroom risotto. I stuck to spaghetti with a tomato sauce. Luigi sauntered off with the menus.

'I love my magnifying glass. Thank you so much. I've already put it to good use.'

'That's what it's for.'

I opened my purse and passed her a wrapped gift. 'What the hell is this?'

On the way here, I'd had to buy something, anything.

I watched as she unwrapped it. I felt quite tense, but her face broke into a soft smile. 'Oh, Booby. Adorable!'

It was a small china dachshund dog, with tiny puppies. I knew she collected anything and everything related to dachshunds. She carefully wrapped them back up in the tissue, placed them in the box and popped it in her purse.

I broke the sad news about Sophia Spark.

'Poor woman.' Beatty said. 'Guess that's why you jumped at another case?'

I nodded. 'These office overheads sure bite you in the ankle.'

She chuckled, heartily. 'You know you can always work for me. I could squeeze Barney in, too. I don't have to keep telling you, do I?'

I smiled, touched. 'Thanks. It's a great safety net to have.'

But one I would never fall back on. I could never risk Beatty Falaise being officially enmeshed with me. If I was ever caught, she could be in trouble as some kind of accessory.

I changed the subject. 'The new case is a tough nut to crack, all right.'

She raised a brow. 'Go on. What's said in Luigi's stays in Luigi's. You know that'

'I'm working for Sonia Parker.'

Beatty whistled. 'Top-of-the-league defense attorney.' She said she knew of her reputation. Rich clients, and a killer-diller in court.

'You know about Ronald Hunter?'

'Jeez, you're on that case?'

I nodded. 'I feel more like an errand girl than a PI. Sonia asked me to do some things. If she's got an angle, she's not sharing it with me.' I would avoid telling Beatty about the huge risk I had taken with the watch. She would be angry I'd been so stupid.

'Do *you* have an angle?' Beatty eyed me over her glass of wine.

I shrugged. 'I don't know. I kinda like the wife for it.'

Beatty put down her glass. She pulled down her tortoiseshell spectacles to see me better. 'Linda Hunter? You think *she* did it?'

'She's the only one with motive. Hunter was not exactly the faithful type. Even Sonia says the killing feels personal. Linda did it and framed Dolly Perkins.'

'Stabbed to death in bed? It's certainly got that touch. Did he have a lot of affairs?'

'I'm not sure. Dolly and another one who I believe fell pregnant by him. I just found out about that girl. I haven't even told Sonia yet. And he was making a move on his latest secretary.'

Beatty whistled. 'Jeez. You've been busy.'

I explained the little Sonia Parker had deigned to share was that she believed the prosecution would maintain Dolly was inventing the relationship, that she was the instigator. 'One may have been paid off. She's not gonna talk to anyone. So far, the press hasn't even reported that Dolly was Hunter's mistress. But unless we can make any of these girls talk, or find a witness who can testify Dolly and Hunter were together, it's dicey.'

'Well, maybe one of his other girls could have done it? Gone nuts with jealousy?'

'I thought about that, too. But one's just given birth in a clinic, and the other hated Hunter's attentions.' I added that if there were more girls, I might not have time to root them out.

Beatty shrugged. 'Well, if Parker can get any of them on the stand, it would help establish he was a creep. If she wants to implicate Linda Hunter.'

We met each other's eyes.

Beatty smiled as Luigi came over with our plates. 'Risotto for Signora Fa-lay-zee, and for Signorina Sla-a-tee, spaghetti.' The way he pronounced Slate sounded like 'slutty'. I concealed an involuntary giggle, but I think Beatty noticed.

I did my best to arrange my face into what just looked like a happy smile, pleased to see such a lovely meal. Anyway, I was ravenous, watching Luigi sprinkle parmesan cheese over our steaming food.

After he left, I picked up the thread. 'The trouble is, the prosecution could maintain Dolly was just jealous, saw other women like the secretary as a threat. Lost it. Sonia doesn't tell me much, but it seems like she doesn't want to give Flannery any more ammo. Anyway, I have no idea of her game plan.'

Beatty leaned back. 'Someone's giving herself an education in criminal law!'

'Want to know the biggest lesson so far? These lawyers are cold fish. You never know what they're thinking. Even if they're friendly, they're secretive.'

'True, but they pay well. You've done great to land this job.'

I smiled, touched by her praise.

We ate in silence for a while. Then Beatty looked up, a porcini on her fork. 'I'm guessing you've considered any of her friends having a beef with Dolly Perkins, setting her up?'

I nodded, chewing. 'Even looked into it. The only people she knows are a swing band and a roommate. She seems to care for Dolly, understand her. The band all seem to like her. Particularly one girl, Zetty. Guess who's Zetty's boss is? Floriana Luciano. Small world, huh?'

Beatty knew about the little assignment I had done for the beauty entrepreneur.

'The only thing I've got now is the Ronald Hunter funeral.'

Beatty nearly dropped her fork. 'You're going to that?'

'Did a deal with Martell. She knows the Hunters and she's taking me on condition I tell the trustees Sophia Spark is definitely dead, so Martell can write the ending to her movie!'

'Just like Martell to look out for *numero uno*. But Booby, you've got to be careful. A helluva lot of reporters will be outside.' She gave me a meaningful look. 'Does Randall Lauder know about all this?'

'No. He's away. And what's the point of him giving me a detective license, if I can't use it?'

Beatty eyed me. 'His idea was for you to do cases that don't attract attention.'

I shrugged, twisting spaghetti on my fork. I could never tell her we were having an affair. I shrugged, acting nonchalant.

'I won't tell him. Just seeing it from his perspective, is all. I know you'll be careful.'

'I will. By the way, that's another thing. Don't you think Linda Hunter's kind of rushed into burying her husband? It's like she wants to start '46 single! Maybe she's got her own fancy man.'

'Some folks like to get it over real fast. Religion, maybe.' Beatty put her fork down. 'Ever wondered if somebody could be framing Linda Hunter, not Dolly Perkins?'

I stared at her. What was she getting at?

'You mean the real killer wants Sonia to go after Linda Hunter, and what, Dolly's like some kind of diversion?'

'Why not?'

'But everything points to *Dolly* being set up. Dolly was sleeping with him. She discovered the body. And she ran away. Predictably.'

Beatty took another glug of wine and nodded. 'True. But it feels too simple.'

'Sonia doesn't see Linda Hunter as a suspect. Never has. So if somebody is trying to force her in that direction, Sonia isn't playing ball.'

Beatty gestured for me to expand.

'Sonia's argument is Linda Hunter would just divorce if she was desperate. And she could have an alibi. So no need to kill Ronald. But I guess she might change that opinion after I tell her about the other girls.'

Beatty said, 'Cases like this have a funny way of suddenly flipping.'

She topped our wine glasses up, her heavy bracelet jangling. 'Still, Parker's an excellent lawyer. I get why she's keeping her cards to her chest about her defense strategy. Frustrating for you, but you can always vent to little ol' me.' She winked.

'I will. I'm so glad you're back.' This just came out. Beatty's face softened with a smile. 'Leave no stone unturned, however pretty the path, remember?'

'Sure, if I was allowed down any paths of my choosing. Sonia Parker's leash is pretty tight.'

'Parker just doesn't know how good you are, is all. You don't need to tell her every single thing you do, not until you've got something concrete for her. The number of times a client's told me how to run a case! If I'd stuck to their instructions, I'd be nowhere.'

I smiled, grateful. Beatty was encouraging me to have faith in myself as a professional woman.

She'd sensed Sonia was wearing me thin.

I asked, 'You don't know anything about Linda Hunter, do you? Any tidbits you can share?'

Beatty blew out a puff of air. 'Nothing. I mean, I've heard of her. Who hasn't? The papers are on fire with the Hunters.'

'It must be terrible to be in the public eye, you know, when something like this happens.'

Beatty shrugged. 'Price of fame and fortune. Can't have it all.'

32

'Probably some third-rate star. A hanger-on, no doubt.' Martell muttered dismissively.

She sat behind the wheel of her gleaming red car. We were in a long, slow-moving line of expensive cars heading towards the Hunter estate. Police had cordoned off a large section of the road, in which the public were gathering. A crowd of middle-aged women, children, older people, and wounded veterans, most waving US flags.

Hunter was beloved by many.

Out of nowhere, reporters dashed past our car. I instinctively pulled the veil of the hat down, but it didn't matter. They weren't looking at us. Their prey was the monster of a black car creeping behind us.

More reporters ran past, frenzy in their eyes, cameras at the ready.

I gave a quick look behind. The press were swarming like flies on the car. I said, 'I can't tell who it is.' I wouldn't recognize anyone anyway.

As we got closer, a flunkey in a gray uniform piped with white stopped our car. Martell gave her name and he directed us to a side enclosure, rather than enter the main drive. Only a few of the most expensive cars were allowed inside the gates.

We looked like a pair of elegant black widows. I had on a little crepe and silk black dress I'd bought in Manhattan about six months ago, when I was planning on a more glamorous life. It had a high neck, with black soutache around the bodice, shoulders and wrists. The waistline felt tighter than it had when I bought it.

The hat Martell lent me was pillbox style in black satin, with a twisted sculpture at the back giving it more drama. The tulle veil was soft and fine. It fell to below my chin and draped onto my shoulders—dramatic, yet effective.

Martell had insisted I borrowed one of her coats instead of wearing my jacket. The one I now wore was tailored and waisted, in the finest wool, and edged with a full black fur collar and cuffs.

'That's more like it,' she said, approvingly, before we set off.

I hadn't had the heart to tell her I normally avoided wearing fur. She wouldn't understand, nobody ever did. I had the odd fake fur item, but even then, I never really wanted to look like I was content that an animal had had a miserable life and death, just to make me look good.

On this occasion, I could only hope the victim would feel honored to come to such a swanky funeral.

But now, its soft fur close on my neck felt hot and cloying.

Let me go, it seemed to be saying.

Martell suffered no such remorse. She outshone me, wearing an enormous dark brown fur stole around her shoulders. Her suit was of darkest aubergine satin, almost an inky, dead-of-night purple. Her hat was an elaborate wide-brimmed number in black and purple stripes. She too had a fine net veil, but it hid less of her face.

She switched off the engine and glanced at me. 'You are Mary, my cousin from San Francisco.'

'Do you have a cousin called Mary?'

'I do. She pens dreadful romantic novels she can't get

215

published. Had the gall to ask me if I'd adapt one! I was obligated to have a look, but what drivel. Couldn't get beyond three pages. I'd pay for her to vanity publish if it got me off the hook. Now, I had to drop Linda a line you were coming with me. She'll be surrounded, but we'll get a chance to give her our condolences in person.'

'Okay. I'm a failed novelist called Mary. Anything else I should know, in case she asks me?'

'Oh, don't worry. She'll forget you the moment she's met you.'

A large oil painting of Ronald Hunter dominated a vast oak table at one end of the ballroom. It was a strange reunion. I felt as if I knew him.

On each side of the portrait, two blue and white Chinese vases held magnificent floral displays of white roses, lilies and ferns.

The room heaved with over one hundred people, crammed onto the parquet floor. More spilled out into the grounds. All in all, three hundred members of the elite of Los Angeles and beyond were here to pay their respects.

If only Lauder could see me now.

A string quartet provided somber background music. Servants in black uniforms and white starched aprons lined another long table, serving tea, sandwiches and cake.

There wasn't a drop of booze, annoyingly. I needed Dutch courage.

'Linda's over there.' Martell subtly nodded at a huddle of people in black, surrounding a woman we could barely see. Only the top of her honey-colored head was visible. 'I'd heard she'd gone blonde,' muttered Martell. 'She is going gray, so probably a smart move.'

Martell rattled off names and roles of important-sounding men: the mayor of Beverly Hills; the police commissioner; studio bosses; presidents of golf clubs, museums, and water companies. She even knew military figures, of which quite a few were here.

She was a social encyclopedia and I was soon lost. The faces blurred into one. What on earth had Sonia expected me to see or do here? It was just too crammed.

No lesser mortals like Pauline, of course. She'd been axed from the script.

'Who's that?' I whispered to Martell, looking at a glamorous fifty-something woman with silver blonde hair in victory rolls. She was defiantly ignoring the dress code in a bright orange-and-black striped dress, an enormous corsage of orange and yellow flowers across her breast.

'Lady Hester Swannington, Hunter's first wife. I can't see the daughters, but they're here somewhere. Maybe outside with the kids.'

'Lady? Is she British?' My stomach knotted.

No English toffs today, please.

'Married to a Brit aristocrat. Was. He's dead, too.'

'That is some outfit! Hell hath no fury like a first wife scorned, hey?' I muttered, trying to be witty.

'Oh, I'm sick and tired of that first wife crap. And I didn't think you'd be one to peddle it, Elvira.' Martell snapped, ratty all of a sudden.

I'd obviously touched a nerve. 'Came out wrong. I meant, good for her, you know,' I mumbled, eating humble pie.

Martell eyed me, only half-appeased. 'Yes, it is good for her. And I'll tell you why.' She explained that after she'd been dumped for the younger model Linda, Hester married Charles Swannington, even older than Hunter, who had promptly died. Before the war, she divided her time between the Upper East Side and Gloucestershire, where the British family estate was. She'd let the Brits use the stately home for convalescing RAF officers and had no intention of going back to a sodden, miserable isle.

Martell pointed out of the huge arched window at a bunch of kids, tearing around the grounds in an unseemly manner.

'See the kid on the sidelines? Harvey. Hunter and Linda's child.' The other kids, probably Harvey's nieces and nephews who were of the same age, were clearly doing their best to ignore him.

Out of nowhere, Brad, Hunter's driver, appeared in the grounds. He was in a dark lounge suit and derby hat, and almost fitted in. Soon he and Harvey began kicking a ball around. The other kids now got interested. Maybe Brad had a good side, sticking up for the lonely kid.

'So Linda Hunter inherits the lot?' I muttered.

'Oh, it will all be carved up somehow. All the children have trust funds. Nobody's gonna starve. Now, let's pay our respects and then I really should say hello to some people. You'll be okay, won't you?' It wasn't really a question.

Martell led the way through the crowd, and I followed.

Linda Hunter was magnificent as the beautiful yet tragic widow, in a long black silk dress with a severe mandarin collar and a simple gold cross around her neck. She looked like royalty, a medieval queen, the most elegantly dressed here. Her hair was a woody blonde, in neat long waves that reached her shoulders. There was something of Veronica Lake in her demeanor and style.

I almost jumped at the sight of the man next to Linda, his arm protectively around her waist. A much better-looking— and living—version of Ronald Hunter.

'Rufus Hunter?' I asked, my voice low. I recognized him from the paper.

'Uh-huh. How can you tell?' Martell replied, sarcastically.

'They look like an item.'

'A golden couple,' Martell concurred.

Linda suddenly saw Martell approaching. She gave a small smile and stepped away from Rufus's arm. A pair of older women homed in on Rufus. He watched, guarded, as Martell and I reached Linda.

Her lipstick was very red. It looked identical to the one I'd dabbed off the wall. She looked drawn, and her expression wasn't quite as empty as it had seemed to me in the newspaper photograph. If she hadn't killed Hunter, the murder must have come as something of a shock.

Martell was all syrupy, fake sincerity. 'Linda, my darling, what a terrible ordeal for you and Harvey. This is Mary, my cousin. I wrote you about her coming. We so appreciate being here on this saddest of days.'

'I'm truly sorry for your loss.' I said. Linda and I shook hands. I'd kept my gloves on. Her grasp was weak.

'You're the romantic novelist?' Linda tried to peer at my face through the veil.

'Trying my best! My books aren't everybody's cup of tea.'

Martell eyes burnt into me, askance, from under her veil.

Linda Hunter said, 'I love romantic fiction. My cousin

219

Dwight's starting a book publishing company. I could introduce you. He's here somewhere.' She looked apathetically around the room.

Martell jumped in. 'Oh, Mary's already promised her debut novel to a small company in San Francisco, haven't you, dear? It'll be out next year.'

'Well, I'll make sure to get a copy. What's it called?'

'*Impossible Dream*,' I muttered.

'That's an original title.' Linda said, without irony.

She wasn't the brightest button in the box, but she was no killer. I just knew it. She looked like a model but at heart was just an uncomplicated girl next door. Married money, because she'd grown up surrounded by it. It was her misfortune that she married a bounder. But did she even know it?

Maybe she was as naïve as one of the heroines in my—in Mary's—slushy novels.

I felt Martell's finger jab me hard in the back. 'Come on, Mary. Linda's got the whole world to talk to.'

'And it's Mary who?' Linda asked. She wanted my surname! I froze. 'I'm sorry?'

Martell laughed. 'Look at her, she's so tired from the trip! Mary Saunders. Or you were, the last time we spoke!' Martell tittered.

'Mary Saunders. I'll be sure to remember it. Have you had something to eat?' Linda said. Martell said we hadn't and dragged me away.

Martell and I walked off, bickering under our breaths about whether she had told me the surname or not. 'Well, never mind. But you see? If you think Linda Hunter's a murderous Medea, you really are a romance novelist.'

'Medea?'

'Oh, it's from Greek mythology. You probably don't know the classics.'

Her snootiness was misplaced. I had been taught Greek and Latin for several years at a grammar school in London, in a former life, in another world, when I had been given my one chance of becoming respectable.

A chance I blew, of course.

The fact Martell was so sure a streetwise PI wouldn't know Greek myths annoyed me. I suddenly wanted to show off my education.

'I know exactly who Medea is. Why her?'

'Oh, she was the first husband-slayer that came to mind.'

'I think you mean Clytemnestra. She killed Agamemnon. Medea killed her kids.'

Martell ignored this, her eyes lighting up. She waved at someone. She said she would find me and we could leave after that.

I headed for the long table, wondering if I could manage a piece of cake and a cup of tea with gloves and a veil on.

What are you thinking! Work the room. Find something! Anything!

I turned around and headed back to the baronial wood-paneled hall with two stags' heads on huge wooden mounts.

Off this was a vaulted hallway, with stone tiles. Portraits of men, alongside lamps and small brass plaques lined the long walls, punctuated with mahogany doors with colossal carved frames.

Nobody was around to prevent me from gawking at the Hunter clan, so I slipped down the hall.

The clan turned out to be mainly several portraits of Ronald Hunter in various guises. The first, him in pose, in a tuxedo and bow tie. He wasn't averse to tooting his own horn, obviously.

I peered closely into his eyes. The painter had even got the stubby fair lashes right. I whispered, 'Look, buddy, I know you weren't much of a gentleman. But who killed you? Help me out here.'

Hunter's greedy eyes danced right back at me. Nobody would recognize the look of a predator but me.

I moved on to the next painting. Linda Hunter, posing in such a way her profile seemed to be looking at Hunter's. A matching pair of portraits. She wore a peach satin evening dress and a diamond choker. Her hair was darker than her new shade of blonde.

'Randy says that Flannery is one of the best detectives the department has. The case against her will be watertight. And then it will all be over.'

I threw myself against the wall. A young woman's voice, coming from a room further down the corridor.

A calm and poised voice.

Randy? Randall? My Randall?

Was I in spitting distance of The Fiancée?

33

My stomach lurched. My mouth was full of sawdust, but still, I edged towards the half-open door. I had to hear more!

'I know. But I was thinking, could it be *them*, not her? I'd hate for an innocent person to...you know....' This was Linda's voice.

'She's hardly innocent. She sounds demented.'

'Yes, but...'

Them?

'Look, the cops know what they're doing. Soon you can move on.' She lowered her voice. 'You've waited so long for this. So has Rufus.'

What? Rufus?

I had been right. Rufus and Linda were in love. She'd married one brother and fallen for the other.

It hit me, like a wave. Rufus. It had to be. He coveted his brother's wife and killed him. At least paid somebody for the hit. But was Linda in on it?

Linda let out a heavy sigh. 'I've got Harvey to think about. He's not himself. Not to mention the gossip. Sometimes I just want to take him back to Texas and disappear. Forget about everything.'

'But Rufus?'

'He'll get over me.'

'The path of love never runs true. Take me and Randy. You think my folks approved of my future husband being a cop? It even took me a while to accept he wasn't after my money. But he's a good guy, the one for me. You just have to give it time, sweetie. You've been through so much. You've got to be strong, for the trial.'

'I know you're right.'

'I am. Forget about what other people think. You've done nothing wrong!'

'Randall's been so kind. He doesn't know yet about Rufus, does he? I don't want him to think ill of me.'

'Of course not, darling. I promise you. That's between us girls. He'll understand in time, when everything's out in the open.'

My mind raced. The Fiancée was in the room with Linda Hunter. It was her. I knew it. I had to remember every word they were saying.

'I'm so sorry this has ruined your holiday. Will you thank Randall for me?'

'Thank him yourself. He'll be here any minute.'

Lauder. About to show up. This couldn't get worse. He'd see through the getup, the ludicrous veil. He would mentally yank it off and he would be mad, but without saying a word.

That steely cold anger. No scene, just the silent freeze. Later, we'd have it out.

Well, this time, the tables would be turned. He'd find out *She* knew more about the case than he did.

And she sounded like a condescending bitch. Was he blind?

Footsteps. A servant was heading my way, very surprised at my odd positioning against the wall. I quickly spun around, peering at another portrait. This was of little Harvey, about three years old, sitting on Linda's lap.

'Ma'am, this is a private area.'

I walked towards him, so the women couldn't hear me. 'Oh, I had no idea. Just looking at the portraits,' I said, quietly. 'Beautiful paintings. So sad.'

I pretended to sniff under the veil and lifted a hankie under to dab my eyes.

'My condolences, ma'am.'

I passed him, nodding in gratitude. 'You're very kind.'

I reached the main hall. The front door was wide open. Should I dash out now? Would Martell be ready to go? I could risk a few seconds more trying to find her.

I hovered just outside the door of the ballroom, trying to spot her. My mind was still racing.

Rufus, the good-looking younger brother, now my prime suspect! There were also some enemies knocking around—the *"Them"* Linda had referred to.

And to top it all, fate had served up a nice kick in the guts for me, stumbling into Lauder's other life.

Lauder knew about "Them", but he was happy to go with Dolly as prime suspect, according to The Fiancée. Even odder was that he was singing a very different tune to The Fiancée about Detective Flannery.

Was "Them" the reason why Lauder was at the Hunter residence the night of the killing? It surely had to be. I smelt the stagnant odor of blackmail.

Somebody was putting the squeeze on Linda or Hunter, or Linda and Rufus, and Lauder had gotten involved. Roped in, or willing aide? I had no idea. He might not even know about Linda and Rufus, as The Fiancée claimed. Maybe his help was off the books. Maybe the Fiancée had instructed him to help her friend Linda who was in a bit of a pickle.

Hell of a lot of maybes, as usual.

But if any of these scenarios were accurate, of course Lauder would have rushed over to see Linda, to allay her fears, or help her somehow.

My world and Lauder's had collided, irrevocably. Everything about The Fiancée made me sick. Her syrupy uptown voice, her confident snobbery.

She was a snake, only out for herself. I could sense it.

Did he really love this woman? Was he dumb, or ambitious, or both?

And if he did love her, what on earth was he doing with me? Or did he know deep down she didn't really respect his social status and I was some kind of secret revenge?

But had I been any better, once upon a time? I'd accepted a proposal from my gangster boyfriend, Billy. At sixteen, I was looking for a sugar daddy, a man to give me a roof over my head, nice frocks and an easy life.

I didn't know what love was, back then, and I still didn't. Romance, in the classic sense, now just felt like a quick fix. A glass of champagne in the course of a long, boring night. The high is nice but doesn't last, and when it wears off, somehow reality is even grayer than it was before the bubbles.

Focus on the damn case!

The Fiancée knew Linda was having an affair with Rufus. She promised Linda that Randall didn't know. A lie? Surely if Randall did know, he would quickly suspect Rufus? But what about The Fiancée? Did she really not suspect Rufus?

Was everyone happy for Dolly to go down, the innocent in this?

All to protect money, status and illicit love?

She was their pawn.

Lauder. I really wished I could talk to him now, that things hadn't spiraled out of control like this.

In another world, we could crack this mystery together by just being open. Ironic. Until we had muddied the water by having sex, we had been more open with each other. There had been a brief window of truth, a certain sincerity in our affairs.

Before, he had definitely been less protective of me and seen me more as an equal partner. And yet, it was the comradely feelings that had led us into bed.

Big mistake.

Is this what men do? They screw you, then they think they own you?

He had been the one to change, not me. He had ruined it.

Telling me about his vacation, banning me from the case, giving me stupid trinkets. And now, the developments in this case were twisting the knife in the wound. Hearing The Fiancée's voice. Learning that she considered herself better than Lauder, that maybe her family still did.

I didn't want to feel sorry for Lauder. He was a big boy. He knew what he was doing. Surely he would know he was a second-class citizen to The Fiancée's clan?

Maybe he really was just out to better himself.

The ends justify the means.

I fought an intense desire to turn back, to stumble into the room and take them by surprise. To confront the bitches. 'You know very well you could be sending an innocent woman to her death and you don't give a damn either way.'

And my parting shot to The Fiancée?

'Hi, you're looking at one of Randy's principles!'

I could do that, couldn't I?

I'd enjoy that bomb dropping, even if I were standing right under it.

No. You can't! Do your job and leave!

34

Martell was deep in conversation with one of the important-looking men. She saw me looking at her and she looked right through me with a *Not now* expression. Schmoozing her way into another Hollywood deal, no doubt.

I turned right around and walked out. She would soon figure out I'd left.

I went back through the main hall, out of the front door and down towards the wide stone steps.

With a bunch of reporters waiting at the other side of the main gates, cameras at the ready, and Lauder's car about to arrive, I was in something of a jam.

The devil and the deep blue sea kind of jam.

I saw a woman standing at the foot of the stone steps. She was around forty-five, in a black astrakhan swing coat and a black dress. Her eyes were hidden by dark sunglasses. She wore a turban style hat, with a neat astrakhan strip around the edge. Gold earrings in the shape of roses were visible underneath the hat. She looked stylish and self-possessed, even if fetal lambs sliced out of their mother's wombs had helped with the sophisticated look.

She glanced at me. 'Valet's on his way. Shouldn't be long.' Her voice was tired, and rather sad. Was she one of the few genuine mourners?

I realized she thought I was joining the line to collect my car. I coughed, acting a little embarrassed. 'I don't suppose you could give me a ride? My cousin's not ready to leave and I've got to be someplace else.'

She looked me over, thought about it, and nodded. 'I'm going to Westwood Village. Any good?'

It was totally the wrong direction, but escape was the only thing that counted right now. 'Perfect.'

A dark red car with a beige soft top rolled up. The valet jumped out and opened the doors for us. 'Ready?' the woman asked. I nodded.

We got in and set off, the wheels crunching down the drive. 'I'm Vivienne, by the way.'

'Mary. Mary Saunders.' I said. 'I only just met Linda. She's a friend of my cousin Martell. I didn't know Mr. Hunter personally, but I'm so glad to have had the opportunity to pay my respects.'

'I'm sure the family appreciated it.' I noticed she didn't say "Linda" but "the family".

'You're a friend of the Hunters?'

'I used to work with Ronald. I was his secretary, when he ran the firm.'

'It must have been a terrible shock for you.' I tried to keep calm. Had she been victim to a few fondles herself, or had his lewd behavior only manifested itself in his later years?

'I just can't believe it..' She dabbed her eyes.

I grunted in sympathy. 'Did you work with Ronald for a long time?'

She nodded. 'When he handed over the business to Rufus, so he could focus on the foundation and other things, I figured it was time for a change for me, too.'

Was it her decision to quit working for him or was Hunter just ready for fresh meat? Did "other things" mean politics? Running for mayor?

'You probably knew him better than most people in there. I'm so sorry for your loss.'

Vivienne turned and smiled. 'You're the only person who's said that to me. Thank you. He was a big part of my life for years. A secretary is behind the scenes, almost a second wife.'

I smiled. 'I bet. Did you stay in touch?'

'Oh, not really. He was so busy. He cared so much about our injured boys. I hope it all goes ahead now he's....' Her voice broke a little. 'I hate to say the word. Gone.'

'He sounds like a hero,' I said, comfortingly.

'Oh, he really was. Ronald was a true American hero.'

'I heard he wanted to buy a department store? Why, if he retired to do other plans?'

She smiled, wistfully. 'I read somewhere that was Linda's idea. Guess he just wanted to indulge her. I wonder if she'll buy it now.'

We drove a long in silence for a while. I admired the lovely houses, in manicured gardens. They would always be a dream for people like me, just like the Bel Air mansions were, but these were more homely. I said, 'Did you know Hester well?'

'Sure. And the girls. They were adorable when they were little. It's just awful, losing a father in that way, at any age. And, of course, for Linda, too, losing a husband. But I don't really know her.'

'She's much younger than him, isn't she?'

'Yes. But I can understand the attraction. Placid. Hester wasn't exactly a walk in the park.' She raised her brows meaningfully. 'Hunter needed a woman to support him. Hester just wasn't the type of woman to live in a man's shadow.'

'She looked kind of...theatrical?'

'That's Hester! She loved throwing parties. Huge affairs. They tired Ronald out. He was such a busy man and he just wanted weekends to be calm. Still, I hear she's done okay with her English Lord.'

'Ironic, considering Linda's the actress.'

'To be honest, when I heard he was marrying her, I thought he was making the same mistake. But they seemed happy. This must be terrible for her.'

I didn't say Linda was being well comforted by Rufus.

We drove on. Vivienne displayed more anguish than anyone else about the death of Hunter. The invisible secretary who probably knew him best.

She certainly seemed more cut up than Linda, or the first wife in her firebird outfit, or anyone else, for that matter.

Yet again, I found myself musing on men and women, secrets and lies and their sordid affairs. Men who fought for their countries, were lauded as heroes, yet got up to no good behind their wives' backs.

The old double standard. A woman's honor and reputation could be destroyed in a heartbeat. Married or not, she only had look at another man to be finished.

Surely, to be truly great, a man should be honorable in all departments? Defending the nation shouldn't confer a license to harass women.

I still had no real take on who Hunter was. To Martell, he was a bore who liked women in their place. To Vivienne, a true hero and a good boss. To his other secretaries, a serial molester, maybe rapist. The guy clearly had wanted the world to revere him. His foundation for veterans, a solid platform for his political ambitions.

But these were goals that put him in the public eye. Surely he could be brought down if he didn't watch it? Maybe he loved risk. Thought the rules didn't apply to him.

Did Hunter just see women as objects, something his money could buy? Or was he a man who just loved the company of women? Or was he addicted to sex? A man with such severe compulsions to screw anything that moved, he couldn't help himself? Had he been born on the wrong side of the tracks, he'd be a rapist doing a long stretch in the slammer. Being rich, he could get away with spreading his seed.

Except somebody had gotten fed up. His wife.

Maybe I was cutting him too much slack, theorizing it was a sick drive. I was no shrink. But one thing experience had taught me: a born liar will never admit it.

Vivienne pulled up at a red light. I looked out of the window at an art gallery. The painting in the window was a watercolor of Paris and I felt a rare pang of nostalgia.

I asked, 'So you changed your job, after leaving Mr. Hunter?'

'Yes. I run a beauty parlor. *Vivienne's of Westwood*. There are some cards in the glove box. I have some wonderful new treatments, why don't you come in? You've got beautiful skin. I hope you're looking after it.'

I smiled, opening the glove box. Sure enough, there were some pretty pale blue cards with gold lettering and a thick stripe around the edges. As I reached for one, I spotted something else inside.

A pot of cold *Oliverelle* cream.

'Oh, you use *Oliverelle* products at the salon?'

'No. That was a gift.' The lights changed and she accelerated. 'More like a sweetener. The owner of *Oliverelle* wants to buy me out. Floriana Luciano. You know she's got a string of beauty parlors? But none in Westwood, so she's after my spot.'

Floriana Luciano again. Something stirred in me. Was this what Beatty would call gut instinct? I said, 'You weren't interested?'

'I never found Mr. Right, so a girl's gotta support herself, right? All the same, Mrs. Luciano made me a pretty good offer. I'm tempted, but what would I do with my time?' She smiled, a little wistfully. 'Do you have a job?'

'Oh, no! My husband's just back from overseas and we plan on starting a family.'

This just came out. Martell's fault for not giving me the whole story about her cousin.

Vivienne grimaced and I knew I'd been tactless rubbing in my married status. Maybe I should have stuck to the romance novelist persona, but I just couldn't be bothered to talk about corny plots.

She drove on in silence.

But our conversation had fired something up. A spark on an overloaded electrical wire, that could fizzle out or set the whole cable ablaze. Zetty, Dolly's best pal in the band, drove for Floriana Luciano. Dolly was sleeping with Ronald Hunter. Vivienne used to work for Hunter. Floriana Luciano had targeted Vivienne's shop.

Just two degrees of separation between Dolly and Vivienne.

A very tenuous connection. Probably a whole lot of nothing. Floriana was just ambitious and seeking prime real estate for another store in her chain of beauty parlors.

I had a lot to brief Sonia on. She would, of course, decide everything that came next.

Pauline and Agnes. They could be used as evidence that Hunter was not such a devoted husband.

Linda and The Fiancée. Linda had been talking about "Them"; that could be something Sonia wanted me to look into. Linda had even suggested whoever was "Them" could have committed murder.

Rufus and Linda's love affair. Surely this would trump everything now for Sonia? I had no idea how the Hunter fortune was carved out, but if Rufus already ran the business, surely whatever Ronald left Linda would pad out Rufus's gains?

The one thing Sonia Parker wouldn't learn from me, of course, was that the friend Linda Hunter was confiding in happened to be engaged to the vice cop she wanted me to look into. I wouldn't exactly be lying, no worse than I already had. I could just say I overheard Linda talking to somebody. And either Linda was putting on a big act, or she was totally complicit in the murder.

Vivienne interrupted my thoughts. 'Well, this is my place. Can I fix you a coffee? Call you a cab?'

I looked up at the pretty beauty parlor, occupying a prime corner plot. It had big curved windows, a white and blue striped canopy, some white orchids in the window. 'What an elegant shop.'

'Thanks.' Vivienne's pride was genuine.

I sensed her loneliness. I was tempted to join her for a coffee. But a chat on a return visit, when she was lathering a mask on my cheeks, might pay more dividends on Hunter. If I asked too many questions today, she'd smell a rat.

I assured Vivienne I'd be back soon for a beauty treatment.

35

Sonia exhaled. 'All very interesting.' She finished her cigarette and stubbed it out.

Joseph jotted a few lines down on his notepad and then looked at Sonia. They exchanged a look that spoke volumes to each other and said absolutely nothing to me.

'What?' I said.

Two blank expressions met my eyes. I was getting to recognize this mode. A kind of *We don't like the question so we're looking at you to be polite but we're also looking* through *you, so you know we're not going to answer* expression.

All very odd, and not how the rest of the human race went about things.

It was early evening. I'd called Sonia from a payphone in Westwood Village and told her we should meet. Urgently.

She had told me to get down to the office *pronto*.

I'd jumped in a cab. The driver was none other than Sal, a female cabbie who had just dropped off somebody in Westwood. She was full of concern when I said I'd come from a funeral party. I took off Martell's hat; seeing life through a black net veil was getting tedious. It was a relief to shake off Mary Saunders.

Joseph had made a pot of coffee and we all sat down. I had set out all the developments over the past two days: Willa's take on Dolly and that she didn't know about the affair; Agnes's baby, who might be Hunter's; and the big discovery at the funeral party—Linda and Rufus's secret love affair. I mentioned Linda's revealing conversation with her friend and my blackmail theory concerning Linda, Rufus and the mystery "Them".

'Rufus looks guilty, from where I'm standing. He's got the strength. He's in love with Linda. He'll make a packet anyway, even more when he marries Linda. Framing Dolly would be a cake walk.'

They both absorbed every word with impassive faces. Joseph jotted notes throughout. At no point had Sonia scowled or interrupted.

Lastly, I had told them about my ride with the devoted former secretary Vivienne and the tenuous but odd link, through Floriana Luciano, with Dolly and the band.

Now we were huddled around a table, and the cups of coffee were half drunk. It was time to deliver my neat conclusion. 'Linda Hunter's either in on it with Rufus, and double bluffing to her friends to keep up some act, or she doesn't suspect Rufus herself, so she's even dumber than she looks.'

Sonia drummed her fingers on the table. Today, her nails were a divine scarlet.

I couldn't resist a question. 'So where next for me? Rufus, or 'Them'?'

Sonia answered with a question of her own. 'Did you get a look at this friend of Linda's? Know who she is?'

I shook my head, lying. 'No idea at all. She sounded hoity-toity.'

'Hoity-toity?' Sonia asked. 'What do you mean exactly?'

'Well, you know, smooth, educated voice. Definitely an uptown girl.'

Shut up about The Fiancée!

I had skated onto thin ice, my eyes open. I wanted to kick myself.

Treading carefully, I sipped my coffee. 'If there was some kind of blackmail by "Them" that could be why the vice cop was there on Christmas Eve. So, I should look into Rufus next, surely?' I risked sounding like a stuck gramophone.

'No. Your services are no longer required,' Sonia said, crisply. She folded her arms.

What! I nearly dropped the cup. 'Excuse me?'

'I no longer require any more work.'

Was I being fired? Joseph was scrutinizing his notes with great intensity.

'But I've got some great leads. The girls. The brother. Blackmail! I mean, nothing conclusive. What if Minski did it?' I blurted out.

'There's been a development and you have done enough.'

Enough? To make a difference for Dolly?

'What development?'

She smirked. 'I can't divulge. Consider yourself released from our agreement.'

Sonia was noting something down. 'By my estimation, we owe you eight hundred dollars plus expenses. Oh, nine hundred, isn't it? I doubled the fee for that first evening? Itemize your expenses, but any...payoffs...should be put down under 'miscellaneous'. Okay?'

My bill. I was being dispensed with. Just the investigative help who should know her place.

'Sure,' I said, feeling anything but okay.

'Good.' Sonia stood up and I had no choice but to follow suit. But the rebel in me blurted out, 'But Dolly? What's going to happen to her?'

'Joseph and I have work to do, so if you don't mind?'

Suddenly the buzzer sounded. Joseph got up and went to the intercom system. A gravelly voice said, 'There's a Mr. Malloy in reception. Says he's a private investigator.'

'Send him up.'

Malloy? Another PI? A *man*?

So I *had* just been fired. They were bringing in a guy to replace me. Sonia the queen bee wanted to maintain her rightful status, surrounded by drones.

Joseph, relieved the ordeal was over, offered his hand. 'Happy New Year. For tomorrow.'

'You, too,' I muttered, unable to meet his eye. His handshake was warm and strong. A shake of pity, not comfort. I had liked Joseph, but he was on her side.

Sure, I'd made a stack of money that would keep me and Barney afloat for a few months. I'd bought a little time. But Sonia Parker simply didn't rate me.

Wait a minute. I stood still. 'What about Dede? Has she agreed to you letting me go?'

Sonia turned. 'Dede's aware of the situation.'

No answer to that!

Sonia escorted me out of the office, back along the powder blue carpet that I would never see again.

'What about Minski's files? And the handkerchief?' I said in a low voice. Sonia said she would send Joseph to collect the files and I should destroy the handkerchief. 'Burn it. We won't be needing it.'

'But...' I stammered.

'No buts.' She smiled, gently pushing me towards the elevator. 'Everything's covered.'

The illuminated buttons showed the elevator was on its way up, no doubt carrying my successor.

'I'll take the stairs,' I said, darting off towards the door. I had no intention of meeting Mr. Malloy, my replacement.

No, sirree.

I sat in the parking lot beneath Sonia's office, feeling a total failure. Obviously, she'd hated my approach from the beginning.

Or she'd just hated me.

She had the power. She was my client. Dolly was her client. And Dede had agreed that I should leave the case. Why? Had Sonia told Dede I was useless? Had I annoyed Alberta that much? Had June told Alberta about my tactless handling of Agnes?

I lit a cigarette and instantly burst into a fit of coughing. I stubbed it out fast, the nicotine producing a vile surge of nausea. My lungs felt on fire.

Did everybody think I was just not up to the job? Even worse, that I was a liability?

I started the engine and reversed.

Calm down!

Surely June and Alberta couldn't be behind it? They were my friends, if I had any in the world. Surely it was all Sonia's prejudice against women PIs. Maybe she thought a male PI would be better at getting access to Rufus's business affairs. She hadn't ever shared any of her strategy with me.

I couldn't go running to Beatty like a child. Frankly, however I explained it, it would sound exactly how it was: I'd been fired. Beatty would be surprised by the twist in events and I couldn't bear her to suspect even for one second I'd somehow screwed up a well-paid job.

Her doubt that I could work at a high level was not something I wanted to experience right now. She'd try to hide it, but she would think she'd got it wrong about me.

Suck it up!

There was only one person I wanted to see. One person who I needed to tell that I'd tried to do my best.

Dolly.

Sonia Parker wouldn't like it, but screw her! I could do as I pleased now. I still had some of her flashy business cards in my purse. Alice Lucas could visit Dolly.

I would say my own goodbyes to the case.

36

The huge white marble building of the Hall of Justice achieved its intention: intimidation. A monolith that stood for power, for order, for the establishment.

I kept Dolly's face in my mind's eye as I walked beneath the marble archway to the entrance, through the vast lobby and towards the elevators.

My heart was beating fast. Attorneys, judges and cops proliferated like flies on a corpse. This white palace was their rightful domain. I was the imposter, the creature to be swatted. My blood and guts would stain that pristine marble.

Head high, shoulders back! No lowered head!

I had to calm myself down. It was okay. Alice Lucas, law-abiding citizen, was here to see her client.

And Elvira Slate, legitimate human being, was here to see a girl just like her.

The elevator doors opened and people flocked out. I double-took. Zetty, in a dark hat. It was almost a relief to see someone from my world. But she looked lost in thought, and didn't see me. Should I call out? Then the bellhop leaned out and said 'Up, up.' I dashed in the elevator.

He just nodded when I asked him for the floor for the women's jail. A few men in suits strolled in beside me, talking about a football game, and up we rode, floor after floor.

One of the men looked me over and tried to make conversation about something or other. I smiled and nodded, not hearing his words. He gave me a funny look.

I was relieved when they got out on the sixth floor, heading for the District Attorney's office. The bellhop called out, 'Up, up,' but nobody else got in. Up we rode. The bell pinged and the hop nodded to me. 'Women's Jail.'

I thanked him. I pushed through some double doors. Inside, a hexagonal shaped office, with several guards. At the front desk, a guard was issuing visiting passes.

'Who are you here to see?'

'Dolly Perkins.' I showed him Parker's company card.

'Popular lady. You want an interview room? It'll be a wait.'

'Not really. Just a quick word.'

He looked me up and down, asked me if I was carrying a firearm, to which I replied no. He didn't take my word for it, of course, and checked my purse. Then he gave me a pass and told me to go through another door. Dolly would be brought in shortly.

Seeing her amongst other prisoners would be better anyway. I wanted her to see me as a friend from now on. This could be the first of many visits to her.

A high barred gate blocked the corridor to the cells. Women's voices, yelling and crying, echoed through barred chambers.

I'd walked corridors like this for the best part of five years.

This was the third time I had ventured into a place of incarceration for Dolly's sake. Her pull on me was powerful. An unbreakable bond of sisterhood, that made me unable to say no to risks I didn't need to take.

Helping her felt like a mission, not a job.

After a while, another guard appeared. This was a woman, stocky, devoid of makeup and wearing a permanent frown that said, *You're trash*.

243

'This way,' she growled.

She led me to the visitors' block, a large box of cement and bars in which about seven female inmates stood around the sides talking to visitors through barred hatches.

Dolly was lurking aimlessly at the back. Her pale face found mine in seconds.

The guard yelled, 'Inmate Perkins. Come forward.' She shot me another hostile look. 'Hands down at all times.'

Dolly approached one of the barred hatches. She had lost weight and her eyes seemed even more bulbous. I noticed now, for the first time, that one eye looked in a slightly different direction.

'Hi, Dolly.' I kept my voice low. 'Good to see you.'

She looked confused. 'Miss Parker send you here?'

I shrugged. 'Look, she doesn't know I'm here. Better it stays that way.'

'Why?'

'I'm off the case. I just wanted....' I met her eyes.

What did I want? Now I was here, under false pretenses, I felt selfish. Had I really come to check on her? Or was I looking for validation from someone who had absolutely nothing to give? 'She's working so hard for you, and I just wanted to say, I'm gunning for you, too.'

Dolly's eyes lowered. 'Should be outta here by now. Thought they'd have got his wife by now. She did it. She never loved him. I'm here, all alone. Only trash for company. Everybody's forgotten me.'

'Zetty hasn't. Wasn't she just here?'

Dolly blinked. 'Everyone except Zetty. She's my pal.'

'Somebody framed me real good. I know it was Linda Hunter, but nobody's gonna touch her, are they? I'm finished.'

'You can't think like that.' Linda, the wholesome wife, was her fixation.

It probably helped her cope. I didn't have the heart to tell her Sonia didn't consider Linda Hunter a suspect and neither did the cops.

'Just remember you're in good hands.' My words sounded as hollow as they felt. She must sense she was an easy target and nobody was interested in real justice.

Dolly moved slightly closer, her voice lower 'Hey, you found a hankie? At Ronald's?'

'How do you know about that?'

'Miss Parker and all her questions. Asked if I remembered touching a hankie? Then I remembered, sure I did!'

I nodded. 'Taken care of, don't worry about it.'

'No, it's not like that! If I get outta here, can I have it? Only thing I'll have of my Ronnie.' She lowered her voice, eyes filling with tears. 'When I was a little kid, in the orphanage, I had a little rag. Curled it round my finger and thumb and sucked on it. I still do it; don't tell nobody.' She wrinkled her nose, in a cute way.

Lots of kids in my orphanage would suck their thumbs for comfort. Cold comfort, as it turned out, as they all got caned if they couldn't break the habit.

I gave her a soft, conspiratorial smile. 'I'll keep it safe for you.' What harm could it do, not burning it, as Sonia said? I was no longer under her orders.

'Give it to Zetty. Now you're off the case. She's going away today to her bosses place, but she'll be back. I should be going with her! I ain't never gonna sing again.'

I smiled. 'When you get out, and you will, I'll come see you sing. And I'll buy you a drink after.'

'You're real nice. You got any kids?' Dolly smiled at me.

'Screaming brats are not my thing.'

Dolly fiddled with her fingers. 'A place like this makes you think real hard about life. What you deserve. Say, you think God's punishing me? Taking my child like that?'

This was a turnaround. 'What? No! That's jail, messing with your mind. You gotta stay strong.'

I felt a surge of anger. Incarceration was a tumor. You went in alive, if a little in shock. But you were still fighting, blood still pulsed through you, you still had some vitality. But little by little any self-worth would be eaten away. The cannibalistic tumor took it all, taking over your body, your brain, and your thoughts.

Soon, you became an empty shell. A dead woman walking.

I could see it happening to Dolly.

'You've done time?' She was asking.

And how. Almost five years.

I said nothing. This could get back to Sonia, so I just shook my head. 'Hang on in there, Dolly. You're gonna make it.'

'Every time something nice happens in my life, it goes bad, anyway. So what's the point in hoping anymore? What's the point of getting out?

'Better than dying in here.' But was it? I'd escaped death and my life was one big struggle.

Dolly's voice was echoing my grim thoughts. 'Is it? I ain't so sure anymore. I'm just so tired.'

37

'You've had enough, lady. Time to go home.'

'Leave me alone!'

It's the bartender and his twin, both in the same black apron and fury in their eyes. Quadruple anger. Hey, you looking at me? I don't care. I hate twins, anyway.

Twins, double trouble. Double dose of shit.

'I just want to go to sleep.' The booth's so soft. I could just lie here. If only they would just leave me alone! I clutch my purse closer to me.

'Someone you can call? Pick you up?'

'Just a few hours. Please, sir.'

I curl up on the soft base of the booth.

'Oh, no, you don't. Get out of here, or I'll call the cops.'

They'll go away. The jukebox is playing something smoochy. I like it.

Ouch. Rough arms under me, dragging me up!

'Just let me sleep, goddamn you!'

'That's it. On your feet!'

People's faces. Staring. Screw 'em. The bar rushing past, a man's face laughing at me. Green lamps, dancing in circles like a kaleidoscope.

The oaf's now shoving me up the stairs. My feet trip. I want him to stop. 'Gimme a break....' My legs are limp, a rag doll in a dog's mouth. I feel a shoe come off. 'My shoe!'

'Now scoot!' he shouts, shoving me hard.

I hurtle forward, crash-landing on my knees and hands. Wet

concrete slabs scrape my skin. The sidewalk? A shoe lands next to me. My hands, my face, my bare legs, all lashed with rain like bullets. Where's my hat? A gust of wind plasters my hair into my mouth, my eyes. I can't see a thing. I somehow get up, and everything's spinning.

Where am I again? Lost. I'm dizzy.

Dolly's face. The prison. *I can't help you!*

Is this Downtown?

Mikey's. I know that bar. He'll give me a drink.

Rain pelts my eyes, my cheeks. Reverse tears. Pretty funny.

Where's Mabel? The Hall of Justice? I can't remember. I lean against the wall, under a striped canopy.

The rain's heavier. Large raindrops plip-plop in unison off the curved hem of the waxy canopy.

I can just walk home, can't I? No law against that. But I'm so tired, so hungry. Where's my purse?

Here, under my arm. *Sheesh!* It was there the whole time. I laugh. 'You stupid cow, you're sauced.'

Lauder. I should find a payphone, right now. I want to be with him now, in bed, in the Astral. He knows we should be together. What's wrong with him? I should tell him right now! He didn't go skiing with *Her*, so he can be with me now. He can make up some bullshit to tell her like he usually does.

I don't even have a number for his house. Asshole!

I know. I can call the LAPD, tell them all about two-timing Detective Randy Lauder! Let's hear what they have to say about that, huh?

Mikey's has a payphone.

Here's a doorway. Mosaic tiles on the porch. Nice and dry. I can just rest here for a bit. I slide down on the floor. Hard like a rock, and cold. My mouth, it's a trashcan. God, I need a drink. I'll go to Mikey's next.

Everything's spinning again.

I'm just so tired.

'Who's the father? You must tell me, Jemima.' Lucinda Seldon's face peers into mine, her voice is as sharp as it can get. Which isn't very, as her pity seeps through her plummy accent.

'Oh, stop asking me. I already told you, I don't want it. Just get rid of it!' I wail at her. My body hurts. Everything hurts.

'He might want to make financial arrangements for your child. It's only fair for him to be informed; you may not be released for quite some time.'

I stare at the dull ceiling in the hospital ward. I can't mention Billy's name. Him and his mobster pals double-crossed me and landed me in jail, but I'm not crazy enough to risk their revenge if I talk. The cad doesn't deserve to know he has a child.

'I don't know who he is.' There, I'm a loose floozie, too. Satisfied?

Right now, I hate the whole world and if I had a gun, I'd shoot everybody and everything in sight. Even Seldon.

Seldon's eyes are now full of anxiety. 'Matron told me you haven't fed her.'

'Some char will do it for pennies. She's not mine.'

'You will need to sign a birth certificate.'

Jemima Day. Address: Holloway Prison. I suddenly laugh. 'You know where I live. Here. And you choose a name. I really don't care.'

'You're not taking your child's welfare very seriously, Jemima. I urge you to reconsider, for her sake.'

'All right. Get her out of this hole of a jail, out of this slum of a city, and find some respectable people to have her.'

'And what's going to be her name?'

'Kettle.'

My cat, Kettle.

'Be serious. You cannot call a child Kettle.'

I turn on my side, away from the doctor. I wished Kettle was here now. He's the only one I want to see now. I so miss my Kettle.

'You choose a name. I'll sign whatever I have to. Just stop talking to me about it.'

'Shutting reality out is not the best way to cope, Jemima.'

'Send me to the loony bin, then!' I growl. Why won't she just go away?

'I'll be back to see you later. Try to think more clearly. I know it's a very difficult time.'

38

I suddenly woke up, sheets drenched, heart pounding. I felt sick, full of a sinister dread.

A dream. Forget it.

Something—everything—hurt. My knees. My head.

I sat up, propped against sumptuous pillows and looked around. Sunlight poured into a room through half-open drapes. Did I die last night, and was this heaven?

I had never seen this room before.

Twin beds, with golden velvet headboards. The other bed was made up, but not perfectly; somebody might have slept in it. Both beds had a luxurious eiderdown of gold, blue and white, matching the blue rose and gold wallpaper. Ornate brass sconces. Nightstands with small gold lamps with parchment shades.

The room had a rich and feminine style, classical, not modern.

A hotel room? It felt impersonal, but expensive. Brand-new and unused. Nothing tired and stale about this place except me.

I peeked under the eiderdown. Somebody had put a nightdress on me. My roommate, perhaps? A long, soft white cotton affair, with straps tied over my shoulders. White satin daisies were embroidered around the bodice, which was fastened by three round pearl buttons. Definitely one of mine.

What the hell did you do last night?

My mouth was so dry. I cried out as I slid out of the bed.

Agony, as if I'd been kneecapped. I pulled up the nightgown. Both knees scraped and raw. Did I fall down?

A few things came back. Sonia, then Dolly. Feeling low, I'd hit a Downtown bar. I must have gotten very drunk. But how did I get here, and more to the point, who brought me?

My clothes were folded up on a padded chair. No beret. But my battered purse was there.

By the other bed, a small case. Padlocked. No initials, just couple of old tattered travel labels. *Roma. Paris.* Who the hell it belong to?

I dared to look at myself in the beveled mirror.

Mascara was spread all over my lower lids. My hair was a straw bird's nest.

Was it a man? Did I have sex? The last thing I remembered was hitting the gimlets like they were going out of fashion. Oblivion called like a hot date.

A cold shiver ran down my back.

Lauder. Did I call him?

I hobbled stiffly over to the window and peered through the nets.

The room was on the second floor of a white building. My window ledge was painted green. Below, a paved side terrace with large terracotta pots with small palms, young olive trees, and yellow and white flowers. Pretty. Beyond that, a parking lot with a thick hedge, the rest partially hidden by trees.

I could make out a few cars. A cream and brown coupe. And another, a larger, dazzling white beast.

Beyond, a beautiful vista I'd never seen before. Magnificent cypresses, palms, eucalyptus trees, rolling grounds with stony paths. I could almost smell the breezy citrus air from here.

One path led down to a glimmering patch of water. A lake? I strained to look around the corner of the window. I could make out a small rowing boat tethered to a simple jetty.

In the far distance, a glimpse of the sea, dark lilac against a bright, pearly white sky.

My room was on the side of the building. The front of the building would have magnificent sea views.

A hotel? It didn't look like any part of LA's coastline I recognized, not from Venice to The Colony Club in Malibu, which was a pretty long stretch.

There was a short rap on the door. 'Hello?'

I froze. No weapon. My mobility severely limited thanks to bashed-up knees. Impeded by a nightgown. Great. There was a vase. I grabbed it, brandishing it.

I'd just have to take my chances. I braced myself.

The door opened. Alberta breezed in, carrying a dark brown overnight case. She had on a pale cream linen dress with red buttons, red espadrilles and her hair was clipped back. Fresh as a daisy, but no smile. 'So, you're alive.' Then she looked at the vase. 'Put that thing down.'

I sighed. 'What's going on?'

'What's going on? You tell me.'

'Alberta, I have no idea where I am or how I got here.'

Alberta closed the door behind her, set the case down and perched on the velvety chair.

'You're in Santa Barbara now. We brought you here on the bus. Sal the taxi driver found you sprawled in some gutter. She took you to the hotel in the early hours.'

'Sal found me?'

'You were all boozed up, hollering like a crazy woman.

Caretaker woke me up to deal with you.' Her eyes expressed irritation and concern. 'You don't remember a thing?'

I sat on the bed, meeting her eyes. 'No. I don't.'

Santa Barbara. 'Is this Floriana Luciano's place? Did she see me in that state?'

Alberta rolled her eyes. 'That all you're worried about?'

'She's a client.'

'Then maybe you shouldn't have gotten drunk like that. Anyhow, relax. I told Mrs. Luciano you had to get real drunk to trick a cheating spouse. All part of the job.'

I groaned, head in hands. 'She'll never believe that.'

'Best I could do, and she laughed.' Alberta pointed at the case. 'I packed you a change of clothes, things from your closet. For today, and for the party tonight.'

'We came here on the bus. The band's bus?'

'You snored and dribbled your way through the journey. '

'How embarrassing.'

'That's not the point. Wanda wasn't too pleased about you coming along for the ride. In case of trouble. Neither did Earnestine.'

I had no idea what she was talking about. 'What trouble? Who's Earnestine?'

Alberta shot me a derisive look. 'Earnestine's our driver. I know you don't know nothing about our world, because you don't have to, so I'll spell it out. Wanda toured with the Honey Duchesses through the Jim Crow States. I wouldn't do it myself, too much harassment. You know what the cops down there would do to us if they saw a white girl travelling with us? Especially a drunk one? Wanda isn't of a mind to tempt fate, especially when she don't have to.'

254

I must have looked blank.

They'd taken a risk by taking a sauced, self-pitying sap on board.

Alberta looked me straight in the eye.

'But I guess if it don't affect your life, you don't even see it?'

She was right. I was ignorant. Arriving six months ago, I was so caught up with my own misfortunes, my own survival was top of the agenda. Still, the segregated coaches on the Super Chief from New York had shocked me. I remembered the "half-caste" and black kids in reform school. As juvenile offenders, we were stuck in the same boat. Everyone got beaten, everyone got starved, everyone shared the same internal scars of being unwanted. But the darker-skinned kids got something else—abuse simply for the color of their skin. They were the easy targets when the real culprits of some so-called misdemeanor couldn't be found, or the staff just couldn't be bothered to find out the truth.

I'd hated the unfairness, at the same time as feeling lucky that was one less thing I had to suffer. My white skin felt like a pass.

'Wanda, she wanted to stow you in the bootleggers' hatch. It's an old bus with space under the floor for hooch. Figured since you were full of liquor, seemed kind of appropriate. But I said, "Shoot, Wanda, she's practically unconscious. What if wakes up and panics, starts hollering again? Or she throws up and chokes on her own vomit?" So we laid you on the seat and hoped for the best.'

I was ashamed of putting the band in a risky situation, but my defenses were up. Defenses to ward off a deep dread, now welling up in me. I said breezily, 'Well, I didn't ask anyone to do anything. You should have just left me in the hotel.'

She snapped. 'That attitude, wish we had. But you kinda gave me no choice.'

255

'What?' Now my stomach lurched. 'I got hammered, that's all. Don't you ever get stewed?'

Shame of unknown sins wasn't pleasant. Knowing you'd screwed up was one thing; you could always make amends. Not knowing *how* you screwed up was sickening.

'Sure, I do. But not like that. That's for cowards.'

'What did I do?'

Alberta gave me a penetrating look. 'You didn't *do,* thanks to us. Said you were going to take your own life. Told me how you were going to do it, too. Your pistol, your morphine pills. Every darned means at your disposal. I heard every last one of your sad ass blues.'

Blood drained from my face. Every last one of my blues? Some instant knee-jerk bluff kicked in. 'Just drunken bullcrap,' I muttered. 'Should've left me to stew.'

What the hell did you say last night?

'Next time, I will.' With that, Alberta got up and headed for the door. 'Say, if you're so fine and dandy, make your own way back home. You'll have to hitch a ride. We ain't going nowhere for a few days.'

She was angry; I didn't blame her. I was mortified. I watched, paralyzed, as she opened the door. She had done her best to help me out, the band had taken a risk, and I couldn't even thank her.

Do it now!

I jumped up. 'Alberta, wait!'

Alberta came back in, fed up. 'What?'

I said, 'Please close the door. Take a seat. I need to say something.'

Alberta sighed. She thought about it. 'I'm all ears and standing is fine.'

I started to pace the room. 'I'm sorry I burdened you. I'll

256

apologize to Wanda, to all the band. Yesterday kicked me hard. Sonia Parker fired me. I guess you and Dede know about it? So I went to see Dolly in the County Jail.'

I paused. This was hard.

'Remember you said me and her were the same? Well, you're right. She's lost all hope. So I guess I did, too. I hit the bottle. I was a fool.'

'So, quitting a job turns you into a bum rollin' around in the gutter?'

'I didn't quit, I was fired.'

'Parker's words?'

'She said my services were no longer required. And then a guy PI showed up to take my place! She never did like me. Not one word of praise the whole time I worked for her!'

'Well, boo-hoo. First thing, that don't sound like firing to me. Second thing, if I waited for praise from any crummy boss I ever had, I'd be waiting till a black woman is President of the United States. What's the matter with you? Me and Dede thought you had gumption.'

'I don't know. I wanted to do a good job. Help Dolly.'

'What if the cops had picked you up in the street? We don't want any trouble at the hotel. Ain't no flophouse for drunken degenerates.'

Degenerate. Her words hit hard.

I looked down. 'It won't happen again.' Was I more of a mess than I realized? The truth was, I had no grip on myself when drunk. The past could bite me again. Could I ever really trust myself?

'Whatever I said, forget it. You won't be hearing it from me again.'

Alberta thought for quite a while before she spoke. 'Forgotten already.'

I sat down on the edge of my bed.

Alberta looked at her watch. 'Take a shower. There's a connecting bathroom through there. Jewel and Carmen are on the other side.'

She pointed at a door I hadn't noticed.

'Am I sharing with you?'

'No. With Zetty. She uses this room when she comes here with Mrs. Luciano. We're all on this floor. Servants' rooms, but they look mighty fine to me. Some guests are next floor down, most are staying in town. Anyhow, I gotta rush. Band practice.'

At the door she turned around. 'And you can quit fretting about Dolly. Word is, she's gonna be released soon, all charges dropped.'

It was a bucket of ice water in the face. 'What?'

Dolly free? Impossible.

Alberta gave a wry smile, opening the door. 'But keep your mouth shut with the others. Even with Zetty. We don't want to jinx it. Who knows? Maybe you did do something good.'

39

'Ah! Miss Slate! Welcome to Villa Rosa! I'm so happy to see you again!'

Floriana Luciano pulled me towards her, laughing heartily. It was more of a bear hug than an embrace. A bear who rolled in divine meadows: her fragrance was lime flower, lilac, lemon and rose.

She looked stunning as ever in cream linen pants, a leather belt made up of twisted woven strings of leather in lilac, black and pink. On top, a crisp pink blouse with bishop sleeves and a pleated bodice. Jet-black accessories—bangles, earrings, and a necklace—gave the ensemble drama and definition. Her almond-shaped eyes were luminous, edged in kohl, her large hazel irises a darker, more golden version of her supple skin. Her hair, like carved bronze, was piled high on her head, with elaborate curls and rolls.

Oliverelle earned its good reputation if it helped you look like that in your sixties.

She certainly looked a lot more relaxed than the last time I had seen her, when a launch of one of her products had been sabotaged. I'd helped find out who did it. She hadn't liked the answer, but she'd liked my fast style.

Now she linked her arm in mine. 'So, I hear everything about your dedication to your job last night! Getting so drunk! You naughty girl. I hope you fooled the cheating louse! You must take a hang-over infusion. A very special botanical mix!'

Her grin told me she hadn't believed a word of Alberta's bogus explanation.

'I'm in Zetty's room. I hope I didn't disturb her.'

'Oh, not at all! Zetty is very easy. She does not mind! You would have your own room of course, but we are a very tight squeeze. Most people have to stay in town.'

We were standing on the ornate marble and terracotta tiles of the sunny entrance hall. The double front doors were wide open. A huge marble curved staircase led up to the upper floor. Marble columns supported the upper balcony.

It didn't feel like winter at all. It felt like a fresh spring morning in a Mediterranean paradise. 'Maybe you stay a few days?'

Could I? Life was looking up. The news about Dolly's imminent freedom felt like a lead weight had been taken from my shoulders, something I'd been carrying around and had gotten used to. I could stand up straight again. It was beautiful here; I could stay forever. But I had trustees to meet, bills to pay, and a sleuthing start-up to make good. I could call Barney when he was back and tell him to set up the meeting with the Spark Trust. Oh, and take down the Christmas tree.

'Sure,' I said.

'Perfect! My hotel and spa will be the perfect retreat for all the busy ladies from Los Angeles. Santa Barbara will be a wonderful town again!'

'You know, maybe just say to anyone I'm just a friend. Not a PI. I'd like to just forget about work.'

'Of course. I can say you are a nose, not a nosey parker!' She burst out laughing.

'What?' I didn't get the joke.

260

'A *nose*. You help me test my new perfume? Nose? Very funny!' Then she stopped laughing. 'But maybe then people ask you too many questions about my business and you cannot answer. So yes, just a friend.'

'Will you live here all the time?'

'No, no, no. I come and go. My beauty business is very big now. It takes up so much time. I love the city, but here my heart belongs.' She tapped her chest. 'I grow olive, almond and lemon orchards, my Sicily. Many trees! And my darling Antonio rests here, he is waiting for me, but I tell him, 'Not now, you must be patient. I am not ready to join you yet!"

I knew Floriana was a widow, but I had no idea how Antonio Luciano had died.

'Is Simonetta here?' I was referring to Floriana's daughter. A model and the face of *Oliverelle*. If appearances could deceive, Simonetta's were the pinnacle of treachery. On the surface, the spoilt rich daughter, but underneath, a lawless, risk-taking and fiery spirit.

'Of course. She will be so happy to see you, too. I tell her to be very hush hush about you. *Hushissimo!*'

We both laughed. *Hushissimo.* A new mantra for life?

Floriana was utterly magnetic. Standing near her felt like standing in sunshine. Her warmth, her smile and her generosity—were those the secret ingredients behind her vast wealth?

If so, I would never get rich.

Floriana suddenly rattled off a speedy command in Italian to a passing maid, a slight girl with a sallow thin face, dressed in a black dress and white lace apron and cap. The maid nodded, hiding a sullenness under the veneer of obedience.

I would be a fool to idealize Luciano, for all her *joie de vivre*. She was successful because she knew exactly what she wanted, dished out the orders and would let nothing and nobody stand in her way. Maybe making everyone feel fantastic was all part of the strategy, but she could only get so far with that. The rest took gumption and a love of power.

'Go with Valeria, she will give you breakfast. Enjoy the rest of day. Ask for whatever you need. And look nice for my party! My beauty salon can fix your hair, in the spa building over there. My guest, there is nothing to pay.'

'That's very kind.'

'Not at all. Next year, no war, no more death. Just life! Tonight, we celebrate it, together!'

The maid escorted me in silence to the dining room. A large fresco covered the walls. Olive trees, countryside birds and flowers.

The room opened onto a vast terrace, with wicker and glass tables and chairs. Flowers, in sprays of white, green and yellow blooms, spilt out of crystal vases. The terrace overlooked the sea, beyond gardens lined with phoenix palms.

At least I had showered and was feeling less delicate. I didn't feel too out of place, thanks to the silk crepe floral dress Alberta had packed for me. It was as if she knew what I'd need to blend in.

After she had left me earlier, I had rummaged through the case. She had thought of everything—makeup, jewelry and underwear. Even red nail polish. I didn't deserve it, but she had my back, for some reason. Pity, probably. I needed to make it up to her, somehow.

And at the bottom of the case was June's red velvet dress.

There were also some peep-toe red suede sandals with gold buckles which I had never seen before. They looked my size.

The perfect party outfit. All I needed now was a red rose in my hair. Could Villa Rosa come up with the goods? I decided I would take a stroll.

But not quite yet. I wanted to sip black coffee on the terrace, bask in the sunshine and feel the breeze on my skin.

40

Gazing at the sea, I knew Alberta had been right.

Getting out of the city was more than a good idea.

The salty air of the Atlantic Ocean filled my lungs. My spot looked down across the gardens, through the wilder landscape, over the lake and beyond, to the rippling expanse of sea.

A whirring sound suddenly broke the peace. A steady line of dirty trucks bouncing down a back road that wound up behind the main house. As they parked, Mexican men unloaded boxes and crates. In the sweltering heat, they carted them up the stone steps that led towards a huge circular tent erected on a high lawn—the scene of the party.

I thought of the band, rehearsing somewhere. They, too, had driven for hours, setting off at dawn. I bet even Zetty wouldn't be off duty later.

Everybody was hard at work except me. I had nothing to do and it felt odd. I looked away from the scene, turning back to the ocean again.

In London, I'd be polishing the glassware for toffee-nosed guests, at a bash like this.

America enabled me, a white woman from low origins, to better myself. Here and now, I was free to enjoy myself, enjoy the surroundings like a guest, while everyone else was hard at work.

Alberta's words. *You're lucky.*

She was right.

I had the right color skin. Dolly could manage it, too. We

were poor white girls, but our lives and our futures could be different. We *were* both lucky, we could break into different worlds, be different people, play different parts.

What Sonia Parker had managed to pull off for Dolly, I had no idea. I couldn't imagine how I'd helped.

But mission accomplished. Part of me didn't even care about the details of any deal that may have been made. Ronald Hunter didn't deserve to die, but it wasn't my job to find his killer. That worthy task fell to Detective Flannery, who seemed to have come to his senses about Dolly.

Or he had found the right killer. Only time, and the press, would tell.

I silently wished Dolly well. I didn't want to see her again. Meeting her had pressed on a big button called Pain.

I lit a cigarette. It tasted foul but I gritted my teeth and smoked it all the same.

Maybe I should quit next year. My first New Year's resolution in five years. In prison, resolutions were pointless. Survival was the only game in town.

I inhaled. It already felt smoother. Ironic how another drink and another smoke could strip away the pain they inflicted.

The wind was getting up. At least the Mexicans would cool down.

With nothing better to do, I decided to stroll around the grounds.

You name it, Floriana had it. Several annexes formed the spa, the beauty parlor, and an indoor swimming pool and steam room. All the buildings echoed the Mediterranean style of the main house, painted in white with green and terracotta features, connected by tiled terracotta paths and fat palm trees. Beyond the buildings were tennis courts, riding stables and a paddock. Between me and the lake were substantial terraces, edged with tall cypress trees, that spread out around the main house. These included a croquet lawn, a rose garden, a maze and a Romanesque outdoor amphitheater.

Antonio's mausoleum was tucked away somewhere.

Floriana was expansive. She wouldn't stop here. This estate would not be the pinnacle.

A new shop in Westwood Village wouldn't be enough, either.

She was the right role model, at the right time. I needed to move on from everything negative in my life.

Lauder. Self-doubt. Fear of failure.

And tonight was the night to let go, to celebrate the end of a year that had ultimately seen me, and millions of others, right.

I was alive, not rotting in some hole in England, where I'd never been happy anyway.

I hadn't been blown to pieces by a bomb. I hadn't been hung, or gassed to death.

I had a life to live, a lover to forget, and friends who gave a damn enough not to leave me wallowing in hell of my own making.

I would thank 1945 with style and welcome 1946 with a great big kiss.

41

The lake was further away than I'd appreciated. After some huffing and puffing, a glimmer of water appeared in the distance like a mirage. To get to it, the path crossed a small bridge that led into some kind of small forest.

The dappled light and shade gave a subdued, gentle light but crossing the forest also took longer. I was about to sit down and rest when I glimpsed something. A metal fence?

I went nearer. Yes. Thick mesh was held in place by strong wooden posts, creating a perimeter to the lake area.

'She cannot be dead, can she?' The unmistakable voice of Floriana.

'We did everything you said, didn't we, Zetty?' This sounded like Wanda, sounding like she was trying to reassure.

'Yes, Boss. She ate everything up. Even the feathers. Here, I try.'

Who or what ate feathers? I crept across the carpet of dried out leaves, trying and failing not to make a sound.

When I got getting closer, I stopped. I could make out some figures.

Floriana and Zetty stood near what looked like a case for a long and wide musical instrument. Nearer the fence, a good few feet away from them, Wanda hovered.

I bent down, and edged through undergrowth for a better look.

'No, Zetty. No stick! Do not hurt Olivia!'

Olivia? Floriana and Zetty now peered over the case. Zetty held some kind of branch, her face one of pure intent. 'Okay,' she said, opening the lid with extreme caution.

Suddenly Zetty and Floriana leapt back, in shock. The lid shut down fast. Everybody burst out laughing. Nervous laughter.

Wanda said, 'Critter's got some fangs!'

Critter? Fangs? What the hell was inside?

'She is alive. My baby girl, welcome to your new home.' Floriana sounded ecstatic. 'You must release her. Now!'

'All right, boss. You better go behind the fence.'

Zetty easily picked up the case, under her arms. One strong woman. She carried it to the edge of the lake and gently placed it down.

Floriana called out 'I stay, to watch.' She tiptoed closer, unable to keep away.

A mother hen.

Undergrowth blocked the sight of Wanda retreating. I heard the squeak of a gate opening and closing.

I took it as a preventative measure.

Zetty suddenly tipped the box on its side, so the lid flopped onto the ground. She wore a gun holster, under her shoulder. Dressed for emergencies.

Then I saw why.

A silver gray alligator, about four feet long, slithered over the prostrate lid of the case. The sun illuminated an impressive row of fangs.

Floriana was over the moon. 'So beautiful, aren't you? Come on, Darling! Go to your new home. It's very nice, and wet, after horrible hot bus!'

Was this all part of the job? Bringing an alligator on the bus, from L.A. to Santa Barbara? Was it one of the conditions behind Wanda even getting a bus?

Was Wanda, lining her own pockets with this freaky delivery? Had it been stowed in the bootleggers' hatch?

But if the cops had stopped and searched the bus, and found a carnivorous reptile, never mind a drunken white woman, what price would Wanda have to pay? Was shipping a reptile even illegal?

Floriana's fee would be good and cover all eventualities nicely.

The alligator was in no hurry to get into the lake, frozen half-in and half out of the case. 'Go my darling! Dinner comes later!' Floriana squealed, with encouragement. The alligator's eyes seemed to roll in Floriana's direction in a *I don't want to, Mommy* kind of look. After a few second's deliberation, it clambered over the narrow rocky shore and headlong into the water.

Its eyes remained visible, just above the surface. Released, and free.

Wanda said, 'Can we go now?'

Floriana was speaking in Italian, to Zetty. I couldn't get much but it was clear she wanted to finalise some plans for the evening, and had Zetty got everything ready?

'*Si, si*,' Zetty said, rather glum, heading back to Floriana.

I kept very still, lurking in the undergrowth. Luckily the women took another path. I wasn't keen to hang around so near to the lake, but presumably the fence was secure enough to contain darling Olivia.

I had to give the women a few minutes ahead of me. Suddenly strolling around the grounds and standing on the jetty had lost all appeal.

Instead, I rather fancied getting my hair done in the beauty parlour. Hopefully the trip wouldn't get any more bizarre.

42

At four o'clock, I emerged from a long and stupefying session under a hot hairdryer. A new woman, with a Betty Grable poodle hairstyle.

Floriana Luciano's philosophy—to have and do whatever she wanted, including keeping alligators as pets—was ultimately responsible for my new thatch of glossy honey blonde curls that looked so shiny and soft, but were in fact brittle as fuse wire, thanks to several thick sprays of lacquer.

I was relieved I would be doing June's beautiful dress justice. Honoring it in a way she would approve.

Besides, you only live once.

And the rigid hair lacquer meant at least nothing would fall out of place when I slipped the velvet dress on.

I still hadn't found a red rose. Maybe one of the Charms could spare a few fake flowers.

As I entered the lobby, Wanda emerged from a side door that said *PRIVATE,* carrying a brown envelope. Her pet-smuggling fee? She had rollers in her hair under a headscarf. She gave me a withering look. 'Look who it is. Sleeping Beauty.'

'Wanda! I want to thank you for bringing me here. I know it slowed you down.'

'Alberta's idea. I had nothing to do with it.'

'Well, it's your bus, right?'

'Uh-huh.'

'Well, it was real kind of you to let me travel with you.'

She put a hand on each hip. 'Alberta says you're a private eye?'

'That's right. New to town, new to the job.'

'Why did you get so drunk?'

'I'd had a bad day.'

'What kind of business were you in before sleuthing?' Her eyes were not altogether friendly. And it was a funny question. Was she suspicious about me? Or just curious?

I said, 'I was in the wife kind of business. Then I got promoted to the widow department.'

She gave me a *Shit happens* look.

I shrugged it off. 'Why do you want to know, anyway?'

'Like to know who's on my bus. Alberta says you're okay. I'll take her word if you don't do anything else to embarrass us here.'

'I understand. I promise I won't. But let me assure you Mrs. Luciano likes me. I've worked for her before.'

She wasn't about to be impressed anytime soon. 'If you say so.'

'Look, I've apologized. What else do you want me to do?'

'Get your own ride home. There's a station in town. You can take the train.'

Wanda headed for the service elevator. She really didn't want anything to do with me.

When I got back to Zetty's room, she was lying on the bed, smoking, cradling an astray in her hand. She was staring up at the ceiling, forlorn.

The case was open. Her olive and green formal gown was slung over the chair, carelessly. A pair of gleaming gold sandals had been kicked off and lay on the floor, alongside the hairpieces.

Now a trombone case lay open by the bed. I'd never seen one so close. Impressively large.

She glanced at me and nodded without smiling.

I tried to cut through the mood with a beaming smile. 'Hi! I'm Elvira. You must be Zetty. We met at Joyce's? And before, as a matter of fact. I saw you one day, when you were driving Mrs. Luciano.'

'I know who you are.' Her voice was heavy, disinterested.

'I really appreciate you sharing your room with me.'

'Why you do that to your hair?'

'You don't like it?'

'You look like poodle.'

'That's kind of the idea,' I grinned.

Zetty shrugged. Chat wasn't going to flow with her either. Clearly my drunken antics hadn't gotten me off on the right foot with any of the band.

'Say, what a pretty frock! This what you're wearing tonight?' I knew of course, but I was getting desperate. I went over and pretended to admire the dress.

Zetty grunted and then inhaled. 'I like to play jazz. Dresses? I don't care so much.'

'Shall I leave you in peace? You practicing?' I glanced at the trombone. I really wanted to paint my nails and have a rest as my hangover was raising its ugly head again.

'No. There are things on my mind.'

Dolly. It had to be. Zetty was in despair but Alberta had banned me from saying anything. I couldn't put her out of her misery.

'Well, look on the bright side. Sometimes things just turn out fine when you least expect it.'

Zetty didn't look very convinced. I decided against probing. Time for my nails.

I rummaged around the suitcase and extracted the red nail lacquer. I sat down on my bed and put the bottle on the nightstand.

'There is lady in the salon for this. Why do it yourself?' Zetty pointed at the nail lacquer.

'Oh, I know. But I was in there for an age already, having my hair done. I was about to go nuts sitting there. I'm just gonna touch it up.' I smiled at her and started varnishing. 'So, how long have you been Mrs. Luciano's driver?'

A pause before Zetty shrugged. 'Many years.'

Then she leaned over and pulled the drawer of her nightstand open. She took out a revolver and began examining it.

I gave a nervous laugh, especially when she vaguely pointed it in my direction. 'Hey, er, I'm kinda nervous around those things.'

She eyed me, checking the barrel of gun. 'Relax. I know what I am doing. You know I am Floriana's bodyguard? Not only driver.'

She spun it around in her hand, like one of those cowboys in a movie. Just to make a point.

I laughed nervously. 'Oh, I didn't know that.' I blew on my nails.

Zetty gave a cynical smile. 'Signora Luciano need protection. '

'Well, she's a very wealthy lady,' I said. 'Could be a target for hoodlums? You ever had to handle anything like that?'

Zetty didn't look up. 'I take good care of her. And Simonetta.'

'When did you learn to play?' I nodded at the trombone.

'I play trumpet too. My father love jazz so I learn as a child. You play?'

I shook my head. I couldn't sit in here making small talk. 'Hey, I think they're serving tea in the dining room. Wanna come?'

Zetty shook her head. 'We eat in the kitchen. Dining room's for guests only.'

I blushed. Of course. The band weren't guests, they were employees, if only for one night. And we were all quartered on the servants' level, as plush as they were.

I was halfway between a guest and an employee. Floriana had been okay with me attending the party—but she accommodated me in Zetty's room.

I stood up. Zetty looked up, twiddling the gun. 'Your hair. It is like my friend's. So you make me feel sad.'

Like Dolly, again.

I left the morose Zetty alone, and went back downstairs to grab a sandwich. I was starving and it was quite a few hours till things got started.

I marched straight into the dining room. A few guests had arrived early, dominating the middle of the room. Five men, their backs to me.

I recognized the type instantly. All had the unmistakable expensively tailored, unsubtle and swanky suits of the gangster brethren.

Nobody else was around except Valeria the maid, setting out a salver displaying cakes on a corner table, obviously for the new arrivals. She kept looking at them warily.

She finished what she was doing, then noticed me and gestured to a table. Then she wheeled her trolley through the double doors to the kitchen, pushing them open with her back.

A man moved to the side, revealing a short woman standing

with them. Her back was to me, as she chatted to a squat man in a black pinstriped suit and a fedora, the shortest and stockiest chap in the bunch. I couldn't see her face.

I didn't need to. A shiver ran down my spine.

Maureen O'Reilly.

A nightmare come true.

What do you do now? Run?

Suddenly, the doors swung open, Alberta, Jewel, Carmen and Bertha came into sight, sitting around a small table inside the kitchen. There was another woman I hadn't met before. She was tall, slim, wearing a red check shirt, and denim pants, her hair in a turban. She wasn't laughing, unlike the others. She was staring at me, bemused. Was this Earnestine, the driver?

A few caught sight of me. 'Hey, Elvira! Get in here!'

Alberta waved me in. Jewel called out, 'No liquor, just tea!'

Through the closing doors, I gave a fake smile and sent Alberta a *in a minute* gesture.

Really, I wanted to throw up. Maureen O'Reilly turned around and grinned at me.

Delight? Or malice? I couldn't say.

The double doors were now shut, closing off the view into the kitchen. The gangsters' laughter now replaced the noise from the kitchen.

I was alone with Maureen O'Reilly and a bunch of mobsters.

Maureen broke away from them, coming towards me. They didn't notice, lighting up cigars, heading for the table with the cakes.

Run!

'Well I never, if it isn't Jemima Day.'

43

The serpent had snuck into paradise and she came with brittle green eyes and a lilting Irish accent, tainted with south London.

Maureen O'Reilly. Here? In Santa Barbara, a million miles away from grim south London, didn't make any sense. She didn't belong here.

Lauder's warning, about my compatriots crossing the pond. And here she was.

Maureen O'Reilly had been my first surrogate mother after Violet, my real parent, went AWOL. Maureen was on the periphery of a gang of female thieves, the Forty Elephants. Her bouts of drunkenness meant they couldn't rely on her.

Maureen found me begging on the Old Kent Road, filthy and starving, and took me in. At last she had found somebody more wretched than herself.

To me, a street urchin, she had seemed like a goddess.

It started out well enough. Maureen had a little basement flat in Manor Place, Walworth. The dirty kitchen windows were lined with empty gin bottles, out of which dusty dead flowers drooped.

I slept on a small, moth-eaten sofa, luxury to me. She fed me, dressed me, even fussed over me a little. My pitiful clingy attachment to her felt like love.

But as with all false goddesses, things soon went wrong. I came to dread the jolliness that came too quick, along with pink cheeks, and then despondent moods that lasted for days.

The drinking sessions always ended up with the same tirade. Coming to England had been a terrible mistake, she would return to Derry. More angry lamentations about the men who had used and abused her.

I got wary around her—one second I could be the scum of the earth, just another parasite feeding off her, the next I was the only person she could depend on.

Relief came in the form of Maureen's sister, Bernadette, who worked at a tearoom in Kennington. Bernadette would come around with ginger parkin and custard tarts that the shop hadn't sold. I remember seeing concern in her eye for me, the charge of her drunken, criminally minded sister.

How I wished Bernadette would take me with her each time, but she never did.

In her sober state, Maureen was no Bernadette. I was merely a handy accomplice, one she put to work. I had to steal for my living and give most of what I'd pinched to her.

Her one goal in life was to land a rich man. Until that happened, every day was an ordeal, for which more booze was the only consolation.

I would spend hours trying to cheer her up. My stomach would be twisted in knots because cheerful Maureen had turned into a gloomy ogre. Would cheerful Maureen ever come back?

Now, in Santa Barbara of all places, she was back, all right. But my infantile allegiance to her was long gone.

Wearing a pink dress and a hat with paper roses, older and plumper, to a stranger she would seem a kindly type. She looked older than her years, the damage of booze.

Her green eyes twinkled at me. 'You know, we all thought

you were a goner. And here you are safe and sound in California. Thanks to our blessed Lady—Mary, Mother of God.'

Her eyes swiveled upwards as she made the sign of the cross. 'How I prayed you were safe! All grown up into an elegant lady!'

A dry lump lodged in my throat, waiting for the punch line.

Sure enough, her thin red lips split into a coy smile. 'There was a lot of readies on offer for news of your whereabouts, Jemima. If you'd like to stay looking so well, you and me need to have a little chat, don't we?'

I straightened my back and gave a hollow laugh. 'Last time you saw me, the Old Bill pinched me and you let me take the rap. I was just a kid. I got two years in reform school, thanks to you. And now, all these years later, first thing you do is put the squeeze on me?'

'Oh, no! Don't say that! I'm over the moon seeing you safe. Look at you!'

She sounded almost genuine. Was it possible she wasn't the evil bitch of my memories? Had time softened her?

Maureen went on. 'I did time as well, duckie, if it makes you feel any better. I blame myself for not taking better care of you. But I was a drunk and I neglected you something awful.'

Duckie. She used to call me that. She had regressed at the sight of me as quickly as me. I had pent-up grievances, while she had regrets.

'But you can't say I didn't give you an education of a sort. Skills you can depend on. I bet they've come in handy once or twice over the years?'

She was right. Maureen had taught me how to be a pickpocket, a con and a thief, and a whole lot more. Her

278

favorite lesson had been how to play men. I was young, but the message stuck.

There was also another irony to Maureen's betrayal. Reform school led me to Gwendoline, my foster mother, the only person who had really cared for me.

Maureen lowered her voice. 'Do you realize who you killed back in London, Jemima? If the mob knew you were alive, they would have your guts for garters. I can get word out that I found out how Jemima Day died. But it's risky for me, so it's only right you make you make it worth my while.'

This woman can destroy you. Don't trust her.

I glanced back into the dining room. The short, stocky guy looked like the muscle, hanging slightly back while the other men talked. 'One of them your fella? The muscle?'

'My Roberto works for the Colombo family. That's him.' She pointed to him. Proud wife.

Colombo. The name meant nothing to me.

She explained they had arrived in Los Angeles a few days ago by train from New York.

'So what, this is a vacation?'

'Oh, no! Stefano Colombo, that's the tall one inside, he's establishing the family business in Los Angeles. Given us a lovely home.'

So they would be living in Los Angeles. Not good, not at all good.

'And you know Mrs. Luciano?'

'Gawd, no, duckie! I've just been dragged along for the party! A little perk. What are you doing here?'

She wasn't going to learn I was a private detective. Floriana wouldn't let it slip.

'Oh, I get beauty treatments at her salons.' I lowered my voice. 'It truly is the land of opportunity here. I dug up a golden nugget. A movie producer!'

Roberto may have made an honest woman out of her, but Maureen would relate to a gold digger. One thing I knew about mobster hierarchy was that henchmen didn't often get a share of the profits. I wanted Maureen to know I had means.

'Why the new name? Elvira?'

'Liked the sound of it. Elvira Jones.'

No way was she getting my surname. I leaned forward, lowering my voice. 'I'm never going back to Blighty. I messed up bad. So I'd be glad of your help. Maybe we can come to an arrangement. I've got plenty of lolly.'

She touched my arm. 'It's the best thing. I can keep you safe.'

'Don't say a word, not even to Roberto, until we figure it out. If anyone asks, say we just met.'

She smiled. 'Certainly. Mum's the word.'

'It's gonna get pretty wild tonight. Say you and me have breakfast tomorrow? I want to hear all the gossip.'

'I'd like nothing better.' She smiled affectionately again.

Maybe she had changed, and I should trust her to help me shake off the mob? If she could reinforce the lie Jemima Day was murdered, as she claimed, I could continue to live in peace.

Don't be a fool.

'Seven o'clock, so nobody sees us? We can go for a stroll, a great way to start the New Year.'

By the lake, I wanted to add, but didn't. My mind was already making the leap.

I should kill Maureen O'Reilly.

44

I remembered it like yesterday. My escape from a bitch of a prison warden, at Waterloo Station in London. I had been given probation, was being sent to a Land Army farm, but I had no intention of sticking it out.

I fled to south London, to my home territory, seeking out Billy. Seeking answers, seeing payback. But my first stop was Betty's, a dress shop. Betty was a Sicilian seamstress. I'd just wanted to look pretty again after five years of feeling squalid, and she helped doll me up.

And it worked. Billy and I had a strange reunion, the same night as Victory in Europe.

Maybe freedom went to my head. I slept with him but didn't get any answers. He grudgingly offered some money.

Then the killers came. They didn't give Billy a chance, shooting him dead while I was hiding in the bedroom.

So I shot them.

One had been barely twenty. His dead yellow eyes still haunted me. I watched the life flood out of him and thought he was too young to die.

It turned out he was too important to die.

Betty was the only person who knew I was going to Billy's. She would have seen my mugshot in the papers the next day, as an absconded parolee. And being Sicilian, she would hear in no time about the triple killing in the apartment above the pub.

The law had no qualms about making it look like I had

mown down the three of them. The fact of my running was enough to pin it all on me.

To them, I was the deranged escapee, a desperate fugitive wanting vengeance. The wronged woman made insane through incarceration.

Then I ran to LA, only to be busted by Lauder. He had contacted Scotland Yard and found out I was wanted for the triple murder as well as absconding. We did our shady deal. Instead of handing me over, I would work for him.

Lauder told the British cops that Jemima Day was found dead in the Coachella Valley. That was supposed to nip in the bud any pursuit of me by anyone—authorities and underworld.

The boy, Paolo Salvatore, was a mobster boss's son. He'd been interned in a POW camp in Orkney, released the same week as me. The other man I had slain had been young Paolo's muscle.

Paolo Salvatore had been too young to die.

But like with Maureen, it was him or me.

Zetty wasn't in the bedroom when I returned. Then I heard the shower running.

I quickly pulled open the drawer in her nightstand. The revolver was still there. I shuddered. Could I really do it?

I caught sight of something else, under the gun. A faded photograph. It was taken at a fair distance and showed a woman and a boy in front of a stone house.

I peered more closely.

Zetty? Incredibly, yes. Much younger and happier. She was holding the hand of the small boy with dark hair and olive skin, like her. He had to be about two years old.

Zetty's clothes were like those of a peasant woman on a postcard. Her hair was tied back under a headscarf. She wore an embroidered apron and a long gathered skirt.

It hardly added up. Zetty was now a henchwoman and a member of an all-girl band.

Why?

The village houses were stone. Was that a minaret in the background? Billy had shown me pictures of Sicily. This didn't look like the same place at all.

I couldn't waste time wondering about Zetty's origins. I put the photo down, picked up the gun and checked the chamber for bullets.

If Zetty had a long night and needed a longer lie-in, I could discreetly borrow it myself tomorrow.

Maureen and I would promenade to the edge of the jetty. One quick bullet in the brain, and Maureen would be gone.

There could be no evidence of her going into the lake. I'd have to strip her. Floriana's alligator might appreciate a quick and easy meal. Take out special of vintage gangster's moll.

I would return Zetty's gun, then leave.

Who would care about a bodyguard's woman going missing?

Floriana wouldn't, and she definitely wouldn't want the sheriff's men poking around her property.

Maybe I could be the source of a rumor that Maureen was seen walking off the property, or paying one of the Mexicans for a lift?

No. I couldn't do that. Roberto might shoot everyone of them dead. They didn't deserve to pay for my crappy past.

The shower stopped running. I quickly lay on my bed, to look like I was resting.

I was pathetic. My ruthless survival instinct was all bluster. I was lying to myself. How could I commit the cold-blooded murder of a woman who tried, however badly, to raise me for a while?

Maybe people do change. Maureen was softer. She had been a bitter drunk. Now she had a guy who loved her.

She couldn't have racked up many years of happiness.

No. You have to do it. You or her!

The bathroom door opened and Zetty entered, a towel around her head. She glanced at me. 'Oh. You are back.' Then she did a double take. 'Are you okay?'

I must have looked as sick as I felt.

45

That night, Wanda gave it everything she had for the assembled hundreds of guests. The band looked stunning on stage in their olive dresses, belting out their new repertoire.

Wanda couldn't regale the crowd with her patter as freely she could at Joyce's. She introduced each song in a quiet and dignified manner and thanked the audience when they applauded. Even so, she still held the room of movie stars, movie producers, fashion moguls, gossip columnists, mobsters, and businesspeople in the palm of her hand.

The Charms were awesome. But the boys were coming home and surely all-girl bands would have to make way. There wouldn't be such demand for all-girl anything—bands, taxi drivers, factory workers—now the war was over. What would happen to all these women?

Wanda had grit, looks, and surplus talent. She wouldn't give up. She just needed to be discovered.

I looked around at the crowd. Maybe somebody would be impressed?

Most of the guests had come in from Los Angeles, some had come from Santa Cruz and San Francisco and others had even flown down from New York. Clearly this party was the place to be.

The tent itself was like a swanky nightclub on the Strip. The canopy was lined with white satin, punctuated by enormous chandeliers. Around the sides, strings of white fairground lights resembled glowing ropes of pearls. Eight fake Corinthian columns supported hanging garlands of green and yellow flowers—daisies, roses, dahlias and olive sprigs—and elegant sprays of the same blooms stood on each table.

The atmosphere was electric. I studied the other members of the band. Alberta was enjoying herself. She knew Dolly was free, she had limited opportunity to play in her life, and she was letting rip.

If Bertha, Carmen and Jewel were exhausted, they kept up a good front.

I felt a pang of envy of their love for their playing, for their passion for something creative. I had no idea what it felt like, but I still envied it.

Only Zetty was frowning.

Maureen wasn't among the Colombo gangsters on the other side of the tent to me. Was she classed as too low in the pecking order? Probably. I'd seen Roberto, Maureen's husband, smoking outside and gathered from his stance that he was on look out, not a guest.

Was Maureen stuck in her room for New Year's Eve? Was it that she could come along for the ride, but at the destination, she was put in her place?

Floriana had put me on a "young" table with her daughter Simonetta, who had flung her arms around me. There were also four dashing young male actors who were the life and soul of our table, and easy on the eye. They were all signed to the same major studio, and kept the table entertained all night with Hollywood gossip. Lastly there were two businesswomen, a beauty magazine editor, and Deborah something, the owner of the Starlight modelling agency.

During dessert, Deborah took an interest in me when I told

her I lived in the Miracle Mile Hotel. She was looking to move her agency to mid-Wilshire from Downtown, and did I know if the owner was open to renting an office?

I gave her Dede's name. It was ironic that Alberta, who was on stage entertaining the crowd that very moment, could give her an answer then and there.

In another world.

Deborah asked questions about the hotel and its residents. I did my best to answer, wondering how a model agency might be of benefit to a fledgling detective agency.

And then it came. A loud bang, violently ripping through the tent.

The band stopped playing, frozen on stage. Silence, followed by more shots. The guests screamed, everyone jumping under the tables. Desserts flew everywhere. I crouched down and crawled behind a column, my hand landing in a meringue. I peered around.

A masked figure, a gun in a gloved hand. Tall, thin, a dark cap over his head. He stood by one of the tent's side entrances.

His line of fire went straight to Stefano Colombo's table. He fired again, and a volley of shots flew back in reply. Roberto ran into the tent, aiming at the shooter.

Another loud bang came from an altogether different direction.

The stage. I spun around.

Zetty! Fury in her eyes and jumping off the stage, she fired her revolver at the gunman. The other band members were cowering behind the drums and the double bass, now lying on the floor of the stage.

Another blast and Zetty was thrown backwards, a bullet searing through her chest.

287

I turned back to see the shooter, also hit. Clutching his arm, he slipped out through the tent.

Mobsters were surrounding the Colombo table, loud voices shouting in Italian. Roberto ran back outside, pursuing the assailant. More gunfire, then silence.

The petrified guests stayed under the tables. Women whimpered.

Floriana was the first to stand up, cautiously. She called out for Simonetta in Italian. No answer. Floriana called out again, more desperately. Someone shouted back that Simonetta had gone to the powder room before the shooting started. Floriana's relief her daughter had escaped the bullets was palpable.

Slowly, guests started raising their heads.

I ran over to Zetty. Alberta and Wanda were bending over her. 'She's bleeding!'

'I'll press on the wound!' I said. My fingers gently tried to stop the blood flow, but it surged like warm water through my fingers.

You couldn't save Billy, either.

I shook the image away. A grim-faced Alberta sat next to Zetty's head, stroking her hair.

We met each other's eyes. We were losing her.

Floriana swooped in. 'My Zetty, my Zetty! No!' She leaned close to Zetty and spoke in Italian very fast, stroking her face. She looked up and screamed at a waiter. He nodded and ran out of the tent.

'A doctor is coming. *Santa Maria, ti prego.*' She looked desperate and torn, whether to stay with dying Zetty or see to the Colombo mob. Duty came first and she got up.

A crimson stain seeped over the entire span of Zetty's green embroidered bodice. Her eyes were flickering, manically. She was desperate to say something, vainly attempting to twist her head to meet Alberta's eyes.

'Hush, honey. Don't move, don't talk.' Alberta was soothing.

'Where's that doctor!' yelled Wanda. She marched off. Jewel, Carmen and Bertha clung to each other, sobbing.

Zetty's skin felt cold and clammy. Her face contorted in agony.

'Hush, now. Take it easy.' Alberta was soothing but it only seemed to make Zetty's anguish worse.

'Okay, honey. What is it?'

Alberta and I leaned closer to Zetty's face.

'Say to Dolly...I sorry...'

Zetty, even now, was still torn up about Dolly. Alberta looked decisive—she had to give Zetty peace of mind. 'Zetty, relax, Dolly's okay.'

'No. I...sorry...I kill Ronald Hunter. I kill him.'

With that, her head lolled back.

Zetty just dropped a bomb on the case. I had no time to process it. Somehow, I did have the foresight to casually slip her revolver under my garter. Survival instinct, again.

Floriana rushed back over, with more staff. They surrounded Zetty. Floriana addressed us. 'You can leave. We take care of her.'

Alberta sadly looked at the others. 'Nothing we can do.' They slipped out of a side door in the tent, the one for staff. They didn't want to hang around to be grilled by the Santa Barbara sheriff's boys.

I hesitated. Zetty was not the only victim. Stefano Colombo

was obviously hurt. I had no idea if he was dead or alive. Several of his men were crouching around him.

Another guy burst into the tent, shouting in Italian. Colombo's men looked around. The man gestured outside. But the others didn't move.

Floriana stood up, queen over the commotion. She made a grand reassuring speech to the guests. There had been a tragic incident. She needed to call the police and she understood if anyone had to leave quickly.

When the going gets tough, the tough get going. A surge of rich and important guests surged out of the tent.

Was Floriana purposely delaying her call to the cops, buying her more important guests a head start?

I had to find Maureen.

Think, what are you going to do exactly?

The opportunity to kill her had been lost. I was secretly relieved.

So move!

I could hitch a ride. The guys on my table had fled but if I was quick, maybe I could catch them.

My hands were thickly coated and sticky with Zetty's drying blood. I had to wash but I wouldn't need to change. My red velvet dress didn't show much of the blood on the skirt.

You look good in red velvet.

Outside the tent, Floriana's people shone flashlights over the grass. A trail of blood drops just disappeared in the middle of the lawn. It was like the shooter had been spirited away.

Others were surrounding a body.

A beam of light lit up the corpse's face. Roberto, a bullet through his forehead, his mouth sagging open.

And then a monstrous wail of grief.

Maureen. Running from the house, hysterical, her arms high. She flung herself over Roberto, kissing his lips, his face, even the wound. 'No! No!'

The mobsters tried to calm her, to pull her off. She shook them off, like a tiger protecting her cubs. 'Roberto, Roberto!'

So this was love.

Roberto was the guy Maureen had dreamed of, all those drunken nights in her squalid South London flat. Her knight in shining armor had finally shown up for her, taken care of her, and stayed by her side.

And now he was gone. Ripped from her by the hazard of his profession.

Maureen looked up, tears streaming down her face. She caught sight of me. 'Jemima, Jemima! Look what they've done to him! My baby!'

She had to shut up with the "Jemima". Somebody could hear. I went over to her, and did what the mobsters couldn't, dragged her off him. 'Come on. Let them take him inside.'

Maureen reluctantly stood up. She collapsed into my arms. 'I want him! No, no.'

The ruthless me should kill her now. Take her for a walk. Do it quietly, quickly. But I couldn't.

I couldn't bear to see the betrayal in her already suffering eyes.

I held her in my arms while she sobbed her heart out. My mind wandered. Would the Colombo gang take care of her now? Let her stay in the LA house they'd given her?

Wherever she settled, being a widow and hitting forty would mean one thing. She'd soon be broke.

Destitution meant hunger, hunger meant determination. Maureen didn't have my full name, or my profession. But she knew I was alive and how to locate me. In time, she would hunt me down. And if she fled back to London, she could easily sell me out to the Salvatores to extract a reward from them.

Even in grief, Maureen O'Reilly very much posed a risk to my health.

A doctor ran towards the tent, passing me, followed by ambulance men with stretchers. Maureen followed Roberto's body, slowly carried by his colleagues, towards the main house.

I raced past them. Inside, I poked my head around the dining room. Hoodlums occupied the corner table, a haze of cigar smoke over their huddle. More of Colombo's crew?

One looked up, but I turned away and ran out. The less they got to know my face, the better.

I bumped into Floriana gliding into the hall. Her expression was strange. A mixture of stress and something else. Disappointment?

'Stefano Colombo is injured, badly. My girl Zetty is unconscious. A man is dead. How dare they bring their battles here! The police are on their way. Where is my daughter when I need her?'

'Poor Zetty. Hey, please leave my name off the guest list, if the cops ask for it.'

'The police will not trouble anybody, once I have explained it was a hit. The Colombo family have many enemies. Only they can explain this.'

Floriana could make it worth the sheriff office's while to ignore the majority of guests.

And then I saw it. A fleeting twinkle in her eye? Then it was gone.

'What?' She demanded.

'A bad blow, for the hotel and spa?'

'My business will not be affected.' She touched my arm. 'But sweet of you to worry.' She kissed me dramatically on both cheeks.

I lowered my voice. 'Hey, there's a woman with the Colombos. Maureen O'Reilly? She's married to the guy who died.'

'The one in that horrible pink dress?'

'That's her. If you see her, please give her my number. Only her, not the people she's with. But don't give her my surname, or tell her I'm a PI.'

Floriana raised a brow. 'You know these people already? You are in some trouble?'

Damn, she was perceptive! But I couldn't be honest with her. Not yet. 'Nothing like that. We got chatting. I feel bad for her.'

Floriana mused, looking curious. 'Okay. I will do as you ask.'

I thanked her and dashed upstairs.

Alberta was hurrying down, a coat over her blood-stained dress. She was loaded with cases. They must have been packed up already.

'This is awful. I pray Zetty's gonna make it but what was she saying?'

'No idea.'

Alberta looked warily around. 'We can't talk now; *you* should scram, too.'

Her emphasis on "you", meant one thing. Whatever I'd said

to her when I was sauced, she knew I was in trouble with the law.

'I'll hitch a ride. See you in LA.' We instinctively hugged each other.

Wanda was on her way down, with a bag. She eyed us coolly. Alberta broke away. I went on up the stairs.

'Wanna ride with us?'

I stopped and turned back. It was Wanda, looking up at me.

A peace offering? Maybe because I'd tried to help Zetty. Wanda moved in mysterious ways.

'Sure,' I said. 'Thanks a lot.'

'Then move it. Wash that blood off your hands. Any trouble on the road, jump into the hatch right away. If they find you, you say you snuck on in the dark. We didn't even know you were with us. We'll say show was over and we were on our way out as the shooting started. Period.'

'And nobody says nothing about Zetty,' snapped Alberta. 'Okay?'

I nodded. In my room, I scrubbed my hands and shoved everything in the case. As I left, something made me go back to the nightstand. I pulled open the drawer and grabbed the box of bullets.

The photograph of Zetty and the child. I would take that, too.

Why? Instinct. I had no obvious need for it. Maybe Dolly would. She could take it to Zetty in hospital. Surely the first thing she would do is sit by her pal's bedside.

I heard something, coming from a small door at the end of the corridor. A groan?

Ignore it! You don't have time!

I tiptoed along the carpet towards the door. It looked like a broom closet, or a toilet. Another groan. A woman, crying?

I was torn. The bus wouldn't wait for me. Then a wail of agony. I rapped on the door. Silence.

'Everything okay?'

No answer. Just a whimper.

I turned the handle.

Simonetta, Floriana's daughter!

Her eyes blazed in fury. Beads of sweat dotted her brow and a long streak of blood stained her dark clothes, pants and a black shirt. She was clutching her arm. Kneeling next to her, the maid Valeria stared up at me, too. Caught in the act.

She had a pair of tweezers in her hand, hovering over a violent raw wound rupturing Simonetta's supple bicep. Blood-soaked pads, bandages and disinfectant lay on a tray.

A hasty bullet extraction? Simonetta was the assassin?

Simonetta hissed, 'Get the hell out, or I kill you!'

I slammed the door fast, heart pumping.

Low voices. I spun around. At the far end of the corridor, Earnestine, the bus driver, was being handed a case from someone inside a room. Was it my imagination or did her head spin back to the door too fast?

Carmen came out and shut the door. Earnestine met my eyes as they went down the stairs.

I hurried after them.

46

Silent sadness pervaded the bus journey, each woman lost in her own thoughts. Earnestine put her foot on the gas and the bus hurtled along the dark, deserted roads.

I dozed intermittently. Too wired, too thrown to sleep. I couldn't make sense of the shocking twist of events. Simonetta's hit. Zetty's confession. Was she saying she had committed a *crime passionel*? Odd. I couldn't see Zetty and Hunter together in a million years. And if and when she pulled through, what state would she be in?

Dolly, Agnes and Pauline were all a type: petite white girls, vulnerable-looking. Zetty was lithe, tall, muscular, tanned. An amazon, really. And while her face was striking, it didn't fit the mold for any beauty magazine.

And she wanted us to say sorry to Dolly for killing her man.

Again, the only people linking Zetty and Hunter were Dolly and Vivienne. Dolly, because she and Zetty were close. Vivienne, because she worked for Hunter, and Floriana wanted to buy her shop.

Unless Hunter had been having an affair with Zetty, which seemed highly unlikely, I could see no motive.

And on top of everything, Simonetta had rubbed out Stefano Colombo. Clever to do it at the party, with her mother, Floriana, standing very near Stefano when it happened. That alone meant Floriana wouldn't be blamed. The Colombo clan would suspect an enemy. There would be reprisals. The LAPD would be busy.

Was Floriana herself in on the hit? Or had Simonetta taken things into her own hands? That had backfired spectacularly. Hurting Zetty, a beloved servant, possibly fatally. Was that just a terrible accident? Was Zetty in on it, her gun conveniently hidden on the stage somewhere?

I tried to curl up on the bouncing bus. I needed Beatty's genius brain.

Eventually, the purring of the bus's engine over the long road helped me fall asleep. 1946 arrived during our dreams.

I roused; the bus was coming to a smooth stop. Had we arrived? Everyone else was asleep. I peered outside. The bleak darkness of the wilderness. No city lights, in fact, the middle of nowhere. I could just make out brush blowing in the wind.

Earnestine was getting off the bus. She was stretching her legs, swigging from a bottle of root beer. A break for the driver.

I decided to join her and crept past the slumbering bandmates.

Outside, she nodded to me. 'Can't sleep?'

I shook my head. 'Guess it's New Year now, so Happy New Year.'

She nodded. 'Except it ain't so happy.' She whistled. 'You see it go down?'

I whistled. 'Everything.'

Earnestine offered me a cigarette. I declined. 'Know Zetty well?' I asked.

'Not as good as the other girls. Why?'

I pulled out the photograph and handed to her. 'She ever mention a kid?'

Earnestine used her lighter to see better. 'Not to me. But that boy sure looks like her.'

I nodded. 'That's what I thought.'

She handed the photograph back. 'I guess Mrs. Luciano will tell who needs to be told. What you doing with it, anyway?'

'I thought I'd give it to Dolly. They were good pals.'

'Little Dolly Perkins.' She shook her head. 'Strange kid.'

'Strange? How?'

'I know she can't help it, but I don't think she would look me in the eye even if she could see straight. Still, nobody's perfect.' She didn't sound a fan.

After a pause, I asked, 'So, you've driven for girl bands before, on tour? Like the Honey Duchesses?'

'Oh, no. My first time driving a band. And last. Too much high jinks for my liking. If it ain't cops causing trouble, it's mobsters.'

I laughed. 'So, what, you're a taxi driver, back in the city?'

Earnestine's face split into a wide grin of what? Incredulity? I bristled, it wasn't such a funny question. Lots of women took driving jobs on during the war. 'Yeah, sure, I'm a taxi driver. What about yourself, back in the city?' She asked. I bet she knew already.

'Private investigator.'

'You don't sound so sure.'

I leaned against a post supporting the fence. 'I kind of stumbled into it. It's hard. You think you're getting somewhere, things add up, then they don't.'

'What you figuring out right now?'

There was no harm in telling her. She'd hear all about Zetty's confession anyway. 'Why would Zetty say that? Why nothing about her kid?'

'Guilt? Saving her soul.' She took a last drag. 'Or, maybe it's like a code. Zetty wanted to get a message out to Dolly. A secret message. Something only they understand. What message? That's what you gotta work out, detective lady. I'm just the driver.'

Earnestine squished her cigarette into the dirt with her boot. 'Let's get going.'

47

'Mornin', ladies. Home sweet home.'

I looked up, rubbing my eyes. Wanda stood in the middle of the aisle. How did she manage to be so perky?

A chorus of tired groans from The Charms.

'Happy New Year to y'all. I know we're all hurtin' over Zetty. She's our girl, and we're gonna pray for her.'

Murmurs of assent followed. The bus was parked along the side of a big house.

Alberta got up and came to the back. She sat in the seat in front. I said, 'Where are we?'

'Sugar Hill. Wanda's place. Belonged to her mother, Mimi Carter.'

I must have looked blank.

Alberta said, 'She was a blues singer.'

I nodded, embarrassed to be out of the loop yet again when it came to music.

I'd heard about Sugar Hill in the past six months of living in LA, a thriving black community where movie stars and musicians lived. I could only see the side, but Wanda's house was a grand turn-of-the-century dwelling.

We trooped off the bus. Jewel, Carmen and Nora made for a side entrance, as if it was home.

Earnestine waved at me, 'Good luck, Sherlock!'

I waved back. I had to laugh.

Wanda hovered, looking at me. 'Can I call you a cab?'

I said I wanted to stretch my legs. I could walk to the main street and pick one up.

300

'Momma!' Two of the cutest kids, little girls with messy hair and crumpled nightdresses, ran out of the side entrance and grabbed Wanda's legs. She leaned down and hugged them. 'Hey, trouble times two! What are you doing up at this hour?'

An older woman appeared at the side door, in a luxurious quilted satin housecoat. It looked primrose yellow under the lamp. 'They heard the bus and woke the whole house up!'

Wanda laughed. 'Happy New Year, Auntie.' She turned back to her kids. 'You miss me? I missed you so much I had to come back early! Look, Alberta's come to see you, too!'

They flung themselves at Alberta, who showered them with kisses. Then the kids spotted me and stared.

'Hello,' I said.

'Come on, let's go in now,' said Wanda. She nodded to me. 'See you around.'

'Thanks.'

'Who's that white lady, momma?' asked one of the girls.

'Just somebody passing through. Hey, want to see what I got you?' said Wanda.

Alberta said she was going to stay at Wanda's for the day. She'd see me at the hotel.

I didn't catch a cab, in the end. I wandered through Sugar Hill, marveling at the beautiful houses populating the stunning neighborhood.

It jolted childhood memories. Fragments of my lost past. The homes in which Violet worked, when she traveled all the way to America, searching for a man who didn't want to be found.

My father, who was he? He had fought in the First World

War. He had survived and sought comfort from a woman in London. He gave her false hope, empty promises and a fake name, but that was enough for her to leave England.

Poor Violet. She had stuck it out with a young child, earning a living by cleaning big houses for rich folks and, in her spare time, trying to track her man down.

Just another military man lacking in the honor department. Maybe, for all his courage on the battlefield, he didn't have the guts to say the truth, that he only craved warmth and love for a night or two. Maybe he was shell-shocked and forgot his name.

Maybe Violet just heard what she wanted to hear.

At the end of the day, it was easier to think he was a cad and she was a sap and out of a pack of lies, they made me.

I walked for miles along deserted city streets. The amber light of the streetlamps competed with dawn's rosy arrival. It felt right to be alone for New Year; a waking city was enough company for me.

Nobody was around, the parties were over. Just the odd drunk in a doorway. I'd been that person a few nights ago, but I wouldn't be again. I wouldn't give up on myself.

1946 would be different. No dumb list of New Year's resolutions. I had only two resolutions. To figure it all out—this crazy crime—and to keep my new life on an even keel.

Unlike my mother, I wasn't looking for anybody.

Instead, I needed to say goodbye.

48

Rouge d'Or was a low-key cocktail bar in Culver City. It opened early, closed late and didn't have any special appeal other than always being half empty, and that Lauder and I could meet here safe in the knowledge no one would see us.

Inside, some over-eager interior designer had conceived the bright idea of remodeling the room into the shape of a kidney, with organically curved walls. The bar was a circular affair at one end of the room, and low tables with green lamps dominated the rest. Several payphones edged a shorter curved wall.

The décor was shades of dark red, which usually created a certain sensual mood, even if we met in broad daylight.

I sat on a padded bench which lined the longest wall. Today, it suddenly reminded me of the edge of the membrane of real kidneys. It hit me I would never come here again.

Lauder returned from the bar with two scotches on the rocks. He sat down and passed one to me. 'Happy New Year. Again.'

We chinked. 'How was your holiday?' I asked, knowing he hadn't been anywhere. Would he tell the truth?

'Oh, something came up in the end. Had to cancel.'

'Shame. Nothing bad?'

'Not really.' He glanced around the room. 'Dolly Perkins is released tomorrow.'

I acted surprised. 'Really? Why?'

He looked at me, harsh. 'Thought you'd be more pleased, considering our fight over it.'

'Well, I got over it. Look, I'm tired. Had a long night.'

'Oh, yeah, do anything nice for New Year?'

I had called the LAPD when I got back to the Miracle Mile. I had a code name to use, if I needed Lauder to ring me. He hadn't taken long to get back to me, and we arranged to meet in the afternoon. I looked and felt shattered.

'Look, I've got some bad news.'

'How bad?'

I sipped my drink. 'Someone from my past has resurfaced. From London.'

Lauder put his drink down.

'She's putting the squeeze on me. The Salvatore family had a big price on my head, before word got out I was dead. Her deal is I cough up and she'll tell them Jessica Day is definitely dead. Her husband works for the Colombos. Worked. He was murdered last night, at a party. She's got a house here, so she'll be back. Soon.'

'You were at Floriana Luciano's bash?' Lauder's voice was hoarse. Of course he knew about the shooting already.

I nodded. 'Luciano invited me. I had nothing better to do after you banned me from the case. Didn't think you'd mind.'

I couldn't exactly explain how I'd wound up there, smashed. It was partly his fault, for being in my life in a way he wasn't supposed to be.

'Oh, is that right? A private party in the middle of nowhere with a bunch of organized criminals? So who's the ghost from London?'

'Maureen O'Reilly. About forty. Looks older. And it wasn't just the mob there, if you must know. The crème de la crème of Hollywood was out in style.'

Lauder asked me what I had seen. I described the events of the party, excluding my encounter with the wounded Simonetta and Zetty's confession. He had his notepad out, scrawling everything down.

'Rumor has it the Colombos killed Antonio Luciano. He apparently declined to add heroin to his olive oil imports and paid the price. Wouldn't surprise me if they were putting the squeeze on the widow. Protection money. Colombo died a few hours ago.'

I stared at him. So Simonetta had avenged her father and liberated her mother—for the time being.

'A woman was shot, injured. She works for Luciano. Do you know how she is?'

He surveyed me. 'In a coma. Not looking good.'

Poor Zetty. But she was strong. I tried not to let my emotions show.

'If you kept a low profile, as I repeatedly ask you, you wouldn't have bumped into this Maureen O'Reilly, would you?'

'Quit the lecture. You're right, okay? But this year's gonna be different. I'll play it safe. Besides, it's better we know she's out there already, before I bump into her out of the blue. We can…handle it better.'

He grunted, giving me a strange look with his liquid turquoise eyes. It was stupid meeting here. The ambience was too sensual. I associated this bar with one thing—leaving to have sex.

'Okay.'

'You don't seem very…perturbed?'

'I know exactly where O'Reilly is.'

'What? Where?' I sat back, thrown. All-knowing, all-seeing Lauder.

'Well, she could be kinda useful...'

I butted in, bitter and derisive. 'Don't even think about making Maureen O'Reilly your CI. She's the reason I ended up in reform school. Born double-crosser. For God's sake, don't let her know you know me. She'll destroy you, too!'

'...if she wasn't dead.'

My stomach lurched. 'Dead? What?'

'My colleagues in the Santa Barbara Sheriff's Office pulled her out of the water this morning. Estimated time of death around midnight or just after. Midnight swim?'

I shivered. It couldn't be. No. Had Maureen taken her own life?

'You mean...in Floriana's lake?'

'Found floating face down, near the jetty. No gunshot wounds. A few odd marks on the body. Like bites? Maybe her and her fella liked it rough in bed.'

Then he looked into my eyes. 'Unless you're forgetting to tell me something.'

'What? You think I killed her and this is a bluff?'

He raised a cynical brow.

'No! She just...lost her guy! She must have jumped.' My voice tailed off.

'Suicide? Well then. Panic over.'

That was the depth of Maureen's love. She couldn't live without her knight. She didn't want my money for herself. I bet she'd just wanted to feather her nest with Roberto.

I sipped my drink. *Rest in peace.*

Yet another mother figure had bitten the dust. I felt my eyes pricking with tears. Irrational. I hoped he didn't see. My voice was stiff.

'Where's her body? Will they bring it back here?'

'Guess so. Mobsters look after their own.'

I asked him to tell me if he could find out the undertaker her body would go to.

They never let me see Violet, or Gwendoline's bodies. I would see Maureen. I would say goodbye.

'Why?'

'It's complicated.'

Then Lauder smiled, softly. 'You wearing that necklace?'

I pulled my blouse down a little and hooked out the pearl with my finger. I had put it on again. Why? To see him smile? Now I regretted taking it out of the drawer.

'Suits you. Let's get outta here.' His hand slipped into mine. He squeezed it, hard.

He meant one thing. All I wanted to do was feel him on top of me, inside me...

Stop it! You're the pawn in their game, remember!

The Fiancée. His stupid relationship. I was just a salve to make his life better.

I gulped. My turn to cross the line. 'We can't do this anymore. You're engaged. It's not right. Nothing good can come from this. Let's get back to how we were.'

I didn't recognize my own voice. I couldn't look at him. Speaking straight, for once. A shiver flew down my back. I had jumped off a cliff and was in free fall.

Lauder hadn't expected this. Neither had I. His jaw went rigid. His hand slipped out of mine, like cold water.

He looked at his watch, and then at the door. Escape preparations?

I tensed up. Had I been wrong to think he had affection for me?

He swigged his drink down in one and stood up. 'All right. If that's what you want.'

'Well...' I started to say.

And then he walked out.

49

Sonia and Joseph flanked a bewildered Dolly just outside the Hall of Justice. 'My client has done all she can to assist the Police Department with their enquiries. She has no comment.'

It was the 2nd of January and Dolly was free.

I sat in Mabel across the road, window down, watching.

Dressed in a shabby, oversized dress, Dolly stood between the sharp-suited attorneys. She looked pale and thin, her lank blonde mop of hair covered by a green beret. The outfit screamed "innocent victim". Sonia must have brought the attire in, to milk the vindicatory moment. The Santa-style dress Dolly had been arrested in wouldn't have quite the same wronged woman effect.

Joseph led the way through the throng of pressmen and women towards a big gleaming car. Sonia's car. Voices yelled at her.

'What was Ronald Hunter to you, Dolly?'

'Give us an exclusive, Dolly!' This pushy reporter managed to shove her card into Dolly's hand. But Joseph ripped it from her, as Sonia bundled Dolly in the back of a glossy navy car.

The lawyers were controlling her every move and word. Maybe they didn't want her to say something dumb, to push her luck. Maybe they had another scheme cooking. Some lucrative deal with the Hunter clan for ongoing silence?

The car sped off, Joseph at the wheel, Sonia and Dolly in the back.

Time to go.

I pulled away, to tail Sonia's car. No way would she take Dolly back to Mrs. Olsen's boarding house. So where?

Traffic was light and Joseph drove fast, to escape the buzzards. We sailed through to Hollywood in no time. Sonia's car slowed, signaling, as it neared the Hollywood Hotel. A good decision. Not a dive, but not too swanky either. Sonia would be keeping Dolly here under a false name.

I kept my distance but took my foot off the gas briefly. I couldn't turn into the entrance without risking being seen. As the blue car turned, I noticed Dolly's hair was suddenly dark, and the beret gone.

A wig, of course. Was she changing clothes too? She needed to pass unnoticed. I could imagine Sonia's voice, right now, barking *do's and don'ts* of her new life to Dolly.

I parked on the street and jumped out. I killed a few minutes in the hotel's flower shop which bordered the street. The buckets of dahlias, roses and hydrangeas made a pleasant sight.

I selected a nice bouquet as a gift for Dolly from the cheerful florist. Some pale pink roses, a few white freesias, and some yellow lilies. I paid the florist and told her to keep the change.

A gift for what exactly? Hope? Congratulations? Or sympathy, because Zetty was bad. Did Dolly even know yet? Was I going to be the harbinger of bad news on the day of her release?

As I left the shop, Sonia's car flew out of the complex. That was quick. I bet they'd given Dolly orders to stay put.

But I knew what incarceration did to a person. Dolly would take a shower, change her clothes and go some place, anywhere she could go of her own volition. Just walk, see life. No way, after being cooped up in a cell, would she sit in a hotel room.

I'd give her a bit of time to adjust. It would be rude to barge in.

I bought a paper at the kiosk and sat down, leaving my sunglasses on. I couldn't really focus, as I had to watch the elevators. Floriana's, of course, had made the papers. *New Year's Eve Mobster Showdown in Santa Barbara!*

Another article caught my eye. A Lord Haw-Haw was about to be hung tomorrow in Wandsworth Prison, London, for treason. My stomach lurched.

I lifted my shades to read more. William Joyce, nicknamed Lord Haw-Haw, was American born. The genuine article of traitor; a diehard believer in the Third Reich.

They were busy hanging all the traitors now. I put the paper down and rubbed my neck, gently. I picked up the bouquet and tried to lose myself in the beauty of the flowers.

And there she was, Dolly, a flash of a pink and white, striding out of the elevators. A new dress, and a pretty bonnet hat made out of crisp white straw, with a pink ribbon.

With a bright smile, she handed her key to one of the girls at the front desk and made for the main doors.

I jumped up, about to call out to her. But something paralyzed me to the spot.

Her expression was clouding over. Determination? Not the face of a woman reveling in freedom.

The face of a woman with a plan.

I hid behind the flowers, and turned to look through the doors.

Dolly was on the move, getting in a cab.

I left the lobby, and ran back to Mabel, flinging the newspaper and bouquet on the passenger seat. A few freesia buds fell off. A shame.

Dolly's cab headed westward. I kept a steady distance.

Where was she going? I glanced at the fuel gauge. Soon I'd be running on empty.

Finally, the cab made a series of right turns and came to a stop. We were back where I'd been only three days ago.

Vivienne's beauty shop in Westwood Village.

Straight out of jail she goes see Vivienne, Hunter's old secretary? Customer or friend?

Dolly and Vivienne. Two degrees of separation.

I parked near the beauty shop and got out, taking the paper and bouquet. I wouldn't barge in, just watch for a while. My instincts cautioned it.

Trust them!

Through the window, I could make out an older woman sat under a hair dryer. Vivienne and Dolly were locked in conversation, near an inner door. One sided chat as Vivienne seemed to be doing most of the listening. She was shaking her head. Upset? Protesting? I couldn't tell.

Suddenly, Dolly pulled off her wig. She leaned forward, as if pushing her face into Vivienne's.

I didn't need binoculars to read Vivienne's face. Dolly had dropped a bomb. Vivienne went behind her counter, and sat down, head in hands. Dolly followed. She opened her purse and got out a piece of paper. She slid it to Vivienne, who picked it up, staring at it.

In a flash, Dolly put her dark wig back on, and strolled out.

I lowered my head into the paper, to watch. This time, Dolly walked for a while until she could hail a cab.

Follow Dolly or go to Vivienne? Surely Dolly would head back to the hotel?

I opened the door and breezed in. A sleepy pug sat at the

feet of the woman under the dryer. Vivienne was frozen, staring into space, clutching the paper. A worn envelope.

'Hello, again! I was in the neighborhood.' I grinned.

Vivienne's head was turned sideways.

'Remember me? From the funeral?'

'Yes, I do. It's Mary, isn't it? Mary…?'

'Saunders. Er…is this a bad time? You look kinda shaken up.'

Vivienne shook herself. She turned, just a little, to glance at me. 'I'm fine. Nice to see you again.'

Poor thing, she was making a bad job of pretending. I glanced at the envelope. The writing was loopy and large. I'd seen it before. On the paper Pauline had given me with Agnes's address at the Miracle Mile.

'Not bad news, I hope?'

'No, no.' Finally, she turned to face me. 'So, you'd like an appointment?'

First the writing. Now Vivienne's eyes were familiar. Big orbs of blue. And one looked in a different direction to the other.

The same as Dolly's.

'What I really want is…' I looked around. The woman under the dryer was still engrossed in her book. '…to know if Dolly Perkins is your daughter?'

Vivienne froze, her lips tight. Instinctively, she turned the envelope over.

'Pardon me?' Her voice was hoarse.

I kept my voice nice and low. 'I'm a private investigator. The young lady who was just here, that's Dolly Perkins. The woman who was charged with Ronald Hunter's murder, and released today. Why are you the first person she goes see? You don't look too happy.'

Vivienne slid the envelope under her hand. Her eyes welled up. 'I thought I'd...lost her. Hey, I...I really need some time to come to terms with this.'

'Lost her? How?'

Vivienne dabbed her eyes with her sleeve. She sniffed. 'You couldn't understand.'

'Try me.'

'I had no choice. I gave her up.' She waved the envelope. 'I wrote this, years ago, to explain why. She found it, brought it here. She doesn't understand.'

'You were in the Pineview Clinic?'

Vivienne stared at me.

'Who are you working for?'

'Nobody, anymore. I was helping Dolly's defense. Guess now I'm just curious.'

She processed this, glancing at the woman under the dryer. 'I've got to see to my lady.'

'So, who's Daddy? Ronald Hunter?'

'No, it isn't. Please go.'

'You realize Dolly's been screwing him?'

'You're disgusting! Get out!'

'You were in love with him, weren't you? Enough to organize little vacations to the Pineview Clinic for all those other secretaries. How long were you doing that for?'

'How dare you!' Vivienne raised her voice. We both instinctively checked the lady under the dryer. Still oblivious to the drama. Vivienne hissed at me. 'Yes, I got pregnant, like a fool. To a loser, not Ronald. I told him, and he helped me out of trouble. He was a real gentleman.'

'Gentleman? Really?'

'All those girls threw themselves at him! All little tarts!'

Her cheeks flushed, and I saw her for what she was. A desperate, lonely woman who idolized a man who saved her from disrepute and, for that, she would go to the ends of the earth for him. In her own eyes, she was his wife—his secret second wife that the world would never know.

'Little tarts like Dolly?'

Vivienne couldn't answer that. 'I didn't know about that. Ronald is not her father, that much I swear.'

'So, she's found you. A nice mom-daughter reunion. Why aren't you happy?'

Vivienne came out from behind the counter. She gave a smile to the lady.

'So it's just a coincidence Dolly fell in love with your old boss, is it?'

Vivienne stared at me. 'She came to work for me a few years ago. I had no idea who she was!'

'So what does she want now?'

'She wants...me. To be with me.' Vivienne started to shake.

'Sounds cozy.'

Vivienne's straight eye met mine, desperate.

'She said we never have to be parted again. Says I can sell up now, that I have to!' Horror filled her eyes. 'I think she's crazy.'

50

'Booby, get the hell in here and bring the brandy with you!' Beatty's voice roared out through the walls. She could see me, hovering outside her office, through the two-way mirror. I hadn't wanted to burst in, in case some forlorn spouse was pouring out their heart.

I found the brandy and crystal tumblers in the cabinet opposite the secretary's desk. I put them on a polished pewter tray and went into Beatty's office. She was behind her desk, in what was, for her, a rather subdued outfit. It was a mushroom and magenta woolen two piece. The skirt was heavily pleated, and the cardigan had the fashionable arrow features that I'd seen on the lady at the Pineview Clinic. The only difference was Beatty's arrows pointed upwards to her face.

A *look at me* pair of arrows.

She wore a rope of glossy amber beads around her neck that clashed but it kind of worked, too. Classic Beatty.

When I had called her from the payphone, she could tell something was wrong and told me to head over.

Now I splashed the liquor into the tumblers.

I sat down and took a big swig. Her face was dismayed. 'Like that is it? No Happy New Year?'

I spluttered in shame. 'Sorry!' We chinked glasses.

'Congratulations. I heard through the grapevine Dolly Perkins was released.'

I raised a brow. That was quick. 'Yeah.'

'You don't look so thrilled?'

'I think I've been played,' I said.

'By who?'

I met her eyes. 'By myself, mainly.'

'Intriguing.' Beatty raised a brow. 'Go on.'

I shuffled in my seat, uncomfortable. I explained everything that had happened since we last met. She listened intently. I concluded the saga with my tailing of Dolly. About Dolly going straight to Vivienne and confronting her with the truth—that she was Vivienne's child that she had given up for adoption years ago through the Pineview Clinic. And what Vivienne just told me, revealing her sick and obsessional devoted love. 'Vivienne was the woman who organized Agnes's trip to the same clinic. She was devoted to mopping up his mess in the secretary department.'

Beatty's face was pure distaste. 'What else?'

'Dolly's behavior. She ordered Vivienne to move away from LA with her. Sounds unstable, right? And there's something else.'

I told her about Zetty's bizarre confession, that she seemed desperate to confess, desperate for witnesses. 'She loved Dolly, wanted to save her from death row. She thought she was dying, and it was her last chance.'

Beatty absorbed this, but, like Lauder, was horrified I had been at the now notorious Santa Barbara party. 'Jeez, you sure get around places you shouldn't.'

I wouldn't alarm her further by telling her about Maureen O'Reilly.

'It's sick. But it's over. Should I keep poking around a closed case? I mean, I worked for the defense, and they've won. What's the ethical thing to do?'

317

Beatty let out a long sigh. She put her glass down and took her glasses off. 'All right. Something you should know. You and me are the reason Dolly Perkins was let off.'

'What?'

'I am Linda Hunter's private investigator.'

My jaw hit the floor. Beatty had kept it from me, the whole time. I wasn't sure how I felt about that.

'That's why my boating trip was cut short—Hunter's murder. Linda's been itching for a divorce for a while. I needed proof of these extramarital affairs, so they could come to a quick settlement. I knew about Dolly, Agnes, and quite a few others. When he was murdered, Linda was worried she would be seen as a suspect, particularly if news of his affairs broke. She had an alibi, but not the best. She was with Rufus.'

I was speechless.

Beatty went on, 'When you told me Flannery was running with the stalker angle, I knew he would drop Dolly if he knew all the juice on Hunter. I gave Sonia my files, she did the deal, Dolly got released.'

I stared at her. Beatty let out a big sigh. 'Linda Hunter married the wrong sibling. She soon got fed up with Hunter's roving eye but by this time, she was pregnant and thought she could put up with it. But then she fell in love with Rufus. Little brother has spent years of his life keeping big brother's reputation out of the press, all to protect the family name. As you know, Hunter senior likes young ladies, and he likes to get them pregnant. Dolly, Agnes, a whole run of them over the years, some of the kids are even in their thirties now. There have many payoffs, organized with the assistance of the late Mr. Minski. Hunter's misdeeds never got out.'

Beatty lit her pipe. 'Perv for sure.'

'But how does it exonerate Dolly, the fact there were loads of affairs?'

'Flannery was finally alerted about some blackmail letters. But that's real evidence, and more convincing than a blonde who couldn't lift a finger, let alone wield a cleaver, another in a long line of knocked-up girls. But even there, Flannery's hit a dead end. Minski knew stuff, but being dead don't help.'

Beatty sure had eyes in the police department.

We both sipped our drinks. I asked, 'So what about Minski's death?'

Beatty shrugged. 'Dead is dead.'

If Minski was considered to know too much, or done too much, Rufus Hunter still could have bumped him off. Surely this occurred to Beatty? But she wasn't going to volunteer it.

'So, the Hunters can trust the cops not to leak this to the press? Everything they've hushed up over the years?'

Hushissimo.

'Something for your rulebook. In this town, never underestimate the power of money.'

I met her eyes. 'So I should leave well alone?'

'Perkins is free. Obsession with a mother who gave her up is no crime. Just another sucker who wants love.'

'What about Zetty's confession?'

Beatty shot me a firm look. 'Case is closed. Zetty wakes up? She'd be a darned idiot to confess now her pal's released, especially if she said it because she thought she was snuffing it. Ronald Hunter's still a hero. Injured veterans are going to have better lives thanks to his foundation. Nobody wins if his reputation goes up in flames.'

Had Sonia done a final deal with Rufus Hunter to pay off Dolly for her silence? I felt sick. Whatever, Beatty's words felt like an order, jazzed up with the moral high ground.

She puffed on her pipe, the blue smoke dividing us. 'This sleeping dog needs a nice long snooze.'

The big sleep, she meant. *Do not resuscitate*. She was being loyal to her client, Linda Hunter. And by default, the Hunter clan.

Beatty smiled. 'It's 1946. Move on. Things are gonna come up roses for you.'

51

'What can I tell ya? Free as a bird!'

Dolly sipped her *piña colada* cocktail. Quite the exotic bird, in her expensive dark wig and pale tangerine suit, teamed with a light blue shirt with an orange palm leaves pattern. A necklace of pale blue gemstones around her neck. Her high-heeled shoes were in burnt orange snakeskin leather.

Edith Piaf, gone tropical.

The outfit looked pricey. More Bullocks Wilshire than Tilsons Department Store.

I felt a pang of envy. Was Dolly living the life I was supposed to live?

When I arrived, I had the front desk ring up to her room. Dolly had come down, quite willingly. She was pleased to see me, she said, as she was going out of her mind with boredom. 'Sonia says I gotta lie low. No talkin'. But you're a pal.'

Now we sat in the sunny hotel terrace bar. It was pretty empty, save for a few salesmen, pouring over documents.

I had opted for a black coffee, which tasted bitter. 'I need to tell you something. About Zetty.'

Dolly grimaced.

'I read all about it. Waitin' in the Hall of Justice this morning took *so* long. So I grabbed a paper. Could not believe my eyes. A mobster hit of all things!'

She shook her head.

'Sad life, real sad life. Sure hope she pulls through. You know, it could've been me singing at that party. I could have got topped. God really moves in mysterious ways! He did all this, to make me whole. So, I'm moving to New York. Pursue my singing. I wanna be on Broadway!'

So she wasn't that cut up about her friend. I had been so blind to her self-obsession. It had been there the whole time. 'You hanging on for Zetty?'

'Why? Ain't she a vegetable?'

'Coma, she could wake up.' I opened my purse and took out the photograph of Zetty and the boy. 'I found this. Know who the kid is? Where it is?'

Dolly glanced at it, not really interested. 'Uh-uh. Zetty showed it me plenty of times. That's her little boy. They have these blood feuds in Albania. Some other family wanted him dead! She escaped on a boat to Sicily. '

'Is that where she met Mrs. Luciano?'

'Uh-huh. Mrs. Luciano had her trained up. To shoot, you know.'

'So where's the kid now?'

'My lips are sealed.' She mimed a zip over her mouth. 'But Zetty don't see him no more.'

'Why not?'

'To keep him safe from the bad guys. Mrs. Luciano sent him away, then to school some place. Zetty goes along with it, for his safety. She don't think he could recognize her no more.'

She went on. 'That's why we got a special bond.' She sucked on her straw. 'My momma was forced to give me up. Difference being, not for my own good.'

She offered me a cigarette. I declined. 'Hey, you bring me Ronnie's hankie? That why you came?'

She hadn't taken long to ask for it. That confirmed my suspicions. My green light.

I shook my head. 'Sorry, I forgot. Brought you this, though.'

I got out the lipstick and held it up. Dolly stared, and then grinned. 'What's that? Makin' yourself pretty?'

I twisted the case off, revealing the blunt, squished end.

'This is the same lipstick you used to try to frame Linda Hunter. You got Zetty to kill Hunter, didn't you?'

Dolly froze, straw in mouth. She sat up. Then she laughed, hysterically. 'You crazy?' Natural actress as she was, she couldn't hide her shock.

'And Zetty loves you so much, she couldn't bear you were stuck in jail for something she did, even for you. After she was shot, she confessed to me and Alberta. She'd take the rap, to save your skin. Tell me about your plan, because there's a few things I can't figure out. Like why. Why did Hunter have to die?'

'Plan? You snuck liquor in that coffee?'

'I followed you the day you got out of jail. I saw your little rendezvous with your mother. So me and Vivienne had a little chat.'

As I mentioned Vivienne, her face hardened. Not hate, not love, but something more twisted, something uglier.

'You wanted to frame Linda Hunter, by first making it look like someone framed you. Pretty smart idea, if risky. But you're a risk-taker, aren't you, Dolly?'

'No idea what you're talkin' about. But go on, this sure ain't boring!' Her voice sounded strained despite the attempt at gaiety.

'Maybe you found out from another shop girl in Tilsons what cosmetics Linda Hunter bought that day. How did you know he'd come to the shop? You were real smart to figure that out. I mean, I'm impressed, Dolly. You worked it all out really well.'

I braced myself. Would flattery do it?

Dolly leaned back, sighing. 'Well, ain't you the smarty-pants, too?'

Bingo!

'The evil creep who adopted me, he died suddenly. Few years back. Devil's spawn, that man. A shame, one day he tripped down the stairs and never got up again.' She looked up, staring at me. 'He might have had a little push, mind you. Deserved it, after what he did to me.'

I froze, folding my arms. She was a born killer!

'So I go through his things. Find this letter Vivienne's written to him, around the time I was born. Saying how she loved me but she couldn't keep me, askin' him and his wife to take good care of me. So I came to the city. I just wanted to see her. Was she nice, a good person? And who was my daddy? I finally locate her, took me a bit of time. So I ask her for a job in her beauty parlor, pretending to be broke, didn't tell her who I was. Vivienne don't even recognize her own flesh and blood! So, I'm washing rich old ladies' hair and one day, some girl comes in, crying, real mad at her. Calling her a liar, how she ruined her life. I follow this girl and get it all out of her. How Ronnie got her in the family way, and Vivienne made her get rid of her baby, at a clinic. They used a slimeball PI to pay her off. Got his name too, figure there'll be more girls like her. So I help her, sending letters asking for more, or he'll be dead.'

I stared at her. She was behind the blackmail too?

'As for Vivienne, I find out she will do anything for Ronnie, this guy who don't love her one bit. Get her to tell me all about him. She idolizes the creep! Why? She ruins my life, to be his crummy secretary all her life? He don't even like her that way! She was always too old for him. Then one day, I read in the gossip magazines an interview with Linda. She wants him to buy Tilsons Department Store. So I switch jobs. I knew I'd meet him one day, and I did.'

'Playing a real long game, then.' I sipped my coffee, sickened. Vivienne claimed Hunter wasn't Dolly's father. Dolly believed it too. But what was the truth? Maybe it was a good thing she miscarried.

'Only had to screw him a couple of times. A prick's a prick. Anyhow, I tell Zetty he was just ruinin' all those lives. She don't like that one bit! Moms givin' up their babies, but they get a raw deal outta life anyway? It ain't fair, is it? So we stopped him. He had it coming. Had a better life than most!'

She must have had an emotional stranglehold over Zetty, who could no longer be part of her own child's life. Dolly and Zetty. A cruscading double act.

'And now you want Vivienne to sell up? For the money?'

'Worth a fortune, that shop. And she kept saying no to Mrs. Luciano. Why? To rot near that creep for the rest of her life? Now she's free like me! Besides, startin' out on Broadway don't come cheap. I need acting classes.'

'Is that how you got to know Zetty? When Luciano came to the beauty parlor?'

She nodded. 'Yeah. We'd have a smoke together while our bosses talked. I got her into the band, after she tells me she's a jazz player.'

I resisted the urge for a cigarette.

'What about Todd Minski?'

'That slimeball! Had tabs on him for a while. Figured it wouldn't hurt if Zetty pays Minski a visit, get his files on anyone who's been paid off. She's hidden them for me.' She tapped her nose.

'Zetty killed him?'

Dolly shrugged. 'Maybe he wasn't so obligin'? You don't want to mess with Zetty.' She finished her drink. 'Why do you care? He was in on it, hurtin' all those babies!'

'Why not bump off Vivienne? She's as much to blame, surely?'

Dolly looked at me. 'Kill my mom? You crazy? I just freed her! We can be together now. For the rest of our lives.'

52

Alberta. 'Well, I'll be...' She sat down, in her housecoat, totally shocked. 'Dolly? Zetty? Murderesses?'

'Had us all hoodwinked. Me, most of all. Dolly was the brains, Zetty the loyal muscle.'

'Shoot. I need some air,' said Alberta, standing up again.

We went out onto the balcony and looked over the city. Dusk was falling. Lights came on like twinkling diamonds, one by one.

Alberta spoke softly. 'All those people down there. Secret lives, doing what they gotta do. How many psychos?'

'More than we realize, I bet.'

Alberta said, 'Won't be surprised if I hear her singing on the jukebox one day. She'll go to the top, braggin' and lyin' all the way.'

I nodded. 'Unless...'

Alberta turned to me. 'What?'

'You and Dede paid for her defense. If you want me to report what I know, I will. But only anonymously.'

Introduce myself to the police? No thanks. And I'd been told to stay away from the job by Lauder. Above all, Beatty was now doing the forbidding, albeit nicely. Sonia Parker would feel exactly the same. She'd had a win. I would never work again in this town if anyone knew I'd squealed on Dolly to the police.

Dolly was a bad seed. If there was such a thing as born criminals, she made the grade. But exposing her would cause many lives to crumble. Lives she didn't even know about.

Alberta ran her hand along the top of the wall, her fingers lightly tapping it as if it were piano keys. 'Remember you asked me why we were helping Dolly?'

I nodded.

'One night, about six months ago, Dolly gets chatting to some guy, hanging around one of our shows. He's asking questions about Dede and me, snooping around a few of the places we go. Turns out Dede's pops had paid him. He's a PI. Pops wanted the lowdown on his daughter's private life.'

'So Dolly warned you?'

'Uh-huh. If it wasn't for Dolly and her big mouth chatting to the creep in the first place, we wouldn't have known a thing about it. Earnestine handled him for us.'

'Earnestine?'

'Earnestine Chappelle.'

'The bus driver?'

'Little secret. She ain't no bus driver. Earnestine's like you, a sleuth, but for my people.' Alberta gave a wry smile. 'Why you looking like that?'

'Because...I don't know. I didn't....'

'I'm just a driver,' she'd said. I felt like a fool.

'Because she's good. And *she* don't get drunk on the job.' Alberta raised a brow.

I would never live that down.

'Wait a minute. Is that why Earnestine came to Santa Barbara?'

'I asked her to come. I kinda had my doubts about Floriana Luciano. Didn't want any of us to get in trouble. That's why the bus engine got started as soon as those shots were fired, and our bags were all packed. Ready to split. Earnestine didn't like the look of the hoodlums.'

I stared at her. Earnestine may have seen Simonetta in the toilet. Had she also worked out she was the assassin?

Alberta grimaced. 'Hunter was a big cheese. If we do nothing, the cops might go after somebody innocent. Just to say they got somebody. That ain't good.'

I could sense her anxiety.

'I think they'll drop it.' I actually did, Beatty had implied as much. Hunter's legacy demanded secrecy from everybody.

'What if Zetty comes round? I mean, she is the killer.' Alberta, hugged herself. It was getting cold. 'But I bet she wouldn't have done it if Dolly hadn't got in her head.'

Floriana wouldn't like me to incriminate Zetty. Just like Beatty didn't want me to either. I had to turn a blind eye to protect our clients, and our interests. Murky waters indeed.

'Cross that bridge when we come to it. Till then, if we squeal about Dolly, and she's caught, I reckon she could even pin it on her mother. She knows about all the love children Vivienne made go away. She's stashed files on them someplace. Vivienne's no angel but she didn't kill anybody. And you know what? Dolly could easily make it all stick.'

'Got all bases covered, then.'

I nodded.

We went back in. Alberta put her hands on her hips.

'I'm not so sure I like knowing Dolly's out there, knowing what she does.' *About Dede and me*, she could have said.

That made sense. Nobody needed a psycho knowing their secrets.

'And one more thing. When she said she was carrying Hunter's child, I wasn't so sure. Sol and her were close for a while, just didn't want to spread gossip around. If she had the baby in jail, and it turned out to be a brown baby, it would be given away to strangers. We had a lot of reasons to help her.'

I remembered the 'S' on the lighter.

Then she said something I wish she hadn't.

'Sorry if that's close to the bone.'

'You did the right thing,' I said, shutting out her implication.

53

All I wanted was to sit on June's balcony, looking out, being soothed by the hum of her sewing machine and listening to her prattle about pleasant things.

I parked Mabel and rang the bell. No answer. I was just about to leave a note when the door opened.

A young woman with dark rings under her eyes. She was very thin, her skin like grey oyster shell. She wore a blue pinafore dress and a white shirt underneath. Her hair was tied back under a cream and pale blue striped scarf. This had to be Sarah.

'Hi. Is June around?'

She shook her head. 'No. She will be back soon. Do you want to wait?' Her accent was strongly Eastern European.

I hesitated, remembering Sarah didn't like the company of strangers. 'It's okay, I'm sure you're busy. Say Elvira popped by.'

'Of course. But she will be here very soon. Come in.'

Maybe her suffering meant she could sense a different kind of troubled soul. She opened the door wider. I raised a brow. 'Sure, if it's no bother.'

I followed her up to June's airy workshop.

'You would like some tea?'

'Don't worry about it. I'll wait.' I was about to head for the balcony when I noticed the door to the smaller workshop— Sarah's safe place—was wide open.

And there it was.

A long shimmer of white gossamer, illuminated like a moonbeam against the room's dark walls.

It was most perfect wedding dress, descending gracefully from a dressmaker's mannequin.

I moved towards the room, a moth drawn to light. Sarah followed.

Layers of sheer silk floated over heavy brocade panels. The top had a high neck, a lacy frill around the bust-line. The long train gleamed with tiny pearls. It was a wedding dress I would choose. Now someone else was having it made, and by June.

'That's a beautiful dress.'

'Yes. A lot of work.' Then she added. 'I like to work.'

I met her eyes. Was she married? I couldn't ask. She may have lost family, like Barney had.

'You're very talented.'

A ghost of a smile crossed her lips. 'I was a seamstress in Warsaw. Like June.' She took a slim box out of the pocket of apron. 'Now I must sew all these.' She opened the lid. Inside, hundreds of tiny seed pearls.

Perfect pearls, for the perfect wedding dress.

'Hello! I'm back!' June's cheerful voice rang through.

She bounded upstairs into the room. She wore a wonderful cape in pale mint that set off her ginger hair. 'Elvira! Happy New Year!' We embraced.

'Sarah was just showing me the wedding dress. It's lovely. But bridal gowns?'

'I couldn't say no! The bride-to-be is so beautiful. She's having a huge wedding in April, a wonderful spring wedding. It will take Sarah all that time just to sew the pearls on. The bride-to-be is marrying a detective. He recommended me, apparently! I have no idea how or why!'

Of course. The Fiancée. Lauder had known all about June's ordeal. It made sense. I felt numbness spreading through me.

Move on! Forget him!

'Well, she's lucky you're making it.' I said, doing my best to sound bright.

All three of us stared at the dress in silence. If white meant hope, what did this dress symbolize for each of us?

After a while, Sarah spoke. 'I make tea.'

June smiled. 'Thanks, Sarah.'

The Fiancée had all the luck. She got the pure white wedding dress out of June. I got the red one, now in the basin in my hotel suite, having blood stains soaked out of it. Then I laughed. Genuinely.

June smiled, curious. 'What's so funny?'

'Life. Life is.'

June grinned at me. She said, 'I'm real glad you're happy.'

54

I sat on the beach, looking out to sea. Winter had finally come. The clouds were full and dark, and the winds churned up the waves into white froth, like the lace on The Fiancée's wedding dress.

I hated Lauder, and possibly I loved him too, a warped love from which nothing good comes.

Every cloud has a silver lining. A cliché, but today, it felt very true. If I hadn't got drunk, I wouldn't have ended up in the care of Alberta. I wouldn't have been at Floriana's. I wouldn't have seen Maureen, and I wouldn't have heard Zetty's confession, that led me to Dolly.

I would never be like Dolly.

My pain was also my strength. I should trust myself more.

That would be my only New Year's resolution.

The Pacific Ocean roared back in agreement. The good ocean. The one that took the long way around to gloomy England.

I was born on the Atlantic, and it was my past. The surging, greenish-blue amniotic ocean that had given me life and taken Violet away.

The Pacific held none of my past, just opportunity.

1946 would be a good year.

With that, I headed back across the sand to Mabel, knowing exactly what I would do.

Barney might not like it, when he came back on Monday, but we would visit the pound and get us a cat.

Acknowledgements

I would like to give sincere thanks to the many people who helped to bring *Chipped Pearls* to life:

Sheila Hyde for editing the book and providing insightful notes; Elaine Sharples for typesetting and book design; Cassia Friello for cover design; Claire Jenkins for graphic help; Patrick Altes for endlessly reading drafts, endless cups of tea and love and support.

I was lucky to have encouragement on early stages of *Chipped Pearls* from two novel writing groups, and in particular I would like to thank Louise van Wingerden, Karen Prentice, Emma Scattergood, Kerry Evans, and Andrea Samuelson.

At the time of writing, I am thrilled the magnificent Cinema Museum in London will be the fitting venue for the launch of *Chipped Pearls* and thanks to Martin Humphries and the volunteers for their support.

As ever, thanks must go to all my family and friends who have provided encouragement, love, and for spreading the Elvira Slate word! You all know who you are.

Creating a private detective who is feminist in a noir world has been a big ambition for a long time. Lastly I would like to thank the readers from all over the world who have contacted me to say Elvira Slate is their kind of 1940s woman. This means more to me than I can express here.

Also by Helen Jacey published by Shedunnit Productions

JAILBIRD DETECTIVE
Elvira Slate Investigations Book One

The past
Jemima Day, gangster's moll, jumps probation.
She runs with the mob, the secret services and the cops at her
heels. She's never going back.

The present
Landing in LA, big dreams of glamor fade when she's busted
by an LAPD cop. Soon she's running corrupt errands in
return for him keeping her safe.

The future
On the sly, she investigates a nasty crime, one the cops
ignore. She reinvents herself as Elvira Slate, 1940s
Hollywood Private Investigator.

Can she get away with it?

978-1-9164417-2-9

Lightning Source UK Ltd.
Milton Keynes UK
UKHW022202201119
353920UK00008B/393/P